W9-BLN-860

Peterson

	DATE DUE	
MAR 2 6 1990		
MAY 3 1990		
MAY 1 2 1990		
JUN 2 1990		
JUL 3 1990		
AUG 2 0 1990		
SEP 6 1990		
FEB 1 5 1996		

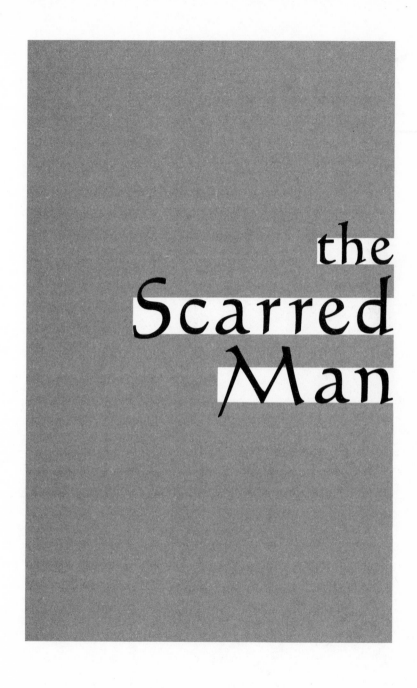

the
Scarred
Man

the Scarred Man

by Andrew Klavan

writing as Keith Peterson

DOUBLEDAY ■ New York London Toronto Sydney Auckland

PUBLISHED BY DOUBLEDAY

a division of Bantam Doubleday Dell Publishing
Group, Inc.
666 Fifth Avenue, New York, New York 10103

DOUBLEDAY and the portrayal of an anchor
with a dolphin are trademarks of Doubleday, a
division of Bantam Doubleday Dell Publishing
Group, Inc.

LIBRARY OF CONGRESS CATALOGING-IN-PUBLICATION DATA

Klavan, Andrew, 1954–
    The scarred man / by Andrew Klavan writing as
    Keith Peterson.
        p.   cm.
    ISBN 0-385-26614-6
    I. Title.
    PS3561.L337S34   1990
    813'.54—dc20   89-35405
                                                         CIP

All Rights Reserved
Printed in the United States of America
January 1990

FIRST EDITION

BG

THIS BOOK IS FOR ELLEN

PART ONE
A Christmas story

Chapter one

I was walking along St. Mark's, past the quaint brownstones and sunken restaurants, the rundown theaters, the newsstands, the boutiques. I was walking with my hands shoved deep in my pockets and my shoulders hunched against the cold. I spared myself nothing. I'd pause beside the shops and gaze at the decorations. Or I'd stand at the corners and stare at the tumbling snow. I did everything but plant myself beneath apartment windows singing "A Poor Orphan Lad Am I." And I'd have done that, too, if I'd thought of it.

It was mid-December, two weeks before Christmas. The world seemed full of lighted windows and closed doors. Visions of TV dinners, of too much scotch, of another holiday alone, danced in my head.

It was Monday, I remember. I was on my way to work, pushing along the wet sidewalk. As I walked I seemed to see the neighborhood's bohemians—the poets and artists; the young, the skewed, the intense, the bizarre—turning into Hallmark cards before my eyes. Here was a radical composer of my acquaintance, hurrying past, humming the standard carols of the season. There was a postmodernist painter I knew, bundled in Norman Rockwell scarves and hats. The editor of the local socialist weekly staggered across the street under an armload of gayly wrapped parcels. And standing at a pay phone was a woman who called herself Randy Trash: the orange dye had been washed from her hair and I could hear her making plane reservations to Minneapolis. I was saddened, I tell you, by the evidence of hypocrisy all around me.

I decided to stop into Ingmar's café for a cappuccino. I went down the stairs and pushed in through the glass door. The place was as it always is: dark, smoky, comforting. Crowded even in the early A.M. Metal tables crushed together. Cups and saucers stained with the residue of coffee. Wire chairs at wild angles. Conversation. Faces leaning toward each other. Mirrored glasses, berets, spiked hair. I weaved to an empty seat and squeezed myself in between elbows.

I scanned the room, hoping for an inspiration. Janice was there, nursing her Monday-morning bloody, a cigarette in one hand, the other pushing auburn hair up under her leather beret. But she'd already told me she was spending Christmas with Kevin. And he was the jealous type. Like, say, the Great Gatsby. My glance moved on to Arnold and Elaine. The two of them were drinking espresso and talking God. They did that a lot: espresso, God. The gold plate of their wire-rimmed glasses glinted in the light as their heads bobbed up and down at each other. Christmas with Arnold and Elaine seemed just the thing if your thing happened to be unbearable Christmases. As I watched them, a hand caught my eye. Toby, my favorite New Wave filmmaker, or No Wave filmmaker, or something. I'd forgotten about her. Toby. Mousey and cute, croissant crumbs on her chin, waving at me. Toby—or not Toby, that was the question. Tempting, definitely, but perchance unwise. I waved. I smiled. I bravely turned away. I saw Carter at the table in the far corner, smoking cigarettes and talking poetry at Belle and glancing black death at the universe. I was just about to turn back to Toby when Peter brought me my cappuccino and I remembered: I'd gone to see Peter play the Cenci in the tragedy of the same name. The only thing I'd understood for two whole hours was that the bastard owed me a big, big favor. I pounced. Peter, I said, how about taking me in for Christmas? But he begged off. He'd told his father he wouldn't bring any friends if the old man wouldn't show any home movies. I sighed and let him go.

A few minutes later I left my cappuccino half finished and headed out. I walked through the snow toward Washington Square.

By the time I got to the office, I was in a black mood. I grunted hello to Marianne and sank down at my desk across the room from her. There I sat, staring at the books stacked up in front of me, trying to work up the energy to get started. I was still working it up at about ten-thirty when McGill came in.

He was about forty-five, McGill, lean and wiry. Always wore a trench coat, always had his jacket open and his tie half undone. His face was sharp everywhere: sharp eyes that shifted, a sharp nose that flared, a sharp chin that he always led with as if he expected you to take a pop at it. All that was left of his hair, the last gray strands, were tangled and uncombed on his sharp pate.

As he came through the door he was grumbling to himself— he did that sometimes—as if he were in the middle of an argument. His overcoat was wet with snow, his cheeks red with cold, his mouth screwed up into an angry slash.

He stopped at Marianne's desk to pick up his mail, then headed toward his office. He waved at me as he came on, his greeting, as always, half a mutter, half a bark.

"Mike. How's it going? Good weekend? Yeah, good."

Then, as he put his hand on his office doorknob, he paused. Now, a whole side of his face screwed up. But the debate lasted only a second. He turned to me.

"Oh, yeah, listen. You wanna come up to my place for Christmas? My daughter Susannah's coming down for the week with a couple of friends. You bring a couple too: She won't get bored with the old man. What about it?"

I managed to get out the word "Sure," and he went on:

"Great. I want you to meet her before I leave for Peru."

Then he went through the door and brought it shut behind him.

Chapter two

The rest was easy: I had only to go home to Charlie Rose.

Charlie is my roommate. We share two small rooms and kitchenette on the fourth floor of a brownstone. Charlie is a radio technician and he works the night shift at a huge news network. It's the secret of our durable relationship: the night shift. I live while he sleeps.

When I walked in, breathless from the climb, he was in the front room, stretched out on his hideaway bed. The window was open, the temperature near freezing, and Charlie, naked, was covered by a single sheet.

"Charlie—" I said.

"Ssh," said Charlie. He stared up at the ceiling. "I'm trying to fry eggs with my mind."

Cursing, I went to the window and brought it closed. "Charlie," I said.

"Ssh."

I stood still and listened. From behind the partition of the kitchenette came the sound of eggs sizzling.

"That's amazing," I said.

"A mind is a terrible thing to waste," said Charlie.

I called out: "Yo, Angela."

"Don't come in," she shouted from behind the partition. "I'm naked."

"What are you doing for Christmas?" I called to her.

"Hey," said Charlie, "I'm working, man. The news doesn't stop for Christmas. America needs to know."

"Want to spend Christmas in Connecticut?"

"Like Barbara Stanwyck?" Angela shouted.

"Sure," I said. "Or not. Can you get a vacation, Charlie?"

"Are you joking? Those buzzards owe me months, brother, months." He sat up, rubbing his face with both hands. "Where am I, by the way?"

"Beats me."

He looked around him, trying to figure it out. A peaceful-looking doke, Charlie, almost beatific, with a widow's peak of blond hair over a soft, lineless face; sleepy, distant eyes. Charlie is almost ten years older than I am, around thirty-four or -five. I want to be just like him when I grow up, but most of the ingredients have been banned.

"Hey," he said. "Connecticut. That's where your boss lives, right?"

"Right," I said. "He invited us."

Angela walked in carrying a plate. She was right: she was

naked. I lost my breath. My hands still remembered the feel of her.

"I fried your eggs," she said.

"You're telling me," said Charlie. "Now could you get me something to eat?"

I spent the rest of that week on Automatic Jolly. Many was the glass of grog that I downed, and many the mulled wine I shared with friends. I went to the church for caroling. I shopped for presents. I gave large handfuls of money away to those beggars I knew by name, and smaller handfuls to those I did not. I became, in short, as good a friend, as good a master, and as good a man as the good old city ever knew.

On Friday I arrived at the office, suitcase in hand. McGill shut the place up a little after twelve. We met up with Charlie and Angela at Grand Central terminal, and, after introductions all around, we all four boarded a train for Connecticut.

The train went through the long tunnel and reemerged to pull away from Manhattan under a slate-gray sky. Charlie, still attuned to his working schedule, was soon asleep. And McGill was soon deep in conversation with Angela. He had his eyes on her all right: They were bright with her, and I couldn't blame him. Angela was long and slender, all leg, and had waist-length straight black hair that framed a small, wry, wicked little face. She was sweet and she knew how to listen—and she was very funny, too, especially when she got on to her singing career. She was on it now: All the stuff about the bars and the bands and the record companies who seemed to her to have made a covenant with trash. McGill peered at her over his cigarette, chuckling the way he did through his tight teeth, squinting and nodding sometimes as if he understood because he had seen everything, which he had. And when she ran out of steam, he had tales of his own to tell, and they were good ones. All about the stories he'd covered and the newspapers he'd worked for in towns and cities all across the country. Angela had big brown eyes in that small face, and they widened at his adventures. And McGill, he loved every minute of it.

All of which left me alone to stare out the window. Which was okay too. It had started to snow, now we were past Stamford, and it was a fine old sight to one who had been long in city pent. The naked branches of the trees were quickly turning to white lace. The house lights, which could be seen beyond the thicket crowding the tracks, glowed warm and friendly. The big snowflakes drifted and somersaulted through the air. It was worth contemplating in silence.

It was a while before I noticed that the conversation beside me had stopped. I turned from the window. Angela had fallen asleep now too, her head on Charlie's shoulder. McGill was reading the newspaper.

I took a good look at him. The old news junky. His whole body seemed concentrated on the page, his stare locked onto the lines like a lover on a lover's lips. I noticed his hands particularly: red, ugly, sinewy hands, which looked like the bare muscle itself. Most of us more or less drape a newspaper over our fingers; but McGill's hands gripped it firmly, as if they were daring you to try to take it away. An old news junky's hands grasping the medicine. I glanced down to see what he was reading. Some story about a death penalty case somewhere, an appeal that had been turned down, and so on.

"How many of those have you covered?" I said.

McGill looked up and quickly folded the paper; set it aside with a laugh.

"Executions?" he said. "Not that many. Too many. Christ, I'm glad I don't have to do that anymore."

And we started talking about the new book, the one on the drug trade, and about his upcoming trip to Peru.

By the time we got off the train in Trent, the snow was falling hard. We drove from the station to McGill's house in his Pontiac. The announcer on the car radio was talking about the storm. Traffic advisories were in effect throughout the tri-state area, he said. He dropped his voice down half an octave when he said it. It didn't sound good.

It didn't look good either. The road ahead was barely visible. McGill, at the wheel, had his face pressed toward the windshield. The rest of us sat hugging our luggage on our knees, trying not to watch as his taut, ugly hands fought against the skids. The car pushed down the unshoveled streets at fifteen miles an hour.

We reached the house, fought our way up the drive, piled in the front door. Angela and Charlie and I—we were slapping each other's hands and shouting at each other like we'd just gotten back from the Donner Pass. Not McGill. While we stomped the snow off our shoes in the front hall and began to struggle out of our overclothes, he was hurrying ahead of us into the kitchen. He was still wearing his trench coat. His shoulders were hunched, his head hung down. His fists were clenched at his sides. As our voices faded and our laughter died down, the three of us could hear him picking up the kitchen phone and dialing.

We looked at each other.

Angela said: "His daughter—she wasn't supposed to come home today, was she?"

I nodded. "Maybe he'll catch her before she leaves."

We heard him hang up the phone. He hadn't spoken. In a moment, he came back into the hall. He peeled off his coat and hung it up. Snow spilled off of it, floated to the floor. He studied the puddles forming at his feet.

"You'd think she'd have the bloody sense . . ." he muttered. He raised his face to us. "What d'ya think?"

"Oh hell, Carl, she'll be fine," I said.

And Charlie and Angela chimed in quickly: "Sure, sure, she'll be fine."

We settled in. The house was a standard Connecticut colonial. Postcard stuff, two stories, solid, lots of wood. McGill showed us to our rooms, and he surprised me. He put me and Charlie together in a downstairs dayroom, while Angela was to sleep upstairs with "the girls." It made me laugh, but Charlie kept his mouth shut about it. He may still have been trying to figure out where to make the connection with the IRT.

He and I unpacked together. Angela went upstairs to do the same. A half hour later we met in the living room. McGill was already there. The room was huge and homey. Lots of easy chairs facing each other, and a sofa too. Lots of coffee tables. All of it on top of an enormous, fading braided rug. Against one wall was a large stone fireplace. Against another was a picture window, looking out on the backyard: a sloping acre with a river through it under willows and elms; woods beyond that, going out of sight. All of it blurred in the swirl of snow. The lawn buried under it. The trees bent with it.

I stood at the window, staring out. There were other houses nearby, I knew, but I couldn't see them. I felt far away from everything.

McGill moved up beside me.

"S'goddamned early, isn't it?" he said.

"What?"

"For a blizzard?"

"Uh . . ."

"S'goddamned early in the year, if you ask me."

"Yeah," I said.

"I mean, it's goddamned December, isn't it? Whattaya call that?"

"Um . . . early?"

"Sure it's early. It's goddamned early."

I nodded.

"Don't tell me. . . ." he said.

"Can I get you a dr—"

"Hell, yes."

I found the bar in the far corner of the room. I dealt out the booze. Then we stood with our hands wrapped around our glasses and stared out at the snow.

After a while we took another tack. We sat down and drank. We talked and were quiet by turns. The quiet turns got longer. In a few more days it got to be late afternoon. Then it was dark. The snow kept falling. The phone didn't ring. Sometimes McGill would get up and go into the kitchen and we'd hear him dialing again and hanging up again. Sometimes he'd ask us if we thought Susannah was all right. We always said yes.

"Where's she coming from?" said Angela at one point.

"Up at Marysvale College. She's a senior there," McGill said. "She's studying to be a teacher."

Angela said, "That's nice."

"Yeah. She's gonna study special education. Like teaching retarded kids."

Angela said, "That's nice."

"Yeah. Yeah. She's gonna bring a couple of her friends along. From school."

"That's nice," said Angela, looking to us for help. Charlie and I were unavailable, however; we were busy staring glumly into our drinks, trying to think of things to say.

Charlie thought of something. "Marysvale. That's way the hell in upstate New York, isn't it?"

"Yeah. Nice area," said McGill.

Charlie shook his head. "Sheesh." He went back to staring glumly.

It was getting on now, close to seven.

"You guys must be hungry," said McGill after a while. "I'm not really . . . I'm not here that often, usually Susannah comes down for the holidays, does the cooking . . . Maybe I can put together something."

He got up and Angela joined him. They both went into the kitchen. As they went I heard him say to her: "Damned thing is: you don't think . . . She knows I look forward to having her here for Christmas, but . . ." And then they went through the door.

Charlie let out an enormous sigh. His head sank onto the back of his chair. "Hey, really, I can't thank you enough for inviting me here."

"Shut up," I said.

"Marysvale, man. That's the fucking North Pole."

"Shut up, Charlie."

"She's history."

"Charlie . . ."

"I mean, jeez."

"Just keep your goddamned voice down."

Charlie shook his head loudly.

"Anyway, she probably stopped," I said.

"Sure. That's right."

"Sure."

"Why didn't she call?"

"It's a blizzard. The phones are down."

"That's right. Sure."

"Sure," I said.

"Yeah. Right."

"Right."

"She's probably in some fucking horrible accident, like

something really unimaginable, you know, like the *National Enquirer* does or something."

I laughed. "Jesus."

"Well, we're all thinking it."

"And how lucky we are to have you here to put it into words for us."

"I mean it, man, I can't thank you enough for inviting me here," Charlie said. "Really."

"Merry Christmas." I tipped my glass of scotch back until the ice rattled against my teeth.

Angela made us some cheese sandwiches. McGill said he wanted to hold off on serving the real food until his daughter arrived. She was sure to be hungry, he said.

She didn't arrive. It got to be eight, then nine. McGill got up twice, to make sure the driveway lights were on. Charlie built a fire: expertly, like the hobo he'd once been. I went out into the snow to have a look at the conditions. The conditions were bad. We were far from a main road and there was nothing out there but white darkness. No cars, no sound, no lights but from the house behind me and another a little ways down the road. The cold was biting; bit through my gloves first, then my coat, then my sweater. Five minutes after leaving, I had to head back inside. All I could say was: "No sign of her." All I could think was: I'd hate to be stuck out there.

At ten o'clock, we watched the local news. At eleven, we watched the news again. The newsmen stood out in the snow like idiots, shivered at the camera and spoke into their microphones.

"It's a record snowfall for this time of year," the newsmen said. "It took weather forecasters completely by surprise."

"Morning takes those bozos by surprise," said Charlie.

There were no deaths reported.

At eleven-thirty, I went out into the snow again. It made me feel like I was doing something. I didn't get very far: about fifty yards. After that I couldn't find the road anymore.

I came back in, stomping the snow off my rubbers. My cuffs and socks were wet through and my ankles stung with cold. McGill, Angela, and Charlie were in the living room, staring at Johnny Carson on the TV. They all looked up at me when I came in as if they expected me to say something. I opened my mouth and stood there silently.

And then we heard an engine.

I was the first one into the hall, but the others were right behind me. They crowded around me as I pulled open the door. We stood together and peered out.

We saw a car's headlights pushing through the snow, inching down the road. We watched. We stared. McGill shuddered. The headlights turned. They inched up into the driveway. They stopped. Then they went out.

We saw the car by the driveway light. It was a little blue Toyota. In another moment its two doors were flung open and three figures poured out into the snow. They were girls—we heard them giggling. We saw them ducking and running in the white blur. We heard them laughing. They shouted at each other and threw snowballs while the four of us stood in the doorway, watching silently.

Finally, one of the girls spotted us and waved.

"Hey, Daddy! Isn't it great?" she shouted.

Then they were running toward us, still laughing. They swept inside: three shapeless bodies swathed in winter clothes. McGill started laughing, too, a tight, gruff laugh. He grabbed each of the girls by the shoulder as she passed him, and the last one, his daughter, he wrapped in an embrace. He wheeled her around in front of the rest of us, displaying her to us, showing her off: a little bundle of brown parka, the fur-lined hood pulled down to her forehead, a bright red scarf pulled up over her nose, and clear, light blue eyes laughing out between.

"Here," he said. "This is my girl, my daughter. This is Susannah." He gestured at us with one gnarled hand. "And here's Angela," he said. "And this is Charlie, Sue." And here —here," he said, reaching out to clutch my shoulder, "here's Michael. Mike North. This is my daughter, Mike. This is Susannah."

Susannah said, "Hello." And then she reached up and pulled down her scarf and swept the hood back off her head.

I was about to lift my hand. I was about to say hello. I dropped my hand. I said nothing. I looked at her. She smiled. I looked at her some more. She laughed and flushed and glanced down and then raised her eyes again. I was still looking at her.

Behind me I heard Angela murmur: "Oh my, North. Oh my, my."

Chapter three

The morning broke bright and clear, one of those perfect mornings that come after a snowstorm. I woke up early to the sound of laughter. I sat up and peeked through the window next to my bed. The window looked out on the far end of the yard, away from the river, where the land lifted gently under the snow-covered trees. There, between the vaunting drifts, Susannah and her two friends were running up the hill with a sled. At the top the three of them piled on board, shouting. One of them fell off into the snow. The two others raced toward the bottom. A second—Susannah—tumbled off, rolling through a burst of white. The third made it all the way down before tipping over at the feet of a snowman. It was a well-made snowman, wearing a watch cap and scarf that looked suspiciously like my own.

I turned to the lump on the bed across the room. "Hey, Rose," I said. "Come here."

He mumbled.

"Hey, Rose."

He clawed the sheet off his face. His eyes were open, but the rest of his face was asleep.

"Hey, Rose," I said, "they're sledding."

Charlie blinked. "Well," he said. "It's a fucking winter wonderland, isn't it?" He pulled the sheet up over his face again.

"Hey, Rose," I said.

"North," said the face beneath the sheet. "I belong to the National Association of Broadcasting Employees and Technicians. If you wake me up before I've slept twelve hours, I get paid short turnaround."

"But Rose—"

"If you wake me up before seven hours, I get to push a screwdriver into your lungs."

He passed noiselessly into another dimension.

I jumped out of bed and started to throw on some clothes. I could still hear them, still laughing. I glanced out the window and saw them toting the sled up the hill again. Dressed, I stepped quickly out into the hall.

I opened the hall closet. As I suspected, my hat and scarf were gone. But I pulled on my jacket and yanked on my gloves and finally—because it seemed to have taken a long time—finally, I stepped to the front door and pulled it open.

And the girls came piling in around me, giggling, shrieking, and slapping at each other with their wet mittens.

They came to a halt when they saw me.

"Hi," said one of them—the long one with the mane of blond hair: Kate. "Going for a walk?"

"Uh, yeah," I said. Damn it, I thought.

"We're just going to make some hot chocolate," said Kelly, the short one; the one with short black hair.

And Kate said: "Coffee too. And biscuits. Sure you don't want any?"

I looked around at them, speechless.

Then Susannah said: "Actually, I kind of think I might go for a walk too." She seemed to think it over while we turned to watch her. She nodded once. "I think I will," she said.

She took me trudging through the snow, up over the hill beyond the river, then down into the woods on the far side. We weren't a mile from the house, but there was nothing but forest here. No one but us. A snowfall hush lay all around. The high branches hung motionless above, gleaming white. Sometimes one cracked, and a tuft of snow tumbled into the drifts beneath with a muffled thump. Sometimes a winter bird sang two shrill notes and ceased, or a squirrel ran suddenly from trunk to trunk and vanished. But then the rift in the silence closed again; the blue sky hung bright over a perfect stillness.

Through this, Susannah walked quickly, her hands in her parka pockets, her head down. I tagged after her, always a step behind, panting a little.

"There's acres and acres of woods back here," she said over her shoulder to me. Her voice sounded very sudden, very loud in the silent wood. "There used to be more."

She'd taken her hood off. I could see her hair. I could see her face when she turned back to talk to me. She was odd-looking. She wasn't beautiful. Oh hell, yes she was, she was beautiful. She had red hair, curly; it bounced down her neck past her shoulders. White, white skin. Those blue eyes: they were just a little crossed, I think, and made it seem as if she were concentrating on something far away. She had a skewed, oversized nose and a lush, cupid's bow mouth, and when she smiled, her face was all cockeyed and goofy. She was beautiful, all right, in her own odd way.

I followed her across a little stream, the edges of it frozen over. She leapt it easily—just one long step. I skittered and crackled and cursed and finally made it across. She had lowered her eyes and glanced up when I came over, as if she were surprised to see me.

"I like to watch the water run underneath the ice," she said. I nodded, breathless.

"We used your hat for the snowman," she said, and turned quickly and headed away from me across the snow.

The woods grew thicker—a maze of rising, tangled white—but there was still plenty of room to walk. The ground rose beneath our feet. We climbed. I saw the snow flying out in front of her boots as I stomped after her.

"It's funny," she called back. "They killed the forests for the horses once. When they had to clear the land for grazing. Then they invented the car and the horse farms died out. The forests grew again. Now it's all part of a state preserve so they can't cut it down anymore." She stopped short. I stopped behind her. She looked around, pushing at her hair with a mittened hand. "Sometimes when I would come here, when I was little, when I was alone, I would be afraid." She glanced at me. She seemed to think that I would speak. I didn't speak. She continued. "I would think there was something, someone, in the woods. Someone following me. When you stood still, you could hear his footsteps getting closer and closer. But when you turned around, no matter how fast you turned, he would be gone: He would hide behind a tree or blend in with the shapes of rocks or with the color of things. He'd be watching you, I mean, but you couldn't see him, you wouldn't know just where he was.

And then, when your back was to him, he would start coming closer and closer again. Until he could grab you." She cocked a red eyebrow at me. "Sometimes, when I was lying in bed at night, I thought I heard him out here, waiting."

She watched me another moment. But before I could answer her, before I could think of anything to say, she was dashing on ahead and I was struggling once more to keep the pace.

When she reached the top of the hill, she finally came to rest. She stood there with her hands in her pockets. She waited till I came up beside her. Then she said: "Look."

I looked. The forest dropped off sharply below us. Over the tops of the winter pines and the dead and snowy elms, I saw the town of Trent. It was laid out in the valley beyond like a picture drawn on the snow and on the blue sky: the houses and the white steeple of the church, and then open land beyond that and more woods running away toward the horizon.

She pointed to the open land: rolling white hills. "That's the Glenns' horse farm," she said. "I go riding there, sometimes. When I was little, I went riding there a lot. I like to ride. I was thrown once, but I didn't cry. Daddy used to take me."

I stole a look at her as she surveyed the vista. A curl of red hair looped over her white cheek and touched the corner of her mouth.

She faced me, caught me watching her. She cocked her head. "Why don't you talk?" she said.

I laughed. "I can't think of anything to say. You keep saying these things—these facts, these things that happen. There's no answer to them."

She frowned. "I was making conversation."

"Oh," I said.

She just stood there, staring at me.

"Did you know the boysenberry was named after Rudolph Boysen?" I said.

"Oh," she said. "Doof. That's stupid conversation."

"You didn't specify."

There was a boulder beside us, capping the rise. Her hands still in her pockets, Susannah leaned back against it. She shook her head.

She said: "Daddy says you're lazy." For a moment, I saw my job pass before my eyes. But then she said: "He says otherwise you could be a great journalist, a famous journalist. He says you'd rather hang out with weirdos and have lots of women, and take drugs all night in St. Luke's Place."

"Mark."

"What?"

"Right neighborhood, wrong gospel."

She considered me carefully. She pouted. Her lips were very thick. She wore dark red lipstick on them. I thought about that. "He also says you're brave," she said.

I snorted.

"He says you were brave about the Sanderson papers."

"Yeah. Right," I said. "Sometimes at night I still hear the judge saying, 'Mr. North, if you don't tell this court who gave you those documents, I shall hold you in contempt and send you to jail.' Then I wake up, and it's only Charlie, standing over my bed, saying, 'Mr. North, if you don't tell this court who gave you those documents . . .' "

"I think you were brave," she said.

Have I mentioned how blue her eyes were? They were so pale that the color seemed to lie beneath the surface of them, like a faraway place you had to travel to. But they were very blue, her eyes, way in there. She kept staring at me with them. A difficult girl to talk to, overall.

She said: "He told me about Scarangello."

"Oh, come on, Susannah, it turned out it wasn't even loaded," I said.

She cast her eyes heavenward, pushed off the rock, and started down the hill. I took one step after her, before she spun around to me.

"Why *don't* you talk?" she demanded.

I raised my hands. "I don't know. What is this, anyway? What do you want to know?"

Her lopsided nose shifted farther to one side as she snuffled. She moved back toward me until she was standing directly before me. The top of her head came up to my chin.

"What's your favorite color?" she said.

"My what?"

"What's your favorite flower?"

"Uh, I don't . . . Jeez . . ."

"That's what I want to know."

I laughed. "All right. Only ask me something normal. Ask me about movies. Ask me what Rick's last name was in *Casablanca.*"

"Do you cry ever?"

"What?"

"In the movies? Do you ever cry?"

"Oh. Well. I don't . . . I guess. I don't know."

"Why don't you ever talk about yourself to anyone?"

Her tone was not challenging; it was hardly a question, in fact. Just another statement like the ones about the horse farm and the frozen stream. She stood before me, waiting for an answer. Her breath formed plumes of mist in the air beneath my eyes.

"Blue," I said.

"What?"

"My favorite color. Blue."

"He loves you, you know," she said. "Daddy. He loves me, and he loves my mother, and she's dead. So he loves me. And you."

I nodded. She cocked her head at me again and her red hair tumbled to one side. I wanted to put my hand on it.

I shrugged instead. "You want the story of my life?" I said with a laugh.

"Okay."

"What?"

"Okay," she said. She nodded briefly, as she had when she'd decided to walk with me. "Tell me."

I gazed at her awhile. Then I shook my head awhile. Then I walked the few steps back up the hill and leaned against the rock and gazed at her some more. And she just looked and looked at me and waited and waited with that lopsided face and the eyes with the blue way down deep inside of them, and I found myself wondering if she'd ever really been afraid in these woods. Or if she'd ever been afraid anywhere. Or if she'd ever had a nightmare even, or even a stray thought that shocked her with its ugliness. Somehow I doubted it. Somehow she didn't strike me as the type.

I nodded. And I said: "The truth is, I don't remember very much. I'm an orphan; you probably know that. My parents . . . died when I was little." I saw her note the hesitation, but she didn't speak, and I went on. "So I was sent to relatives in California. They didn't like me much, so they sent me to some other relatives, who couldn't take care of me, so they sent me to some other relatives, and when the music stopped I was in Florida somewhere and I'd just graduated high school and I got on a bus and I headed north." I paused. I waited for her to stop me, to catch me, to say, "That's not it, that's not any of it." She didn't move. She didn't say a word. "I kept my first name, if it was my first name," I said. "Hey, listen: Have we ever met before?"

She blinked, at least. "What?"

"I say—"

"Oh," she said. "Maybe. You mean, like, on some other plane? Do you believe in—"

"No."

"Oh. Well, then I don't think so."

"What difference does all this make? About me. I mean, I never think about it anymore. Why do you—"

"How did you meet my father?" she asked.

I gave up. I looked into her eyes and had a sudden mental picture: of the stream of her consciousness like a current of clear water. I rode with the flow. "All right. So after one thing and another I got a job on a small newspaper in Poughkeepsie. And the paper started to print a series of articles concerning corruption in high Poughkeepsie places, which is an oxymoron but then so were some of the officials involved. So then, some magazine or other assigned your father to do a piece on Poughkeepsie, and up to Poughkeepsie he came and he stopped in at the little newspaper in Poughkeepsie and he introduced himself to me and we talked for about a half hour and he offered me a job as his assistant—his factotum, he called it—and I packed my bags and left Poughkeepsie forever. That was two years ago. I'm twenty-five years old. I'm kind of partial to daisies, and no—no, I never cry at the movies."

"Have you had breakfast?" Susannah said. "I'm going to make a big breakfast for everybody."

She turned on her heels and kicked away from me through the snow. I pushed off the rock. I walked down the hill after her at my own pace. I think she must have slowed down, because soon I had come up beside her. She glanced up at me and smiled. Her cheeks were red with the cold. She smelled good too.

. . .

"And she has a nice figure," I said. I was lying in bed. An ashtray was balanced on the blanket over my belly. One of Charlie's cigarettes burned down in my fingers. I took a drag. "Definitely nice figurewise. Nice dress. Did you see that dress, Rose? I thought that was a nice dress. Flowers. Flowers are nice."

Charlie stirred under the sheet on the bed across the room. "Hey, North," he said. "Did you hear that disgusting noise?"

"Yeah. What was that?"

"That was me snoring. Now shut the fuck up."

"The thing is, Charlie—"

"Kill me, Lord."

"The thing is: I've gotta find her another Christmas present. I got her a pen. I mean, all I knew about her was she was in school, so I got her a pen. I have to give her something more personal, you know, but not too personal."

Out of the dark came a low chuckle. "You know what that one Kate said to Angela tonight? Remember when she played that Bing Crosby album on the stereo?"

"Yeah?"

"She said to Angela: 'Tomorrow, the boys'll have to go out and get the Christmas tree, so' "—he started to laugh—" 'so we can decorate it at night.' " The sheet vibrated with his steady chuckling.

"All right, all right," I said.

"This is a great place, North. Really. I'm really glad you brought me here."

I nodded at the ceiling. I put the cigarette out in the dark.

"I bet it would look really funny on acid," Charlie said.

Chapter four

All in all, probably, Charlie was right. Probably, that whole week would've looked funny on acid. We got the tree first. Charlie, McGill, and I had to go to a tree farm and cut it down ourselves so Kate would think we were having fun. McGill hung around us, huffing and puffing, all the way out of shape and trying to look like he was doing something strenuous. Charlie sang Negro spirituals. I cut down the goddamn tree. Hauled that sucker over four hundred miles of savage driveway, tied it to the Pontiac despite the advice of my companions, and be damned if I didn't carry it into the house with no less than four women crowded around me telling me where it should go.

We hung ornaments on it that night, and lights. It was brilliant with the lights reflecting off the ornaments' glass. Susannah put the star on top. Angela made eggnog, and, heaven bless her, a liberal hand the girl had. We plugged the tree in and oohed and aahed with the best of them. Charlie built a fire. Kelly played the piano and we all sang "Silent Night." Charlie played the piano and we all sang "Johnny B. Goode." "Silent Night" again, then "Hark, the Herald Angels Sing," and so on.

The next day, the Glenns came over from their horse farm with a horse-drawn sled, and gave us all rides in turn. I went with Susannah and we rode through the town and she pointed and said a lot of things there were no answers to. Charlie went with Angela and the two of them came back five hours later on foot. Kate and Kelly and McGill crowded on together and went off giggling. Charlie built a fire. Angela made eggnog. We played Pictionary. Charlie won.

I bought her a scarf. The next day. It was all I could think of. I snuck into town and got it for her. A blue one with orange designs on it. Angela helped me wrap it, though the whole project seemed to annoy her. She kept tearing the paper and cursing and snapping at me, until I actually thought she was going to cry. But she did a good job. And it was nice enough. It was just all I could think of.

The next day was Christmas Eve. Susannah and Angela teamed up to make dinner. It was a powerful performance, supplying in gusto what it lacked in organization. Even Charlie kept wandering into the kitchen to taste it, which is saying something because *Emmett Otter's Jugband Christmas* was on HBO and he never misses that. I kept hearing Angela in the kitchen scream "Rose!" and then he'd be back in the living room looking sheepish and asking me what happened as if he couldn't have recited the whole show word for word. And then we ate, an experience somewhere between orgasm and apotheosis. Better than actual life, at any rate. And McGill raised his wineglass and cleared his throat and said, "Okay, listen up, then. Merry Christmas, you guys."

"God bless us, every one," I said.

And Charlie said, "Doo-wow."

After dinner, we put the presents under the tree. They spilled out over the living room floor. All kinds of shapes and colors. When we were done, we went to bed. It wasn't much past eleven.

So, finally, 'twas the night before Christmas, and all through the house, not a creature was stirring, except for me. I couldn't sleep. I got up sometime after midnight, dressed, and wandered around awhile. Wandered back into the bedroom and stole another one of Charlie's smokes. Carried it out to the living room. I plugged in the tree. Sat on the floor with my back against an easy chair. Lit up the cigarette and stared at the ornaments and lights. The lights reflected on the wrapping of the packages. I puffed away quietly. Pondered the cosmos, such as it is.

I heard the floor creak and I looked up. She was standing there in the doorway. She was wearing a pink, flannel nightgown with a ribbon tied in a bow around her neck. Her red hair was all tousled and shaggy on her forehead and cheeks. Her eyes were sleepy.

"If you don't go to bed, Santa won't come," she said.

"And if I do go to bed?"

She just stood there, her head cocked, her lips soft, her eyes at once fixed on me and slightly off, giving them that distant, contemplative look. The sight of her put a major dent in my cosmos-pondering.

She said: "Was it awful? Being sent from place to place? Was it really awful?"

I moved my head a little. "Oh, I don't know. The past is past. Like I say, I don't think about it anymore."

"But you told me about it."

"You asked me to tell. So I told."

"But you didn't really tell me, did you? Not really, I mean."

I didn't answer.

"You never tell anyone," she said.

"No. I never do."

"Was it awful?"

I sighed. "It was—I don't know—lonely. It was lonely sometimes. But then, that's life, isn't it."

"No," she said.

"Well." I smiled. "It did start to bother me tonight a little. All of a sudden, I mean. I felt . . . wired. I don't know."

"I think it's awful," said Susannah. "I think it must've been awful."

"No, no," I told her. "You can't dwell on it, anyway. Just tonight. Just tonight, it suddenly . . . I don't know. I don't know."

She merely stood there. She merely stared. I pulled on my cigarette. I watched the tree's lights until they melded into a blurry mass of red and blue and yellow.

"The house in San Francisco where they sent me first—that was really the worst of it," I said. "It was my father's family, I think. I was very little. It was a big house. Lots of money. I remember the curling banister and the chandelier in the front hall. And I remember I was glad the house was so big because I could get away from her, from the way she looked at me. My grandmother. I could never understand why she hated me so much. Tall, duchess-type with eyes that could immolate you. And she had a voice like a snaking wire on a wet road. There were lots of closets in that house and I used to sit in them by the hour, hiding from her, hiding from her eyes. Smelling her clothes and her husband's clothes, and listening to my uncle arguing with her. He was a drunk. The thing was: nobody ever told me anything. About my parents, about why I was there, about who I was. And I can't remember anything. It doesn't seem right, somehow, to have forgotten so much. I don't know." I shrugged. "It just bothered me suddenly."

Susannah was silent. I glanced at her.

"And it shouldn't," I said. "Your father's done a lot for me. I consider myself a lucky man." I laughed once. "Do I sound like Lou Gehrig?"

"Lou . . . I don't know who that is."

"You don't know who Lou Gehrig is?"

"No. Don't make fun of me."

"He was a baseball player."

"Oh."

"One of the greats. And when he was dying, they paid tribute to him at the ballpark and he got up before the crowd and he said, 'Today I consider myself the luckiest man on the face of the earth.' "

"That's a good story."

"Gary Cooper played him."

"Gary . . ."

"He was an actor."

"Oh. So *do* you?"

"What?"

"Consider yourself the luckiest man on earth?"

"I'm a hell of a lot luckier than Lou Gehrig," I said.

She didn't laugh. Her head down, her arms folded over her breasts, she walked slowly across the room until she was standing a little to the right of the tree. Then she looked at me again for a long time before she spoke.

"I want you to feel lucky," she said.

I smiled. "Thanks."

She shook her head. She did the casting her eyes heavenward bit again.

"What?" I said. "What did I say?" Then I looked up. I swear to God, the girl was standing under the mistletoe.

Upon reflection, I came to feel the moment was choice. I put out the cigarette and stood.

"God, don't you—" she said, and I took her by the shoulders and kissed her. I kissed her and put my tongue in her mouth and held onto her, and I could feel her, naked, under the flannel, and I ran my hands all over her, feeling her curve and yield, and I kissed and kissed her.

We pulled away from each other and breathed, hard and warm, on each other's faces. She smiled at me.

"You have this goofy smile," I said. "I just really like your smile."

She kissed me. She whispered: "I have to go back to school the day after Christmas."

I ran my hand up over her waist to her breast. I kissed her eyebrows. "It'll be Sunday."

"Friday."

"Right. Why?" I kissed her cheek. She kissed me. "Why do you have to go back?"

"I have to write a paper. I have a lot to do." I ran my other hand all the way down her back. She closed her eyes. "A lot." I kissed her. She opened her eyes a little. She whispered: "Are you gonna visit me? Will you? Or are you gonna go back and think it was all stupid?"

I tried to think about it. I didn't know. I knew I wanted to die before I stopped kissing her. I pressed her against me, and she pressed back. I knew I wanted to be inside her. That was what I knew.

We began again, our lips everywhere on each other.

"I want you," I said.

"Will you tell me? Will you come?"

"I can't. I can't tell you. I'd lie, I'd say anything. I'd say anything. I don't know, how could I know."

"Know. Lie."

"Yes," I said.

She put her hands on my face and we went down to the floor together, under the Christmas tree, with the colored lights in her eyes.

Chapter five

So then this is what happened on Christmas. First of all, there was screaming; laughing; giggling; shouting. Charlie Rose got out of bed early. Photographers covered the event. We staggered out of our room and found McGill amidst a flurry of women. Then the whole pile of us tumbled into the living room. There was some sort of family tradition about having eggs and toast before opening the presents. This we trampled into the dust. Susannah was cooking the eggs and shouting "Wait for me" and running into the living room to yell at us, and then back to the eggs while we tore into our packages. We were animals. I blush to describe the greed.

I gave Charlie an autographed picture of Richard Nixon, which I'd gotten by writing to the guy. He (Charlie, not Nixon) gave me a lighter and a pack of cigarettes, his brand. Susannah came in and I gave her her scarf and I looked in her eyes and I thought about being inside her. She seemed to like it, the scarf. I wish I could've thought of something better.

Then we ate. Then we drank. Then we ate some more. We sat and talked. McGill told stories and everybody laughed. I looked at Susannah and thought about being inside her. Then we ate some more and drank some more and watched the movie *A Christmas Carol* with Alastair Sim on TV and afterward Charlie held forth at great length about why it was better than the Reginald Owen version and the George C. Scott version and possibly the Dickens version and possibly sex and french toast, all of which seemed to be true at the time. We drank and ate and I could have stared at her until I went blind. She had such a goofy smile.

It got dark. I began to think about her leaving tomorrow. Then I didn't think about it. I thought about tonight, when everyone would be asleep except for her and me. It got darker. Charlie built a fire. I watched the fire grow and the orange flames rising. After a while I fell asleep in my chair. We had gone to bed at four A.M., and I was tired. I woke up and Susannah was asleep in her chair and I sat and watched her sleeping. She woke up and she looked at me. It was getting late. They couldn't stay awake forever.

The first one to go was McGill. I was in the kitchen, pouring myself a mug of coffee when he came in to say good night.

"Merry Christmas, buddy," he said.

I nodded. "Thanks for inviting me."

He paused in the doorway. I watched him. I wondered if he knew. He said: "There hasn't been any time to talk."

"Yeah. Christmas," I said.

"Right, right," he muttered. "No time. I had some things . . ." His voice trailed off.

I raised the mug to my lips, touched my lips to the hot coffee, thought of Susannah. "You don't go till February," I said.

For a moment he didn't answer me. He stood in the doorway, his wiry frame bent, his sharp features pointed downward, the kitchen light gleaming in the last gray strands of his hair. Then he looked up quickly, smiled. "Sure," he said. "I'll see you in the morning."

I wandered back into the living room, hoping the others would soon follow McGill's lead. But they were pretty well planted where they were. They sat motionless, black and orange shadows around the fire. No one was even talking anymore. Conversation was dead. No one wanted Christmas day to be over.

I settled into an easy chair again, felt the heat of the fire run up my side, inhaled the steam from my coffee. Looked at Susannah.

"I know!" said Kate suddenly. "We could tell ghost stories. You know: Christmas and the fire and everything."

I didn't groan. It was Charlie.

"Oh hey," he said. "Let's not, okay?"

Kate pouted. "Come on. Why not?"

Charlie puffed up his cheeks and sighed. His sleepy, childlike face glowed in the firelight, looking the soul of mockery.

Angela turned up a corner of her mouth. "Oh, come on, Rose, it might be fun," she said. I knew the battle was lost.

"Oh, man," said Charlie. "I don't know any ghost stories. The only one I know is the 'The Golden Arm.' "

"Ooh, that sounds good, what's that?" said Kate and Kelly and Susannah all at once.

That clinched it. Faced suddenly with the prospect of telling "The Golden Arm" to three attractive girls who'd never heard it before, Charlie was unstoppable. He perked up at once. He rubbed his palms together and chuckled maniacally. I cursed under my breath. Then Charlie launched into it, and I have to hand it to him: Rose rose to the occasion. He told the story as if he'd just made it up. He stood and acted out the husband digging up the wife's body. He crept back to his chair with her golden arm, peering back over his shoulder at the sound of the wind. The wind: he had the eerie howling of it down pat, and you could hear how the wife's voice sort of welled up under it slowly and mingled with it: *"Whoooooo stooooole my goooooolden aaaaarm?"* When he finally spun on Kate and shouted "You did!" even I jumped in my chair. Splashed coffee down the front of my shirt. And Kate screamed and giggled till I thought we'd have to have her hospitalized.

Charlie sunk his chin on his chest and chuckled. Angela and Susannah laughed. Kelly hugged herself and shivered. It was quiet for a few minutes.

Then Kelly said: "Who else knows one?"

And I heard myself answer: "Okay. I do."

Everybody turned to me. I couldn't believe I had spoken. All I wanted was the quiet of the sleeping house again, the small white feel of her under and around me again. On top of which, Charlie had just told the only ghost story I know. But his performance had inspired me. The little shrieks of the women had gotten my blood up. And so I had spoken, and now there they were staring at me, and I had to say something, fast.

Which is how I came to invent the scarred man.

The moments passed. My mind was blank. I smiled calmly, panicking. Like Charlie, I rubbed my hands together, playing for time. I cast a slow, wicked glance at each of them: Angela with a cigarette held before her lips and her thumbnail pressed to her teeth; Kate and Kelly sitting shoulder to shoulder, two glowing pairs of expectant eyes; Susannah absently rolling the brandy in her snifter around and around; and even Charlie, perched on the edge of his seat with his arms dangling between his knees—all of them: waiting.

I took a deep breath.

"Okay," I said softly. "Listen."

And I began.

Actually, this story is true [I said] so I don't know if it fits the bill. But it's eerie enough in its way. I heard it from a man named Robert Sinclair, who was once a popular newspaper columnist in Chicago. I met him at a party in SoHo in New York. His heyday was before my time, but I'd heard his name in another connection. Eventually the conversation turned to the old days and his work. Sinclair's primary interest had been crime: He had a lot of good stories to tell and he told them with relish—so much so, in fact, that I eventually asked him why he'd left off doing what he obviously loved. We'd had a few drinks by that time and he seemed ready to tell me, though he gave me a good once-over before he started.

"Are you sure you want to know?" he asked.

I said I was.

"Then I'll tell you," he said. "I'll tell you about the last story I ever covered."

This happened, as I say, before my time, twenty years ago or more, but Sinclair remembered it vividly. At the time it took place, he was deeply engrossed in covering the famous Chicago Strangler killings. He was doing the usual profiles of the seven dead women, the police-are-baffled pieces and so on. And what always struck him was that while he was working in the limelight, the story that was to end his newspaper career was beginning in complete obscurity.

In obscurity, it seems, there lived a man named Honeywell. John Honeywell. In fact, he kept a house in a suburb of the city, but he was obscure enough; a drab sort: quiet, meek; gray. He worked as a bookkeeper for a Chicago firm and commuted into the city every day by train. Into the city and out again, that was his life. No wife, no kids, no friends to mention. Like the old song says: nobody knew he was there.

Now, one day, Honeywell was riding the train into work—sitting alone, reading his paper—when a man sat down next to him. Honeywell paid no attention to him at first, but after a few moments he became aware of a peculiar smell: a wet, thick, and bitter smell, thoroughly unpleasant. He couldn't help it: he glanced up at the man beside him. There was nothing strange about the fellow at all. A medium-sized man in a black suit, white shirt, a thin black tie. Pale face, a thin sharp nose, and close-set blue eyes. Thin blond hair in a widow's peak. As Honeywell glanced at him, the smell grew stronger—and Honeywell, without knowing why, became afraid. And just then the man looked up—looked back at Honeywell—looked him right in the eye. And he smiled. Honeywell wanted to turn away but he couldn't for a moment. For that moment, he was mesmerized by the sight of a deep, white, jagged scar that ran from the man's right eye, over his cheek, to the corner of his mouth. The scar seemed to transform the man's whole face—transform it from a nondescript, even pleasant, face, into something horrible. The man's smile seemed almost wicked, and suddenly an odd thought flashed into Honeywell's mind: he thought he knew what that smell was—that smell coming from the scarred man. It was corruption, he thought. It was the smell of evil.

Now, if this were a story, Honeywell would've gotten up and run away or screamed or something. But in real life, you know how it is: he was afraid of being rude, more than anything. He turned away and buried his face in his newspaper—though for the rest of the trip he felt sure the man was still staring at him, still grinning at him—and the smell: he thought the smell would choke him if that ride didn't end soon.

After what seemed a lifetime, the train pulled into the station. Honeywell got off and hurried away through the crowd, leaving the scarred man behind him. He went to work and buried himself in his books and figures. He didn't mention the incident to anyone. There had been no incident. And anyway, he had no one to tell. By lunchtime the whole thing seemed to him to have been the product of an overactive imagination.

As the day drew to a close, Honeywell found himself feeling nervous again. He was thinking about the ride home. He stayed longer in the office than usual. In fact, he stayed so long that, when he looked up from his work, he noticed that the building was empty. He sat at his desk, staring out the door of his cubicle on a small section of deserted hallway. Deserted—and silent. So silent that when he heard hollow, echoing footsteps approaching, he gasped. He sat rigid. The footsteps drew closer. And finally, a cleaning woman wandered past. Honeywell seized his briefcase, stood from his desk, and walked swiftly out of the building and into the street.

When he reached the train station, he saw that the rush-hour crowds had thinned out almost to nothing. Honeywell scanned the faces of the remaining commuters carefully as he walked to his train. When he boarded, he made a point of sitting next to another man, though there were still some seats left empty.

All of these precautions, at any rate, were unnecessary. There was no sign of the scarred man.

Honeywell's house was in a pleasantly wooded part of town about ten miles from where the train let him off. He always left his car nearby, so when he arrived in his home station, he went to the car at once and headed off. It was full dark by then, and his drive took him along a curving, unlighted road. He was still a little nervy, and he was in a hurry to get home.

He was about halfway there when it came to him again: that smell, that man's smell. It filled the car, growing stronger and stronger. Honeywell was terrified. He turned his eyes to the rearview mirror, fully expecting the scarred face to appear there like something in a horror movie. He even cast a glance into the backseat. But it was empty. There was only the smell, filling the car, nauseating.

Honeywell rolled down the window. He stepped on the gas. His tires screamed as they took the curves on the road home. By the time his own driveway appeared before him, he was panting, breathing through his mouth, that is, so he wouldn't smell anymore. He came to the driveway. He spun the wheel. The car turned and his headlights swept the darkened drive.

And for one instant, he saw a figure, a silhouette, captured in the beams.

And then the beams passed on and he could see nothing there but the darkness.

Honeywell backed the car up, swept the lights over the spot again. Nothing. But the figure had been there, he was sure of it. He locked all the doors of his car and sat inside, the lights on, the engine on, staring at the door of his house: judging the distance.

Anyone who had been looking on that evening would've then seen a rather comic sight: a mild, gray little man, clutching a briefcase, racing across his own lawn to his own door as if demons were chasing him. When Honeywell got inside, he immediately turned on all the lights. Turned on the TV for company, the radio for good measure. Up until then he had always been very regular in his habits, but tonight his bedtime came and went and he was still seated in his bedroom easy chair, staring at the television. It was past midnight before he could bring himself to go to bed. Even then, he left the TV on and fell asleep to the sound of it.

The tone of the test pattern woke him. The tone—and the smell. His eyes shot open and he sat up in bed—relieved at first to see that dawn was breaking, then sickened to notice that that odor was everywhere in the room. He sat there with the covers clutched to his chin, with all his senses alert. There was no one in the room, and he could hear no one moving in the house. As the light rose outside, Honeywell told himself that, somehow, that man's smell had gotten all over him. That it was coming from him now.

He got up. And he saw the muddy print of a man's shoe on the floor. On the floor right beside his bed, as if someone had been standing over him.

John Honeywell washed and shaved and dressed as fast as he could, and left the house immediately. It was about five-thirty in the morning when he reached the train station. The place was deserted. The ticket office was closed. Honeywell didn't even know when the first train would arrive. He just stood on the empty platform, clutching his briefcase, staring at the tracks, feeling his heart race and thinking over and over again: *What will I do? What will I do? What will I do?*

Then he heard footsteps. They were coming from the covered bridge that went across the tracks. He looked up. The bridge was covered with a kind of pebbled, plastic sheeting, and Honeywell could see the dark figure of a man crossing slowly to his platform. He watched, motionless, as the figure moved to the stairs at the near end. He saw a man's legs begin to descend the stairs. Then his body came into view. And then his face.

It was the scarred man. Coming down the stairs, quietly—inevitably. Honeywell knew there was no sense running or calling out or trying to hide. He could only stand there, as the smell grew thicker, as his heart beat faster—as the scarred man came on, down on the platform now, walking toward him, closer and closer until the smell of him was overpowering and Honeywell's vision was filled with that mild pleasant smile of his, that smile twisted by his scar into something secret and evil. And the man leaned down to Honeywell, so that Honeywell could hardly breathe.

And in a sweet, confidential whisper, the man said: "You."

And Honeywell killed him.

He dropped his briefcase and wrapped his hands around the man's throat and squeezed and squeezed until the man's feet left the ground and he dangled in Honeywell's grip like a rag doll. Honeywell watched, fascinated, as his hands closed tighter with a strength he didn't know he had, as the man's twisted face turned red, then purple, then white, and his tongue fell from his mouth and dangled there as his feet were dangling.

And when the first commuters arrived, they found Honeywell, still there, laughing and laughing, over the mangled body of a woman.

Well, this is where my friend Sinclair comes into it. The police were thrilled to have the Chicago Strangler case solved, but Sinclair was disturbed by the fact that Honeywell was only charged with one of the eight murders: the last one. Sinclair followed the trial closely, of course. He saw Honeywell's lawyers try to plead their insanity case while saddled with a client who clearly refused to testify. He saw the jury return the only verdict they could—and finally, inevitably, he saw the sentence lowered on the silent, drab little man at the defense table: Death in the electric chair.

A few years later, Sinclair managed to arrange an interview with Honeywell and met him for the first time on Death Row. That first meeting made Sinclair come back again—and again. Over a period of time, he gained the little man's confidence and, at last, Honeywell told him the story I've just told you: It hadn't come out at the trial. The story convinced Sinclair of two things: that Honeywell was, in fact, the Chicago Strangler, and that he was, in fact, insane. He began to lobby in his column for the commutation of Honeywell's sentence, and Honeywell began to regard him as his only friend. So when Sinclair finally lost the good fight, Honeywell offered him the one gesture of friendship he had left: he invited him to witness his execution.

Sinclair was there, then, when they led Honeywell into that awful room. The little bookkeeper looked drabber than ever in his death clothes. As the guards strapped him in to the electric chair, his eyes darted everywhere as if he were trying to record every impression he could of the last of sweet, terrible life. And then they brought out the hood to put over his head. And Sinclair, looking on through a window, saw a movement behind a partition on the far end of the room. It was the executioner's hand reaching for the switch. Honeywell saw it, too, and he turned toward the motion—saw the man hidden from Sinclair's view—and suddenly shrieked:

"Him! There he is! It's him! It's him!"

The guards had to struggle to pull the hood down over his head. They backed away quickly from the thrashing figure. Then the switch came down. And Honeywell died screaming.

Now, Sinclair could have dismissed even this as madness, if he hadn't attended Honeywell's funeral. Because there, at the graveyard—

"Stop it!"

A glass shattered.

Susannah had leapt to her feet, the brandy snifter falling from her hand. Even in the firelight I could see that the blood had drained completely from her face. She was white. She stood there, looking around at us wildly, her hand at her mouth, her fingers dancing over her lips. Finally her eyes came to rest on me. She stared at me as if I were something risen from the grave.

"What are you doing to me?" she said. Her voice was shrill. "What are you trying to do to me?"

"Susannah!" I was on my feet too. We all were. Kate and Kelly and Angela crowded in around Susannah while Charlie and I looked at each other helplessly.

Susannah began to cry, to sob, her head against Kate's shoulder.

"Make him stop," she kept saying—she said it over and over. "Make him stop it."

Angela turned to me. "Jackass, you frightened her."

I said: "I . . ."

"Look at her, she's terrified."

"I didn't mean . . . It was just . . ." I stepped forward—and Susannah recoiled from me into the arms of her friends.

"Stay away from me!" she said. She was sobbing hysterically now. "Keep him away from me!"

"It was only a story," I said. "I made it up. It doesn't even make any sense. There's no Sinclair, no Honeywell. It's all a story."

Susannah eyed me, trembling. "You stay away from me," she said.

Kate said: "Idiot!" And then showed me her back. "Come on, Sue, we'll take you upstairs," she said.

I looked on, helpless, stammering, as the three women led Susannah away. I could still hear her sobbing when they shut the bedroom door.

Chapter six

"Man, you sure know how to tell a ghost story," said Charlie Rose.

"Shut up, goddamnit, Charlie," I said. "Let me think."

We were both lying on our beds, dressed, smoking cigarettes, staring at the ceiling.

Charlie said: " 'It was theee scaaaarrred maaaan . . .' You were great."

"Shut up. Jesus." I shook my head. "She wouldn't even let me touch her."

"Why should she let you touch her?" I didn't answer him. He sighed. "I guess it is a pretty shitty way to end Christmas."

"Oh well, hell," I said bitterly, "I could've guessed that would happen. That was written."

"Nothing is written," said Charlie. He pointed to his forehead. "Except up here."

"Great. What is that—Zen?"

"Peter O'Toole in *Lawrence of Arabia.*"

"Great."

I watched the smoke drift from my cigarette toward the ceiling: tangled spirals spreading out into a white mass.

"What am I gonna do?" I said.

"Why do you have to do anything?"

"Would you stop it? She wouldn't even let me touch her."

Charlie looked across the room at me. "I'm serious," he said. "Why do you have to do anything? So she's a screwed up little burbie, that's the way they grow them out here. It's her problem. Say you're sorry." He took a drag on his cigarette. "Then start looking for another job."

"Oh Christ," I said, "I hadn't thought of that."

"See: I can be helpful."

"It doesn't matter. I don't care about the goddamned job."

There was a long silence. Then I heard Charlie say quietly: "I know."

"What?"

"And I know what you think, man. You think this is what it is."

"What are you talking about?"

"You think it's like snow and Christmas and giggling virgins."

"Leave me alone."

"I grew up in the suburbs, man. I grew up here."

I turned on him fiercely. "Well, I didn't."

"Yeah," he said. "I know."

"You don't understand, Charlie."

"I understand, North, I understand."

"Damn it," I said. "Damn it, what am I gonna do?"

He stared up at the ceiling. He said: "Go home, little brother. Go home where you belong."

We lay together in silence then, smoking our cigarettes down, starting on others. After a while, Angela poked her head in through the door. I sat up.

"How is she?"

"She's all right. She's asleep."

Charlie snorted. "How many Valium did that take?"

"Shut up, Charlie," Angela said.

"Shut up, Charlie, shut up, Charlie. Gonna change my name to Shutupcharlie."

"What happened?" I said.

Angela came in and leaned against the door: a long figure in a red sweater over green leggings. She shrugged.

"You scared her, lover. Your story scared her. Maybe you missed your calling. Maybe Stephen King would be interested in a collaboration."

"Wonderful. I'll probably need the work."

Angela looked at me—glared a little, I thought. "I doubt it."

I moaned. "Oh God, Angela. I made it up, damn it. Maybe they never even had the electric chair in Illinois. I don't know. I made it all up."

Angela wasn't glaring at me anymore. She just gazed at me, kind of sadly, kind of wearily. "Tell her in the morning," she said. "She'll feel better in the morning, tell her then."

I nodded, sighing.

"Merry Christmas, guys," she said.

"Ho, ho, ho," said Charlie.

In the morning Susannah was gone. I woke up at seven-thirty, and she and her friends were just driving away. McGill was standing in the doorway waving. He seemed a little puzzled by his daughter's sudden departure, but that was all. She hadn't told him anything. She hadn't gotten me in trouble with the boss. Later that afternoon McGill and I parted on good terms and I went back to the city to spend the rest of the holiday.

Back home, where I belonged.

Chapter seven

On New Year's Eve I met a girl named Julie. A model of some sort, I never did get it quite straight. She had a great figure, though. And masses of brown curls. She talked a lot but she was always game for something. The weather was bad all that month, and we were thrown together too much indoors. It ended with a hell of a fight.

By then it was mid-February, and everyone on St. Mark's Place—everyone in the city, I guess—was feeling tired of the winter. We threw parties—lots of parties. It seemed to be the only thing to do. There were a lot of smoky rooms filled with people talking, dancing, impelled toward each other by the threat of the cold beyond the walls. There was a lot of loud music battering at the windows while the rain and snow battered back. There were a lot of close encounters, face to face. In the smoky rooms, the way a woman did her eyes, or the color of her eyes, the color of her lipstick or the way her lips moved as she was talking, the curve of her cheek or her nose, or the lines of her body falling away under the line of my gaze —and sometimes all of it at once—would come to me intensely. I'd be talking about art or politics or MTV and suddenly my mind would be stumbling in a haze of need, suddenly the whole weight of the naked winter would be pressing in around me, and I'd be staring at her, whoever she was, and deducing all the warmth of her from the clues of her attractions, and imagining the desolation of the cold night without her. That was the winter, I remember, when the touch of a woman's body in the dark had an even rarer pleasure for me than usual, a special power. It rained and snowed so damned much, and the streets were all so gray and dying-like, that it would seem to me as if the breasts of her and the flow of her belly and the warm inside of her were all there was between me and the brink of something barren and unbearable.

I wasn't at home a whole lot. I hardly saw Charlie or Angela at all. I missed them, but it seemed to me the smart money was on moving fast. McGill was getting ready for his trip to South America, and I was working the street again, finagling my way into the drug scene to get him the names of some suppliers. It was just what I wanted: another world. Crack dens in the dead of night. Everything smoky and dizzy and down. Moving fast, thinking fast, living in the crazy eyes of rocked-out fiends tumbling and tumbling from their nests in the high trees. Home again to the St. Mark's parties, and the warm bodies in cold apartments, and the sleeplessness and the streets again, and the sense of distance from everyone.

Then, after a while, McGill was gone. He took me out to dinner at Doobie's the night before his flight. We sat at a little table by the window, looking out on bleakness and Bleecker Street, the drab Village theaters and poster shops in the drab winter rain.

Mostly, I think, he talked about the book. He congratulated me on my research. He outlined his plans. Told me to take it easy for the month he was away. I don't know what he said. I was hardly listening.

So it seemed to me as if it came out of nowhere: "Tell me something, North. Did anything happen between you and Susannah?"

I didn't move. It was the first time he'd mentioned her since Christmas.

"Like what?" I said.

He spread his hands. "I'm not trying to pry, old friend," he said. "No kidding, I'm not. I just want to know: Did you two get along all right?"

"Sure," I said. "Sure we did. She's a grand girl." He was silent. I couldn't help but ask: "Why, has she said anything?"

"No, no, no. Nothing like that. I just want to . . . I mean, there was nothing . . . ?"

I raised my wineglass in front of my mouth. "What do you want to know, Carl?"

He grinned tightly. He hissed through the grin and shook his head.

"I see I've fucked this up," he said. He rubbed his hand over the sharp stubble on his chin. I watched him as he wrestled with something deep down in his narrowed eyes. "There are things I have to tell you," he said. "Should've told you before." He shook his head again. "Shit."

"Look—"

He held up his hand.

"There're things about Susannah. About Susannah, but the thing is, North—"

"Forget it," I said. I glanced at my watch. "Lookit: it's late. You've got a plane to catch in the morning. Whatever it is has waited till now, it can wait till you get back."

McGill stared at me a long time. But I didn't back down; I stared back. Finally he lowered his eyes to the table, and when he raised them again, they were clear.

"Sure," he said. "It's waited till now, it can wait another month."

"Sure," I said.

"I mean, it's been a nice dinner."

"That's right."

"Sure."

So he was gone, and I was moving fast again through the dead of winter and the life of lovers, and the cold was at the windows, but I paid it no mind.

Then one day, a Saturday at the beginning of March, it stopped. An oversight on my part: I found myself with nothing to do. Stupid of me. There was plenty of rocking going on all over, and plenty of places I'd've been welcome if I'd dropped in. But somehow, by the time I got around to it, it seemed like too much of an effort. I decided to stop in at Ingmar's, have some dinner, and let it be.

The café was crowded, smoky, noisy. A band was playing jazz at the front of the room. A small, nervous flutter had been rising in my stomach. It died away as I found a seat in the crush.

Peter came to my table. I ordered a scotch before dinner. I sat and listened to the band. I felt good—warm—with the shoulders and the conversation and the music all pressing in around me. Peter came back. I ordered another scotch. I caught the eye of a woman across the room, but then turned away. Tonight, as I say, it seemed too much trouble.

So I sat and I listened to the band and I had another scotch, and I thought of the night on the street through the window behind me and I ordered another. At some point the music began swirling in my brain like finger paints and I grew woozy. Peter leaned over me and whispered in my ear.

"North, you don't drink that much, remember?"

"Oh yeah," I said, "I must've misplaced my personality. Calls for a drink."

"North, it's midnight . . ."

"What're you, my watch?"

He shook his head at me. "North . . ." he said. "What's happened to you, man?" And he wove away from me between the bodies.

So I had another just to show him who was boss, and then decided I knew when I wasn't wanted. I lumbered to my feet, struggled into my jacket. I stood still for a moment and took a long look at the dull dark outside. Then I went to the door and pushed my way out.

I started walking. Going home. Watching the pavement. Drunk. Watching my feet moving. Fast, fast, fast they were moving. Oh yes. I was drunk. No doubt about it. Every grain in the concrete of the sidewalk seemed chiseled by the street-lights into the stonework of reality. Every smell—the garbage, and the old rain, and the exhaust of passing taxis—seemed viscous in my nostrils. Every inch of my face seemed alive to the stinging cold. Drunk I was. Drunk. Indubitably.

I stopped. Walking, I mean. I stopped and looked around. I was in the East Village somewhere. I was standing in front of a seedy bar; a green box of a place with black windows. I peered at my feet reproachfully.

"I thought you were going home," I said to them. There was no reply. They carried me inside.

I heard her voice as I stepped into the yellow darkness of the place. It came to me like a bright idea. It throbbed over the empty tables. Down the sodden line of stubble-headed leather-bellies leaning their elbows against the brass rail of the bar. I was in McCullough's. Hell, I knew that. It was the dive where Angela sang sometimes. Sure. There she was, up on the stage, under the spotlight, far away at the other end of the room. I stationed myself at the rail. I ordered a beer. I drank and I watched her.

Oh man, that girl could rock. Oh man, she rocked that night. Rocked it all, all out to the staring emptiness. Some willowy splash of beard was trampolining half mad with his guitar behind her. A wild drummer girl, her hair thrashing, was thrashing the drums with machine-gun speed. And Angela rocked on. Her long body waved like a stream of cigarette smoke and that wicked little face of hers was as wet and hazy as it is when she makes love.

I thought about that. I stared in my beer awhile. I thought about it some more and grew melancholy. I looked at my watch. It was nearly two. She was off at two. I waited.

The music stopped suddenly. The set was done. Angela took a long step with her long legs and came down off the stage. She walked to the bar, leaned in next to me and ordered a beer. I stared at her. She put her arm around my shoulders. She put her face close to mine.

"Ooh, you smell good. Like liquor," she said.

"There's a perfectly good explanation for that."

"You come here for the ambience or to listen to me sing?"

"What is ambience, anyway?"

"It's what they take you away in if you use long words in here." I laughed. Angela kissed me. "It's good to see you, North," she said. "Where the hell have you been?"

We walked back to her place together. We held hands, and when I made her laugh, she leaned against me. I kissed her hair. Her long black hair. It smelled of smoke and shampoo.

She had a studio in a Chelsea brownstone. Two flights up. Sparkling clean and neat. Brick walls and a view of the drunk lying in the gutter below. There was a sofa that folded out into a bed. There were bookcases. There were lots of black and white photos of tree branches and staring faces: I think she got them free at the lab where she worked.

We dropped our jackets on the couch, and I sat down next to them while she went into the kitchen.

"You have a choice," she called to me. "Coffee or get out."

"I'll take it black," I said.

I turned on the tube while I waited. An old movie was on. *Wuthering Heights.* I stared at it.

"Why don't you get cable?" I said.

Angela came in with the coffee. "What? Oh, for Christ's sake, North, turn that off."

She put the mugs on the coffee table. She killed the set with a flick of her wrist. She sat down next to me.

"What are you trying to do to yourself?" she said.

"I haven't decided."

She didn't answer. She looked at me. I watched her breathing under her black sweater. She watched me watch her. My eyes ran down to her lap. She watched me.

"Oh hell," I said. And I reached for her. I took her face in my hands, brought her to me, kissed her for a long time.

"Unfair," she whispered to me. "Definitely unfair."

I kissed her. She came into my arms. I kissed her again, my hands moving over her. She felt warm and soft inside that sweater.

"Let me go," she whispered.

"No."

I kissed her. She pulled away from me.

"Come back," I said.

"No."

We regarded each other across a small wilderness of sofa. Then Angela sighed and turned away. She got to her feet. There was a leather director's chair against the wall to my right. She wandered over to it and slumped into it, her legs stretched out in front of her.

"Toss me a cigarette," she said.

I dug the pack out of her coat pocket, took one for myself, and tossed the rest. I smoked and waited.

"I'm not going to do this, North," she said finally. "Neither are you."

"Why not?"

"You're not drunk enough."

"That's an insult. I'm plenty drunk."

"You're drunk enough about Charlie maybe, but you're not drunk enough to use me."

"Give me a chance."

She snorted. "I mean it, North. I don't do stand-in work."

I snorted back at her. I stood up and went to the window, looked down at the drunk. I blew smoke against the pane.

"What is this?" I said. "Is this the scene where you sacrifice your feelings and send me away for my own good?"

"Yes."

"I saw that in a movie once."

"Good for you."

"More than once."

"Then you ought to have it down pat."

"You're funny," I said.

I heard her shift in the chair behind me. I saw her shadow rise and move toward me on the glass.

"North," she said. She was standing at my shoulder. "You know I could never tell you to go."

"I know."

"So just get out, okay?"

I gazed at her.

"Like, now," she said.

"What for? You're not gonna cry, are you?"

"Goddamn it."

"Okay." I went to the door. I held up my hand to her.

"Hey, North," she said. Her voice broke.

"Yo."

"Just do the whole goddamned lower end of Manhattan a favor, okay? Go get yourself the girl you love."

Sometime after first light, Charlie came home, pried me from the toilet bowl, and put me to bed. I awoke that afternoon in a philosophical mood. Should I drink a gallon of orange juice, I asked myself, or should I rip my face off with a rake? I couldn't say. I couldn't say anything. I could barely move. But I did. I got up. I shaved. I puked. I drank the juice. I showered, took some aspirin, put myself together. Then I went into the front room and woke up Charlie.

"Yo, Charlie," I said.

The lump under the sheet moved.

I said: "I tried to make your woman last night."

"*Bâtarde,*" he muttered. "Though you fly to the ends of the earth, you cannot escape my vengeance."

The sheet fluttered gently with his snores.

"Yo," I said. "I'm leaving. I'll be back tonight. If I'm not back tonight, I'll be back another night. I may never be back. Take my messages."

The sheet shifted again. Slowly, Charlie peeked out. He sat up, rubbing his face. He looked around him. "What day is this?" he said.

"Sunday. March sixth."

He fell back in bed. "Aw, shit," he said, "I had the fifteenth."

"What?"

"We had a pool on how long you'd hold out." He pulled the sheet up, vanished beneath it.

Chapter eight

I walked down to the garage on Bleecker Street. It was a crummy day. It had rained in the early morning, and now the sky just hung there, undecided. As I walked, the clouds opened and splattered a gout of rain on me, then settled in to drench me slowly with a steady drizzle. My soaked sneaker laces lashed the cuffs of my jeans as I walked, until my cuffs were wet through and my shins were clammy. My hair dripped on my forehead. My forehead throbbed. And what if she didn't want me? It was a crummy day.

I got out the company car: an ancient, yellow Mustang. The Sunday afternoon traffic was sparse and I made it out of town without a fight. I bounced up the Bruckner through the Bronx with the gray sky all around me and the gray skyline stretching out in all directions. I felt like the ashy center of it. I had a knot in my stomach the size of a fist.

It was about four when I got started, and I figured I had about four hours of driving ahead of me. For a while, the weather held. It drizzled and then the drizzle died, and then it drizzled again. Soon I was in Westchester with the willows weeping by the roadside and the wet naked hills of late winter trees rising and falling away into a low mist. The traffic stayed light. Only the trucks were rolling in my direction. They thundered by me, churning up the fallen rain, spraying it over my windshield. I squinted through the mess and cursed as the wipers swept it away.

I turned on the radio, full blast. Springsteen and Madonna and Prince. There was a downpour as I crossed over the county line, and I traveled through Putnam at about thirty-five, my nose glued to the glass. As the sun went down, the clouds broke a little on patches of deepening blue. The hills, I saw, were turning muzzy. The mist was spreading over them, snaking into the lowlands.

So the driving was easier for a time. I noticed the knot in my stomach hadn't gone away. I noticed it was bigger now. Then they played an old Jim Croce tune—"Operator"—on the radio.

"Damn it," I said. But I didn't turn it off.

I glanced up into the rearview mirror at my own eyes.

"Goddamnit," I said.

I don't remember when the song ended. I was just aware all at once that the beat was harder and the music wild. The highway rose steadily between the hills. The mist was beginning to creep across it. Sheets and tendrils of it wafted over the running white line. It was getting dark. I put my headlights on and the beams lay blandly in the mist.

And it got darker. And the mist became a fog. Yellow and

thick, it closed in, until the headlight beams were bouncing off it crazily. Now the trucks came up behind me out of nowhere. There'd be an angry roar, then the blank gray wall of the thing sweeping by me, then the suction of it rocking me as I pushed forward, and finally the great gust of rainwater and the blindness. The windshield wipers ticked and ticked. And then there was just the fog.

An hour went by, maybe more. I was going thirty, twenty sometimes. My throat was dry and tight, my stomach roiling. But that was just the effect of the hard driving. And anyway, maybe she would welcome me with open arms.

The sign for the Marysvale exit shot up out of the mist suddenly. The words on the green background were dazzling white in the beams. I rolled off the highway slowly. It was almost nine o'clock.

Now I was in an even deeper darkness on a winding road. The bare branches of maple trees hung over me, the thick trunks of oaks leaned down. The fog gave way in inches before my headlights, regrouping inches away into a solid mass.

Then, the way fog will, it parted. The road appeared, twisting before me. It was gleaming and black with rain. A brick wall lined the road, the drenched grass at the foot of it matted, the branches above it dark with rain. In the sky, I could see now, the clouds were racing fiercely over a gibbous moon.

I came to a gate in the wall. There was a plaque beside it: Marysvale College. I turned and drove through the gate onto a gravel drive. The fog closed in again. I could see it lying sullenly on a wide lawn. Through it I could make out the silhouettes of buildings arrayed in a half circle all around me. I drew nearer, and I saw the yellow lights of windows shining in the fog.

The gravel crunched and spat under my tires as I went

around a sharp curve. And all at once, a figure loomed out of the mist before me.

I hit the brake, hard. The car skidded, swerved, stopped. The figure spun around to me. A face shone suddenly in the headlights.

"Good Christ," I said.

My heart was hammering. I peered wildly through the windshield. The figure was gone.

But I'd seen him. I'd seen him.

It was the scarred man.

PART TWO

A newspaper story

Chapter nine

I jumped out of the car and went after him. I ran about ten steps, then pulled up short. There was nothing. No movement. Not a sound. I stood still with my heart going like a piston. I fought for breath as my eyes swept slowly over the campus yard.

The fog swayed and shifted. Black shadows of buildings and trees appeared and vanished in it. A light in a window blinked on; another died. And in the beams of the Mustang's head-lamps, the gossamer mist twisted and twined with the dark.

I breathed deeply once, trying to get calm, but my nerves were on the rack, stretched tight. I thought I heard a footstep on the gravel. I spun to face it. Then I thought I heard an engine starting down the drive and I swiveled the other way.

The Mustang's engine overrode any other sounds, and I wasn't sure what I'd heard. I wasn't sure what I'd seen. The night seemed barely real to me. I felt lost in it, confused.

I put my arm up against the headlights' glare and walked quickly back to the car. I reached into the Mustang and grabbed my keys. I killed the engine and the lights. The silence and darkness seemed to drop down over me like a blanket. I took a few slow steps along the drive. I paused again and listened hard.

I heard the motor scream before I saw the car. There were no lights. The fender only glinted once as it broke from the fog. Then there was just a roaring blackness plunging at me. I jumped. I hit the lawn and rolled. The car sped by, and its wake of gravel sprayed over me, biting into my skin. Lying in the wet grass, I looked over my shoulder. I saw the brake lights flash red as the car thudded off the drive to avoid the Mustang. I saw the red flash again as the car paused at the gate just before it turned and raced away.

Slowly, I stood. I rubbed my right arm. It ached with the force of the fall. I moved back onto the drive and stood staring after the car.

Again I heard the footstep on the gravel, closer this time.

I spun around. A white phantom drifted toward me out of the mist.

For a moment I could only stand watching it as it floated closer. It floated closer lazily. Then it raised its arm and drove a dagger down toward my chest.

I brought my crossed arms up in front of me, caught the falling wrist in the crux of them. The knife hovered before my eyes.

"Drop it, drop it, Susannah!" I shouted. "It's me."

I heard her cry out: "Michael!"

I saw the knife slip from her fingers and tumble through the air. I heard the clink of it as it hit the gravel. I released her wrist and her hands fluttered out at me, touching my face, running up through my hair, grabbing at my collar. Her face was gray. Her mouth hung open. She gibbered at me breathlessly.

"I saw him. Michael, I saw him, I saw him." She kept saying it over and over.

I fought her hands off, grabbed her by the shoulders.

I shouted at her: "You can't see him. I made him up. You can't see him. I invented him."

I was in no great shape myself.

Susannah looked up at me as if I had struck her.

"Michael?" she said. Her voice sounded small and hurt.

Still gripping her shoulders, I drew a long breath. I fought for control as she stared at me. Then I nodded and pulled her against my chest. I wrapped my arms around her and held her fast.

"I saw him too," I said.

"Thank God," said Susannah, and started sobbing.

We stayed like that a long time.

Then I said: "Aren't you cold?"

She was wearing only a nightgown.

"I don't know," she said.

My arm around her shoulder, I took her to the Mustang. I opened the passenger door and helped her in. She was trembling. Her hands were clasped under her chin.

"Is college always like this?"

She didn't laugh. "I don't know," she said.

I closed the door, walked around, and got behind the wheel.

I turned on the engine. I turned on the lights. But for a few seconds I could do nothing but stare at the spot where I had seen him.

I shook my head. "But I made him up," I whispered.

And Susannah's whisper answered me out of the darkness.

"No," she said. "No, you didn't. I dreamed him."

Chapter ten

"I've dreamed about him for a long time," she said. "The first week I got here—three years ago—that's when it started."

We were in her dormitory room. She was sitting across from me in an old, stuffed easy chair, a tan one. Her legs were tucked up under her. Her gaze was trained on empty space.

I could hardly bear to look at her. I kept thinking about her laughing as she burst through the door into her father's house. I kept thinking about her trudging through the snow in front of me. I kept thinking about her beneath me with the Christmas lights in her eyes. I kept thinking about her body, flushed and electric and alive.

Her cheeks were ashen now. Her lips were white. Her eyes—

it was as if someone had shut off the power in them. Her frame seemed sunken in on itself. Her voice trembled as she spoke, and her hands fluttered together beneath her chin or hugged her shoulders tightly.

"Do you understand what I'm telling you?" she said. "Before you ever told your story, he was in my dreams. My dream, I should say. There's just the one, again and again."

I nodded. I was sitting at her desk, across from her in the corner by the window. It was a small desk. There were notebooks stacked neatly on it. There was a Charlie Brown mug filled with pencils. There was one of those little Tensor lamps bent like a mantis over a picture of her father in a standing frame.

I was straddling the wooden chair, my eyes wandering, avoiding her. I saw the bed against the wall to the right of me: a single bed with a flowery spread on it. Above the bed, a poster was tacked into the wall: Grandma Moses, a winter scene. On the wall above Susannah was a framed print of a Grant Wood countryside. There was a dresser against the wall to my left. It had makeup and perfumes and a mirror on top of it. Beside it was the closet door. And behind me, two teddy bears were sitting on the window seat. They were looking out the window at the drive and the yard.

Susannah said: "I'm in a small space. It's always the same in the dream. I'm sitting in a small space in the dark. Curled up in there. Locked in there. I can't get out. The only thing is: someone's arms are around me. I feel that. It comforts me, the warmth of someone's arms. But we're very close together and I can't move, and I can feel our breaths—my breath and the breath of the person holding me—I can feel the warmth of our breaths because the space we're in is so small."

Her voice was trembling. She had to swallow hard to go on.

She said: "So, we're huddled there together, the two of us.

And we're both so weak. And we're so afraid . . . Afraid of the dark and the small place . . . But we can't get out of there. We can't . . ."

She blinked and brought her gaze out of the emptiness. She looked at me. Her eyes were pleading with me.

"We can't leave," she said to me, "because *he's* out there. We can hear him. We can hear his footsteps, Michael. He's looking for us. He's calling us. We can hear him calling. We can't . . . We can't hear what he's saying but he's calling us the way people call to children. He's . . . beckoning us. He's . . . he's trying to tease us into coming out. He's calling . . . sweetly." She shivered and looked away again.

After a moment she went on—went on unsteadily, slowly finding her way. "We hear . . . we hear . . . his footsteps growing louder, outside the dark place. He's coming closer . . . looking for us everywhere. And all I can see is the dark, and I can feel my breath and my knees pushed up almost against my chest because it's so small in there. I'm so afraid, I'm so afraid of the dark. And then . . . And then his footsteps . . . are right outside. They're moving right outside. And . . . and we can hear him calling." She raised her chin. Her voice changed slightly. It became light and beckoning. "Come out," she whispered, "come out now, come out." She swallowed again, shivered again, clasped her shoulders with her hands again. She lowered her eyes.

"And I'm so scared of the dark that I almost want to go out to him," she said. "I just think . . . anything would be better than waiting here like this." She shook her head to fight off tears. Her red hair flashed back and forth at me. "But I can't go out. The arms . . . the arms around me, they're holding onto me so tightly, protecting me. They keep me from opening the door. And then . . ."

She lifted her face. Her eyes were glistening. "And then the footsteps stop. Just outside. Right next to where we are, they stop, and we can feel him standing there . . . the dark and the waiting . . . I can barely stand it . . . and suddenly . . ." She closed her eyes. Two tears fell from under the lashes and rolled down her cheeks. Susannah drew a deep breath and let the words flow out with it. "Suddenly there's a burst of light . . . a burst of light and he's there: the scarred man. He's standing over us. He's terrible. I try to get away. I try to break away from the arms that are holding me. And then . . . all at once . . . I realize that the person holding me . . . he isn't holding me to protect me. *He's holding me for him!* He's keeping me there for him. And I struggle and struggle, but I can't break free. And I turn to see who it is, who's holding me . . . and it's Death, Michael. It's . . . Death . . . grinning at me . . . It'll never let me go." She opened her eyes. One hand fluttered up to her cheeks, brushed the tears away. "It's Death," she said softly, "holding me there for the scarred man."

She was finished. She sat with her hands clasped together between her knees. She stared at the floor, like a child in the principal's office.

"Susannah," I heard myself say hoarsely. "Susannah, look at you, what's happened to you?"

She laughed. I winced at the sound of it. She brought her hands up and pressed the heels into her forehead. "I don't know, I don't . . ." Her hands slid down over her face. "I don't know," she said. "I used to be so happy."

She began to cry again. It shook her body violently. Her body which already seemed so frail. I went to her and sat down on the chair arm. I held her against my side.

"You were fine until I told that story," I said.

I felt her nod. She said: "Suddenly, I just thought: it's all true. It's all real. *He's* real. He's real, and he's coming to get me."

"Oh Jesus, Sue."

"I know, I know. I even knew I was going crazy, but I couldn't make it stop. I couldn't make it stop. I started to have the dream every night. Every night, I lay awake, trying not to sleep, praying it wouldn't come. I couldn't sleep at all after a while. I couldn't eat. . . ."

"Why didn't you tell Kelly? Or Kate?" I asked.

"Because I knew . . . I knew I was going crazy, and I . . . I couldn't . . . I . . . They'll hardly talk to me anymore." She laughed and sobbed at once. "They think I'm into drugs."

"Why didn't you talk to a counselor?" I said. "Why didn't you call your father? Why didn't—"

Her hands shot up swiftly, viciously, pushing me back. Her face, blotched with crying, twisted, and she hissed out: "Why didn't you come? Why didn't you come to me? Where *were* you, Michael?"

I stood up, averting my eyes.

She whispered: "I kept thinking you would."

I couldn't face her. I went to the window. My fists were clenched at my sides. I stood with my head down, peering up from under my brows at the dark glass. I ran my hand up through my hair.

"You were so afraid of me," I said. "I thought . . . I didn't know if . . ."

"Didn't you know you could always come to me?"

"Ah God, God," I whispered. I had. I'd known.

I braced my fingertips against the window seat. I leaned toward the pane, toward my own reflection: a fragmentary image with night in its empty spaces. Susannah's voice followed me.

"You were the only one I ever would have told," she said. "About the dream, and how it was all real, and how he was coming to get me . . . I wanted to tell. I wanted . . . I was so afraid. But I couldn't stand . . ." I nodded at the window. I knew what she was going to say. "I couldn't stand for Daddy to know I'd gone crazy." She sniffled. She was fighting for her grip. "I would've killed myself before that."

"The knife," I said. I could hardly get the words out.

"I was only holding it."

"Oh man, oh man, oh man."

"It's just a steak knife, I . . . I brought it up from the cafeteria. I was just holding it, really, Michael. Standing where you are, right by the window . . . I was looking . . ."

"For him."

"No. No. For you."

"Oh . . ."

"I guess I was still hoping you'd come at the last . . ." She didn't finish it. "Otherwise," she went on, "I wouldn't even have seen him. He was standing back in the shadows, but I was looking so hard for you I turned out the lights in here and . . . I recognized him right away." Her voice was steadier now. "I was almost glad. He was here. Finally."

"Oh man," I said.

"I took the knife and ran outside. I thought: At least I won't die trapped . . . in the dark. . . . Just sitting there, scared. Just waiting."

I turned around to face her. She was looking at me directly. She'd gotten it out of her finally. Some of it, anyway. There was something alive now in her eyes. Her lips were taut, her fist was raised and clenched as if she were holding the knife again.

I laughed.

"You just charged out there with the knife," I said.

She smiled at me a little.

"Way to go," I said. "Bad, bad Sue."

She smiled and nodded. In one quick movement, then, she

stood up and held her hands out to me. I went to her, took hold. She was trembling.

"Who is he, Michael?" she whispered.

"He's just—"

"How could he be there?"

"He's just a man."

"How can he . . . ?"

"He's just a man, Sue. He has to be."

"I dreamed him. You—"

"Ssh, Susannah."

"You made him up."

"It will be all right."

"Who says, who says? Why will it? Why will it be?"

"Because it will, I know it. It's written," I said. "It's in the Big Book. All right? All right?"

The harshness of my voice stopped her. She studied my face, unblinking.

"Yes," she said then. "All right."

That was all. I don't know whether she believed me or not. I don't know whether I believed me. I could not keep my thoughts straight. I was all fog and reeling. I held her hands and I looked at her for a long time and she looked at me. When I finally did approach her, I approached her slowly. When I finally kissed her, I kissed her gently. I was afraid she would break at first, she looked so fragile. But when I kissed her, I felt her rich lips give and hold, and she felt me, and then we were on each other. We tumbled to the bed together. We undressed each other with hands like claws. And when, finally, I was over her, in her; when, finally, she was crying out to me and thrashing on the flowered bedspread—then I was not confused anymore. Then I knew for certain: I loved her. I loved her, and I told her so, again and again.

Chapter eleven

When I woke up, I heard Susannah singing. I opened my eyes.

She was sitting on the windowsill, gazing out on a sunny day, blue sky. She was wearing my shirt; she was lost and small in it. Her red hair was tousled. Her expression was sad and far away.

She was singing the Cyndi Lauper cut: "Time After Time." She had a thin, sweet voice that trembled on the high notes.

I stirred and she turned to me. She tilted her head. Her lips curled up into that silly smile that made all her features lopsided. For a moment I saw the face I remembered, the Christmas face.

"The fog's gone," she said.

I sat up, ran a hand up through my hair. I looked around the room. "I don't think I'm in Kansas anymore."

She laughed. "Doof."

"What time is it?"

"Eight. We slept almost nine hours." This last she said so happily, it made my heart hurt. I wondered how long it'd been since she'd slept three hours in a row.

I started to pull the covers off me. "I gotta get dressed," I said. "See if I can get to work before noon." Her smile faltered. Just a little. Just in her eyes. But it was enough to let me see that she was still afraid. I paused on the bed. "You're gonna come back with me, aren't you?" I said.

The smile returned at once. She slid down off the sill, came over to the bed and sat on the edge of it.

"Listen," I said. "I've really gotta go."

She reached out and touched my cheek with her fingertips. She leaned over and kissed me. Then she leaned over and kissed me again.

"Here's your shirt," she whispered. "What's your hurry?"

We drove down together in the Mustang. When we got back, I installed her in my apartment. Charlie was sleeping there, a white snoring lump beneath the sheet, a flash of hairy leg. Susannah looked down upon him kindly, like an old friend. I left them to each other.

I walked down to Washington Square, glad to be out in the good weather. Glad to be alone to think things over.

But I couldn't think things over. My mind was racing.

The first shock of seeing him had not worn off. I could still see him: standing there in the fog, sprung to life from my own invention. I couldn't get around it, couldn't get it down to a manageable size where I could begin to make sense of it. Despite what I'd said to Susannah, I wasn't sure I ever would.

I strolled through the park slowly. The March air was cool, and clear for Manhattan, and the place was thick and colorful with the lunch-hour crowd. Mothers pushed their strollers, students carried their books, boys dipped and swirled through the empty fountains on their skateboards, and girls in black leather pointed their hair at the sky. Someone was selling Mickey Mouse balloons. Someone was playing guitar. Plenty of guys in green jackets were peddling crack at the entranceways and corners. Most of them greeted me. Most of them knew me by name. I was glad to be here with all of them.

By the time I got to the old white building across from the park's southeast corner, I wasn't thinking anything much at all. I rattled upstairs in the elevator, leaning against the wall with my eyes closed. When I walked through the office door, Marianne greeted me with a drab look. I plopped myself behind the desk across from her. I put my feet up. I toyed with a pencil. I stared aimlessly into space.

I thought of Susannah. I just couldn't focus on him. So I thought of Susannah instead. I thought of her as she'd been last night when we'd finally pumped and screamed and scratched the ghost of him out of our systems for a while. I thought of her head on my chest, the scent of her red hair. It made me think of Christmas again. It made me think of her laughing. Sledding down the hill with Kate and Kelly. How could they just have deserted her? Or had she forced them away? That must have been it. Slipping into solitude as she watched her old self slipping away, as she watched herself, helplessly, beaten into madness by a bad dream. Of the scarred man. My scarred man. I thought of her screaming: Stop it. Thought of the brandy glass slipping from her hand as I told the story I had made up. My fault. My fault. I had left her alone.

Left her there so he could latch on to her like a vampire, invade her dreams, suck the life from her. But, I told myself, there are no vampires. No goblins, no ghoulies. There are only people. How could he have been there in the fog like that?

Marianne looked up sharply as the pencil snapped in my hand.

"Who the hell is he?" I whispered.

But I could not focus on him.

I called home. Charlie answered groggily.

"This better be good or the whole fucking shop walks," he said.

"It's me."

"I'll kill you."

"Is she all right?"

There was a pause. Susannah came on.

"I'm all right," she said softly. "Let him sleep."

"Are you really all right?"

"Yes. Really."

"Put Charlie back on."

"There's a girl in here," Charlie said.

"Don't leave her alone."

"Over my sleeping body."

"Consider me reassured," I said, and hung up.

That was how the afternoon passed. It didn't pass quickly. I tried to work. I tried to think. I could do neither. I called home. I woke Charlie up. He told me Susannah was sleeping. I didn't call again.

At around four—around four hours after I'd come in—I got ready to leave.

"I'm getting out of here," I told Marianne.

"You'll be deeply missed," she said.

I started to straighten up my desk. I cursed, and stopped. I strode across the room and pulled back the door.

And a man was standing right before me, sudden as a specter.

Startled, I stepped back. But then I got my bearings. It was just a lean, easy figure: a guy around fifty. A thin face stroked with friendly wrinkles. A full crown of white hair.

He nodded and smiled at me, and came through the door. He took one hand from the pocket of his brown, zippered sweater and reached it out. I shook it, looking up at his face. Even with his relaxed stoop, he had two or three inches on me, must have been at least six-four. He had damp, gentle blue eyes, but they took in everything around him. They made a sweep of the room, pausing on Marianne for a moment like a benediction, before returning to me.

Jimmy Stewart, I thought.

"My name is Howard Marks," he said. He had a soft drawl, a rhythm to his speech like a porch swing's. "I'm looking for Carl McGill."

"He's away," I said. "He's in Peru. Can I help you? I'm his assistant, Michael North."

"Peru," he said. He tugged at his ear, smiling wryly at the floor. "Well, that certainly puts him out of reach. Will he be back anytime soon?"

"About two months."

Marks's chin lifted a little. Then he sighed, sagging. "Two months," he said. "Too late."

"Well, if it's important, I have a way of contacting him, but it's sure to take a while. A week, ten days. If you have the time . . ."

"Oh, I have the time, young man," said Howard Marks. "*I* have the time." He shook his head sorrowfully. Then, he said: "Well . . . thank you."

He turned for the door. Then he paused and looked up at me.

As he searched my features he drawled quietly: "But if he should happen to get in touch with you, tell him Nathan Jersey will die in the electric chair in ten days. Tell him the Turner case is finally over."

For another moment, he seemed to study me with those gentle eyes, and for that moment, I felt as if I were being unmasked. I thought he must hear my heart pounding.

Then he smiled again, sweetly, and stepped out into the hall. I heard the rattle of the elevator as it came and went. I shut the door.

"What the hell was that all about?" I said.

Marianne shrugged.

I went back to my desk and called American Express. I left a message for McGill at their Lima office as we had arranged. But he was probably deep in the jungle by now, where coca becomes cocaine. It was unlikely I'd hear from him within two weeks, let alone ten days.

When I was finished, I left. I hit the street in a hurry. I couldn't tell why but there was a little live wire loose in my stomach now. I was jumpy, like a man alone on a dark street. The fog that had been curling through my brain since last night seemed on the verge of clearing suddenly—and seemed to be growing denser at the same time. I wasn't even sure I wanted it to clear. I felt if I didn't start thinking soon, it would be too late. I felt if I ever started thinking again, it would be too soon. As I rushed across the park, I kept telling myself, "Think, damn it, man, think, think." It did no good at all.

Evening was coming on as I reached St. Mark's Place. The light was growing mellow, dying. The trash cans were losing their glitter. The brownstones seemed to grow one-dimensional in the twilight. When I came to our building, I took the stoop two steps at a time. At the top, I reached through the broken windowpane to open the front door from inside. I was still in a hurry as I went up the stairs.

Outside our door, I could hear Charlie singing to a theme song from the TV.

". . . Heidy-heeeeey, freebasing nasal spraaaaaay, gonna staaaaaay, where I can aaaair myyyyyy feeeeeeet . . ."

I went in.

Charlie was on the move. He was getting ready to go to work. As I came through the door, he was just disappearing, shirtless, into the bathroom.

Behind him, the TV was on. Susannah was sitting on the edge of his bed, staring at it dully. Her red hair framed her face in uncombed curls. Her hands dangled down between her knees.

Charlie kept singing more or less along with the set: "Zip-pee-yaaaaaay . . . Baby, come kneel and praaaaay . . . I think this is gonna be the one," he shouted, "where the bird loses his teddy bear, man, and he goes to the Missing Bears Bureau, and all the while the cowboy guy's got it under his hat, dig? It's a gasser."

Susannah smiled wanly. Then she looked up and saw me.

"Hi," I said.

She stood. She came to me. Wearily, she leaned against my chest. I put my arms around her.

Charlie sang: "You can eeeeeeeat my meeeeeeat . . ."

I kissed Susannah's hair. I felt my shirt getting wet. I heard her sniffle.

"My favorite is when these beetles come out and sing, 'Let-ter B, letter B,' man, see, cause they're really bugs . . ."

Charlie stepped into the bathroom doorway, shaving cream on his chin, the razor half lifted. He saw us. We exchanged a glance. He shrugged and went back inside.

"Did you get any more sleep?" I asked her.

She shivered. "A little."

"It's going to be all right," I said. I felt the live wire snaking in my belly. I didn't ask her anything else.

When Charlie left for work, I took Susannah down to Ingmar's for dinner. It was a good night for it. There was old time rock n' roll and it was loud. There was liquor and it was good. There were friends who saw me with her and came by to chivaree. When we were alone, I told her stories: about her father, about the city streets, about anything I could think of.

But after a while the band sat down. The liquor was too much. The friends began to drift back to their tables. And as for me, I looked into her eyes where she was making the desperate effort, and I just didn't have it in me anymore.

I looked down into my drink. She touched my hand.

"I'm sorry," she said. "You really are good, though."

I snorted.

"The North and Charlie show. You could sell tickets. Really."

"If I could just get it clear in my mind," I said.

"I know. But you never can. How can you?" She smiled. I didn't like the way she smiled. "The more you think about it, the more bizarre it is. The more bizarre it is, the more it takes you over." She leaned toward me. "Sometimes . . . sometimes I think that what he is is some kind of incubus. . . . You know? Not . . . not like in some horror movie, but a real kind . . . an idea . . . an evil idea that takes you over . . . that becomes more real while you start to fade away. I've read about it, Michael. It's like . . . like what they call a doppelgänger. . . ."

I looked at her carefully. "A doppelgänger . . ."

"Yes, you see, technically, technically, it's a double of a person, but the point is—"

"He's not a double, it's not—"

"No, no, but the point, the point is, it can take you over, replace you, you see. . . ."

"Susannah—"

"I'm just saying—"

"Susannah, stop it." I took tight hold of both her hands.

"I'm just . . . I'm just . . . saying . . ." She lowered her head.

I sat there for a moment, speechless. A doppelgänger. She had read about it. She had gone to the library to look it up.

"Susannah, listen to me—"

"Michael, I'm so scared."

"No, no, it's all right, I was thinking the same kind of thing this afternoon, it's just . . ."

She stared at me wildly. "Now he's doing it to you."

"He's not doing anything, he's just a man, he can't—"

"Michael, you're hurting me."

"What? Oh . . ."

"My hands . . ."

I let her go. "I'm sorry."

"It's all right."

"I'm sorry."

"It's all right." She shook her head sadly. She touched my cheek. "I know it's hard," she said. "You're just beginning to understand."

"Understand?"

She smiled again. I didn't like it any better this time.

She said: "There really is no other explanation."

Chapter twelve

I took her home. She sat in the beanbag chair. I stood by the window, staring out at the street. I studied the faces of the people passing. I couldn't help it.

A truck rumbled past.

"It's noisy, this city," Susannah said.

"You get used to it."

"I don't think so."

I didn't answer. After a while I said: "I have to go out."

She pushed at her hair distractedly. Her lips trembled. "Am I unbearable?"

"No, no."

"This isn't what I'm like at all."

I nodded.

"Do you think . . . ? Maybe I need a doctor."

"I don't know. If you do, so do I."

"I'm just so . . ."

"I know."

". . . *scared.*"

"Yes."

"I mean, all the *time,* Michael."

"It's going to be all right."

She nodded. "It's written in the Big Book."

"That's it."

"Okay," she said.

"You'll be fine. I'll leave the number and the address."

"I'll be fine."

"The machine'll answer the phone if it rings."

"Yes."

"If it's me, you'll hear me talking. Just pick up the phone and the machine'll shut off."

She nodded.

I kissed her. I headed for the door.

"It's getting chilly," she said. "Don't forget your coat."

I got my coat, and left without looking at her.

It was full dark now. It was chilly, like she'd said. I walked across town and caught a subway. Express to Times Square, the Broadway up to Lincoln Center. When I climbed up into the air, the center was all around me, vaunting white stone and arching windows, appointments of red and gold inside, and outside, the fountain, lit up, with the bright water rising and falling as on a breath. The theatergoers coming out of the buildings, arm in arm. I could hear cab doors clunking shut. I could hear women laughing, and the sound was like bells. I dug my hands into my pockets, hunched my shoulders and headed uptown.

Lincoln Center fell behind me. That and Tower Records and

McGlade's café were the last signs of civilization. Another block up and I came to the network. It was five or six buildings in a row, glass and red brick, faceless, staring.

Charlie was in radio news, and radio news was in the seven-story tower on the southwest corner. I had the security guard call up the news desk, and the assignment editor recognized my name. I was allowed to pass into the elevator.

The newsroom had an old-fashioned feel to it. It hadn't been computerized yet. Newsmen were hammering at typewriters in little cubicles that wound across the great expanse of the place. Desk assistants were running around with long sheets of copy over their arms, dumping a batch off in each cubicle. The editors were at the central desk, smoking, watching TV. And beneath everything was the clatter of the wire machines, muffled because they kept them under glass in a long row against the far wall. Other than that, it was quiet just now. The day's business was over, the night's shooting hadn't yet begun.

I waved to the assignment editor, a long blonde named Barb, and she gave me a big grin and waved back. She pointed at one of the huge glass windows on the wall to my right. I walked off toward it.

I peeked through the window into the studio inside. No sign of Charlie. Just a guy on the phone at a table and then an empty chair before a huge console of knobs and dials and switches. There was a bank of tape recorders against the left wall, most of them rolling. I went in through a heavy, sound-proofed door.

A voice was coming over a speaker.

"We will continue this vigil all night." It was a woman's voice. "And we will hold such vigils wherever the state sanctions murder. We are here in the name of humanity, and in the name of God—and for the good of the state of Florida."

The man on the phone said, "Have you had any word at all from the governor?"

And the woman started talking again while one of the tape machines recorded her for broadcast. I, by this time, was concentrating on the pair of white socks sticking out from under the console.

"Hey, Charlie?" I said.

The man on the phone pointed at the socks.

"Charlie," I said.

I heard a snort—an interrupted snore. A voice rose from under the switches and the knobs. "Is she finished?"

"No, it's me. North."

"North?"

"Come out of there, Charlie. Life's intense."

He grunted again. The white socks stirred. He pushed out from under the console, blinking—I think—behind mirrored shades.

The woman on the speaker said: "If I could find any justification for this, any at all, I would take some comfort from it. But the number of executions has skyrocketed over the last few years, and the streets aren't any safer, people aren't any more secure in their businesses or homes. Less so, if anything. We have made a covenant with death."

The man on the phone waggled his eyebrows at me. I laughed. He said: "Sister O'Connell, thank you very much for speaking with me."

"Thank you," she said.

He hung up with a sigh. He said, "Kill it, Charlie."

Charlie, sitting on the floor beneath the console, felt around for a red button up there. He found it, hit it. One of the tape machines shut down. Charlie scratched his ear. "You want to cut it now?"

"No, we got time. I'm gonna get the D.A. first and have him tell me why the sucker ought to burn."

Charlie nodded. The man before the phone picked it up again and dialed. Charlie looked up at me from the floor.

"Intense, huh?"

"Molto intenso."

He wrestled himself up into the chair in front of the console and dropped into it. He took off the mirrored shades, jacked his red eyes wide at me.

"Have you got a cigarette?"

"Augh!" I said.

"Just joking. Here." He offered me his pack. We lit up. Charlie leaned back against the console, taking a long drag. "So how is she?" he said. I glanced at the guy on the phone. "It's okay. That's Fred Lamarr. He's mechanical."

"Did she tell you, Charlie?" I asked him. "When I went up to see her?"

"What?"

"The scarred man was there."

My friend sat bolt upright. "Not . . . *the* scarred man."

"Yeah."

"Who the fuck's the scarred man?"

"The guy from my story. The story I told on Christmas night, remember? That scared her."

"Oh yeah."

"The reason she was so scared was because she'd been having dreams about the guy. And when I drove into the driveway of her school, he was there. My story, her dream. He was standing right there in the driveway."

"He's probably the parking attendant. Or the avatar of Satan. I'm sure he had a perfectly good reason for being there."

"It's nearly made her nuts."

"Nearly? She's got her feet in Manhattan and her head in Taipan."

Fred Lamarr, who had been speaking softly into the phone, now looked up and said: "Gimme a roll here, Charlie."

I glanced at him. "God, he really does look real."

"I know, it's amazing." Charlie spun to his console and fiddled with some knobs and buttons. A man's voice came over one of the speakers. Beside me, the tape that had just stopped rolling started to roll again.

Fred Lamarr said: "We're taping this for broadcast, okay?"

And a voice coming out of the speaker answered: "Okay. Shoot."

"I feel like I'm just—" I began.

"Hold it," said Charlie.

The voice on the speaker continued: "It seems to me the opponents of the death penalty conveniently forget the reasons the penalty is in force." Charlie, meanwhile, hit the dials: lowered the volume, fiddled with the treble and base. When he had it right, he turned to me again.

"So?" he said.

"So what's it mean, Charlie?"

"It means you are one very powerful storyteller, my friend."

"I feel like I've almost got it, but I'm blocking it, you know? If I can just talk it out."

"Okay," Charlie said. "Let me get this straight here. You tell a story about a guy she's dreaming about and then he shows up for real."

"Right."

He grabbed the front of his face and screamed.

"Helpful, Charlie, thanks."

Serious suddenly, he leaned toward me, gesturing with the cigarette. "Okay, Mr. Sherlock," he said. "Let's get down and do it. When you eliminate the ridiculous, whatever is left, no matter how obnoxious, must be indefinite. What are our options? Right off the top of your head, who do you think this guy is?"

"Um . . . the incarnation of a horror thousands of years old?"

"Good. Okay. I'm talking to a fucking lunatic. Any other ideas?"

"I don't know. He . . . He'd have to be . . . We'd both have to know him, Susannah and me."

"We're cooking. We're hot. How could you both know him?"

"We met him, we saw him."

"So why don't you remember?"

"We just glimpsed him. I got it. He's following her, and she's sort of seen him subconsciously, see, without noticing. Then I spotted him over Christmas and got the idea for the story without knowing it."

Charlie clapped his hands. "That'll be a hundred and fifty dollars."

The voice on the speaker droned on in the background: "Let me just review this crime for you . . ."

I shook my head. "She's been dreaming about him for three years, though."

"Oh come on, man," said Charlie. "That screws up the whole thing."

"Can I have my money back?"

"In the mail, big buddy."

"I mean, the guy's gotta really be planted in her mind, like in her subconscious."

"Uh-oh. Subconscious. Woh. Get down."

"I mean it. It's like: she must've seen him as a kid or something."

"There you go."

"But then, how do *I* know him? I mean, I would've had to

have seen him as a kid too. I mean, she and I—we'd've known each other."

I stopped. The cigarette was halfway to my mouth.

"Okay. Forget that," said Charlie.

"No, wait. That's right."

"How can it be right? It's stupid."

"I'm telling you, I'm telling you." I stood perfectly straight, perfectly still, vaguely aware of the turning reel and the droning voice and Charlie's eyes on me and the cigarette burning in my hand. "I can feel it. Like I knew it all along. We knew each other as kids, we knew the scarred man, something terrible about him, something we had to forget. That's what it is."

Charlie whistled the theme to *The Twilight Zone*.

"And I saw her," I said, staring blindly at the smoke spiraling in front of me. "That must be it. When I saw her, it must have brought him back to me. Or . . . no. I don't know. I don't know. I mean, if we knew each other, then McGill . . . he must have . . ." I heard a rough sound come up out of my throat. I put the heels of my palms against my eyes. "I can't think about this, man. There's too much. McGill, man. I just can't think about it."

Charlie took a long drag off his cigarette. Then he took a long look at me. My hands slid down.

Charlie spoke quietly. "I thought you always said you didn't care about your past."

"Oh, sure, yeah," I said. "But that was bullshit."

"Oh."

". . . and those who commit the worst crimes against society must suffer the full penalty that society has to offer," said the voice on the speaker.

"Well, counselor," said Fred Lamarr, "thank you very much for speaking to me." He hung up. "Okay, Charlie," he said, "let's cut these assholes."

Charlie nodded, put his cigarette out in an ashtray on the console. "I gotta work," he said. "I got O.T. I'll be home late."

"Okay." I stubbed my cigarette too. I stood for another moment, dazed. "I guess I gotta talk to her."

Charlie nodded. I held my hand up.

"Ten-four, camarado."

"Yo."

I walked out the soundproofed door. Behind me, Fred Lamarr was saying, "Okay, I'm gonna take about twenty seconds from Sister Jellybean, and maybe two tens from Fry, Sucker, Fry."

I walked slowly across the room to the news desk. I leaned over a television set to the assignment editor.

"I gave 'em up," Barb said.

"Good for you. Can I borrow your phone instead?"

"Just dial nine."

I picked up the phone and called home. After three rings my machine picked up. I waited for the message to end. Then I said:

"Susannah, it's me."

I waited. There was nothing.

"Sue," I said. "Just pick up the phone."

Still, she didn't come on.

"Sue, wake up," I said loudly. "I've gotta talk to you."

Nothing.

I reached into my pocket, rummaged around for the doohickey, the thing that makes the machine play messages back. I found it, held it up to the handset and pressed the button. I heard the tape rewind.

Then it began to play. I heard a rasping voice. A man's voice that hissed like a snake's.

"Hello, Michael," it said. "My name is Johnson. I'm the man with the scar."

Chapter thirteen

Barb glanced up at me. "My God," she said. "Michael, what's wrong?"

"Ssh," I said with a wave at her.

The voice on the tape went on:

"You saw me last night. But it wasn't the first time. You must know that by now. It's taken me a long time to find you. To find both of you." There was a pause. I heard him breathing. It was not a pleasant sound. "I need to meet with you. Tonight. I can explain everything." The pause was longer this time. I thought he'd hung up. Then he said: "Midnight. The Bethesda fountain in Central Park. Both of you. It has to be both of you or I don't show." And that was the end of the message.

I set down the phone.

"Michael," said Barb, "for Christ's sake, what is it? You look like someone kicked you."

I glanced at my watch. It was eleven-fifteen.

The editor leaned across the desk to Barb.

"Who's Michael North?" he said.

"Him."

"Me."

"Someone's asking for you at security."

"Michael?" Barb said.

But I was running for the door.

The elevator took forever to get down. When it finally hit bottom and opened, I came out as if I'd been shot from a gun. There she was, standing by the guard's desk. Her shoulders were hunched, her arms hung stiffly before her. Her right hand was gripping her left wrist. She looked like she was physically holding herself together.

I took hold of her, pulled her to me. I breathed in the shaggy red hair. "You're here," I said.

"He called, Michael."

"I know. I thought—"

"I was asleep. I fell asleep watching TV, and the phone rang."

"I shouldn't have left. I keep deserting you."

"I woke up and there was his voice, it was like I was in the dream. I just ran. I just listened to him and then I got up and ran."

I held her away from me. "I thought you might have gone to him."

She nodded. She raised her eyes to mine. One corner of her mouth lifted. "I'm all right, see?"

"Yeah."

"I'll be better."

"I'm sorry I left."

"No, no, no, doof. Even I can't stand me."

"I love you."

"But I do want to go. I want to see him, I want him to be real."

"Forget it," I said.

She shook her head, trained her blue eyes on me. "I want to come. I want to see him."

"No."

"He said it had to be both of us."

"Rough luck for him."

Her lips tightened. "You're not going alone, Michael."

"You got that right," I said.

"What?"

"You think I'm going into Central Park at midnight to meet a guy with a big scar on his face who I strongly suspect is a no-good guy? Wrong movie, Susie. I'm not in that film."

For the first time since Christmas, I saw that smile again that threw her face off-kilter.

"Fuck 'im," I said. "He'll come to us."

We stepped out onto Columbus. I raised my arm into the streak of passing headlights. A cab pulled over.

"St. Mark's Place," I told him.

We headed home.

We sat beside each other in the dark of the rear seat. The cab turned onto Broadway and headed downtown. I saw Lincoln Center again. And then the white spire rising from the middle of Columbus Circle, and golden Columbia, triumphant, sailing forth from the corner of Central Park on the memorial to the *Maine*.

"Now you know something," said Susannah. It was that way of stating things she had. There was no answer.

We rolled by the bright marquees of the theater district.

"We've met before," I said finally. "You and me. We must've known each other as children. We must have known him."

I gave her time to think about it. I felt her shoulder brushing against my shoulder as the cab rocked. The lights of Times Square curled out of the endless avenue before us. The billboards, their behemoth faces, soared into the night at either window. The wild neon tilted and circled and rode whirling through the undark. On the electric screen hung from the tower of Number One there were sprays of color. Beneath it, in the lighted letters of the zipper, the day's headlines chased each other around the building's waist.

"I don't remember," she said softly.

"No. Neither do I. But I'm sure."

"You remember something, then."

"No. I just know."

She was silent as the cab crossed Forty-second Street and plummeted into the winding alleylands of the south.

Then she said: "It must have been awful."

"Right."

That was all she said. Herald Square; Madison Square: the rounded wedge of the Flatiron building, the golden crown atop the campanile; Union Square, high-walled and seedy and gray as an old woman dragging her shopping bag over the pavement. Across the farthest border of the top-hatted city, into the East Village, where the rock people live. She said nothing else.

We got out of the cab in front of the brownstone. I stole a glance at her as I let her in the front door. She brushed a shock of hair from her eyes. She was gnawing her lip, inward and thoughtful.

I led the way up the three flights.

When we got to my door, I fumbled for the keys. It took me a moment to get the right one in the lock. I pushed the door in on the darkened, silent apartment. I stood back to let her pass.

She took a step toward me. She looked me dead in the eye.

"Susannah . . ." I said.

"He wouldn't hide anything from me," she said. "I know." She moved to the door.

I opened my mouth to answer. Then I closed it. Then I slugged her.

It was a hard shot with the heel of my right palm. It caught her in the shoulder and sent her staggering to one side, out of the doorway. In the same motion I pulled the door shut and dove across it until I was next to her, pressed to the wall.

"Michael, what—"

"Why isn't the TV on?" My voice sounded like a ghost's.

"What?"

"You said you fell asleep with it on. You said you ran when you heard his voice. Why's it so dark and quiet in there?"

Her lips parted, but she didn't speak. "I left it on. I think, I . . . don't know."

I took her hand.

"Leave us depart," I said.

We ran. We started down the stairs.

Susannah grabbed my arm. "Wait!" I stopped. She whispered: "Listen!"

Below us, I heard the front door open and shut. I stood stock still, listening. Susannah's fingers dug into my flesh. I heard her breath, and mine, and nothing else.

Then, slowly, footsteps started up the front stairway.

I looked up the stairs behind me, up at the closed door of my apartment. Stair by stair, the footsteps neared us from below.

"Uh . . ." I said.

"Just someone," Susannah whispered.

I hesitated another instant. Then I chose.

"We've gotta go back up."

"What if he comes out?"

"Let's go."

I took her hand. We turned and charged back up the stairs. We passed my door. We spun round the corner. Up the next flight. There was only one more after that and we scrambled up it, hand in hand. At the top we hurtled to the end of the hall.

Susannah gasped for breath. "He'll corner us."

"There's a trapdoor to the roof," I gasped back.

It was set in the ceiling, four feet above our heads. There was a ring in it, to pull it open with. The footsteps were now cresting the fourth flight, the flight below. Now they were heading down the hall for the stairs. I jumped. I reached. My fingers scraped the ring. I fell back to the floor.

"Shit, shit, shit!" I said.

"Boost me!" said Susannah.

I bent and set my hands as a stirrup. She stepped in. The footsteps started up the last flight of stairs. I hoisted. Susannah went up the white wall. She snagged the ring. She pulled. It didn't budge.

"Hurry it, baby!"

She pulled again. The door came free with a bang. A wooden ladder unfolded from inside it. Susannah tumbled down into my arms, knocking me against the wall.

The footsteps paused on the stairs a moment. Then they began to hurry up the last few steps.

I shoved Susannah. "Go!"

She scrambled up the ladder. I scrambled up after her.

On the roof, above the night city, surrounded by bright starlike lights and pale lightlike stars, the air was cool and the car horns far away. It was peaceful all around us, and we tore through that peace like a couple of rockets. We raced over the asphalt, hand in hand. We ran without thinking, without looking back. We did not want to see what might be coming up behind us.

We leapt over the curb dividing one roof from the next. We ran across the next. Then we braked on our heels. The third roof, though connected to the second, was quite a ways down. I looked back over my shoulder toward the trapdoor through which we'd come. I half expected to see him framed against the sky, maimed and terrible. I saw nothing. I knelt down and lowered myself onto the next roof. I caught Susannah as she came down after me.

We ran. The cool air burned my lungs. She let out little gasping noises as we ran, hand in sweating hand, the sparkling sky all around us.

And then, beneath us, the abyss opened. A plummeting blackness at our feet. Susannah cried out as we pulled up short, each clutching the other to keep from going down.

We were standing over a restaurant alleyway. I stared into it. It was dark, shadowy. I could barely make out the trash cans and boxes stacked against one wall.

"There's a fire escape," said Susannah.

We ran for it, climbed onto it, ran down, our heels clanging on the stairs and gratings. I hit the ladder at the bottom and rode it as it lowered with a loud rattle. I jumped, dropped onto the pavement below. And in a moment more, Susannah was beside me.

We peered forward, panting. The alley was black. At its end we saw the pale glow of St. Mark's: a shimmer at the entrance of a corridor.

I laughed.

"What?" said Susannah, giggling.

"Do we feel like idiots? Yes or no."

She laughed. "Uh, yes?"

The scarred man stepped out of the darkness, pointed a rifle at us, and fired.

That's a guess, really. What I saw was a shadow rising out of the shadows, a darkness stepping out of the dark. I saw an uncanny light which was not light but flashing blackness, which I believe was the glint of the rifle's barrel in the moment it was raised.

Then I was leaping across the alley, slamming headlong into the wall, crashing down into the boxes and the trash cans, and all tangled with Susannah as I pulled her with me.

And there was nothing in the world but noise, a vortex of sound like the wave that hits you at the beach and sucks you under for moment after moment that might not end: the noise of the gun, the noise of the cans smashing and clattering around me, the noise of the boxes crushing under our weight as we sank into a stinking morass that battered and cut us as we fell.

We hit the ground and it all piled down on top of us, covering us. I was buried. I struggled. Susannah's legs were tied up with mine. I was smothering under metal and offal and wood.

I fought for air, for space to move in. I could not hear, but felt, his footsteps nearing. I could not see, but sensed, the rifle lifting for a clear shot at us as we fought to get free. I was strangling with fear, struggling for a breath, going down again, going under . . .

And then something gave way and I came surging up out of the grave—driving up into the night just in time to watch him blow my guts open.

But he wasn't there.

Even in the dark, even with the others crowding in toward me, I knew he wasn't there. These were people from the street. They were calling to me. They were pushing in around me. They had scared him away.

Behind me now they were helping Susannah to her feet. I heard her crying, breathless, next to me.

We held each other.

"Now we know he's real," she said.

"Yeah." I looked at the open end of the alley. "And that he's smarter than we are."

Chapter fourteen

We called the cops from the street. They met us outside my apartment building. There were two of them in plain clothes. They were driving a cab. Both of them built like eggs. One of them looked like an egg with hair. His name was O'Donnell. The other was a bald egg. His name was Green.

I led them up the stairs. I said over my shoulder: "I have his voice on tape."

We came into the apartment. I switched on the light. From Charlie's unmade bed to the cockroach in the coffee cup, everything was as it had been.

I went to the answering machine. Rewound it. Played it back.

It rolled in silence.

"Uh . . ." I said.

The interview went downhill from there.

"Michael North," said Officer O'Donnell. "Aren't you the guy who told Meatgrinder Scarangello to go fuck himself? Excuse me, ma'am," he added to Susannah.

"Yeah, okay, so what?"

"Well, you think mayhaps this could have anything to do with you getting shot at?"

"No. Hell, no. Scarangello likes me. He sent me a Christmas card."

"Yeah," said Green. "This must have been for Easter."

"It was a guy with a scar named Johnson."

"Oh, yeah, I know him. He has a boil named Sue."

"Could you see him in the dark?" said O'Donnell.

"No, but he—"

"Left a message on your machine, that's right."

"Join me for cocktails and gunplay," said Green.

"You're a funny, funny man," I said.

He chuckled.

"Well," said O'Donnell. "We'll send some guys out to look for the slugs in the morning. Unless you think he erased those too."

I sighed.

"But if I were you," he said, "I'd pay a call on Scarangello and I'd say, 'Pretty please, Mr. Meatgrinder, don't shoot at me anymore. I'll be good.' Then I'd kiss his ring or something. He likes that."

"He'll probably kill you anyway," said Green. "But at least you'll have degraded yourself."

"I'll take it under advisement."

"Good," said O'Donnell. "Why'd you say that to him, anyway, smart kid like you?"

"I was researching a book."

I could still hear them laughing when they got down to the sidewalk.

Susannah grimaced. She was sitting in Charlie's beanbag chair. She slumped forward and dropped her hands between her knees, sighing up through her lower lip so that her bangs lifted on the breath. She swiped at a green smudge on her cheek. "Well, they're not my heroes," she said.

I nodded. "I smell like garbage. You look like shit. Let's go take a shower."

She got it going. The water steamed. When I climbed in, she stepped from the mist like a phantom. I soaped her. Her skin was the color of ivory. When I touched her breast, her neck arched. When I touched her neck, she curled her cheek into my hand.

She moaned a little. "You were great, though," she said.

"Yeah, terrific."

"You were. You were fast."

"He was smarter." I kissed her. "He knew everything."

"Everything?"

"Sure. He scared you out of the apartment with that call, then came and erased the message. Then he just waited for us."

She trailed her hand up my thigh. "He knew we'd come back."

"I guess."

"That's scary."

"He must've gone to the alley." I knelt down in front of her. The water pounded my hair.

She gasped. "He's really after us."

I didn't answer. She gasped again.

"You think Daddy knows something."

I stood, my hands coming up behind her. "I don't know, Susie. . . ."

"I know," she whispered. "He wouldn't lie."

"We were children. He must have been there."

"He wasn't." She pressed against me, slippery.

"How can you say?"

"He's not my father."

I slid inside her. She cried out.

I whispered: "What?"

"I'm adopted," she hissed with the hiss of the water. "I'm an orphan, sweetheart. Just like you."

For another second or so it seemed to matter.

Chapter fifteen

It was two. I was beat. The bruises and cuts from our dive in the alley were beginning to ache and sting. I had a twisted ankle. Susannah had a slash on her arm. I had a black eye. Susannah's knee was bleeding.

I came out of the shower limping. I collapsed, naked, into the beanbag, my head thrown back, my eyes closed.

"I need a drink," I said.

She called to me: "Stay off your foot. I'll get it."

I stayed off my foot. I drifted in and out of a doze that was like music, or like the waves of the sea, or like the music the waves make when they sing. She slipped the drink into my hand. I felt the glass sweat cold against my hot palm.

"It doesn't make sense," I said.

"Oh sweetie, Jesus, let's stop tonight."

She was at my feet. I cracked my lids and saw her there. She was sitting naked on the floor, cross-legged. She was surrounded by all the first-aid stuff she had found in the bathroom. She shook some hydrogen peroxide out on a cotton swab. She swabbed her knee and then her arm. She leaned forward, kneeling, and did the scratches on my leg and my side.

I lifted my drink and sipped it. It went down me in a fiery little spiral. I gasped at the ceiling.

I said: "Why should he want to hurt us after all this time?"

"Be quiet," she whispered. "Drink your drink."

I drank my drink. "Susie?" My voice was thick and amber. I felt the soft cotton soothe a pain in my shoulder.

"Susie."

"Hm?"

"When were you adopted?"

"I don't know," she murmured. "I was little. Maybe two."

"Do you know why?"

"Well . . . I was an orphan. My parents were dead."

"How did they die?"

"I don't know. My father said they never told him."

"Who?"

"The agency."

"Which agency? Where?"

"Michael, I don't know." She breathed it, exasperated. "I never asked."

"At all?"

"No."

"But Susie—"

"Michael . . ." She sat back on her heels. She was looking down at the bottles and boxes of gauze around her. Her hair, wet and dark with it, hung limply down her brow and temple.

My eyes followed the ivory lines of her, curling in along her spine, out along her hips.

She raised her face to me. "I loved them," she said. "They were the parents I had. I loved them. I never asked for the details. Okay?"

I nodded. "Okay."

She brushed her hair back. She smiled at me. Her eyes glistened.

"Okay?" she said again.

I nodded.

She gathered the first-aid stuff into her arms and got to her feet. I watched her carry it into the bathroom.

Then I stood up. It took some doing, but I got there. My ankle was tender. My mind was warm with sleep and liquor. I shook my head to clear it.

As quickly as I could, I hobbled into the other room. My bedroom. That was about all there was room for too: a bed, a closet, a window on a brick wall.

I got my bathrobe out of the closet and put it on. Then I knelt down and reached into the back past my sneakers and my Diplomacy game. I pulled out a shoe box. I'd forgotten how heavy it was. I opened it and took out the .38. McGill had made me get a license for it. I'd fired it a few times. I'd carried it once. I didn't like it much.

I fumbled with the wheel to get it open. I fumbled with the bullets to stuff them into their chambers. I snapped it shut and slipped it quickly into my bathrobe pocket. I stuffed the shoe box back into the closet and closed the door.

I stood and turned and she was in the doorway. She was wearing my shirt. It hung down around her thighs. She was holding her shoulders as if she were cold.

"You have to get some sleep," was all she said.

"I'll sleep when Charlie comes," I told her. "You get in bed now, I'll sit beside you."

She pulled the covers down and climbed in under them. She was blinking hard. I sat down next to her. I kept one hand in my pocket around the gun butt. With the other hand, I stroked her forehead.

"My parents died in a fire," I said.

She reached up, curled her fingers around my wrist. "Poor Michael," she said.

"It was different for me. I could never get anyone to tell me more than that. I'd ask, but that's all they'd say: They died in a fire. They made it sound like something shameful."

"They were vomitaceous doofs," she whispered. She could barely keep her eyes open.

"They were. No question," I said. "But . . . Doesn't this have to do with him . . . with something?"

Susannah rolled over on her side. She lay her head in my lap, her eyes closed.

"I keep having this feeling that I'm blocking it out," I said. "That I know but I won't let myself in on it."

"Mm-hm."

"It all seemed so much clearer when I was talking to Charlie. . . ."

I tried to recapture the clarity. I had an image in my head for a moment of Charlie at the controls, of Fred Lamarr on the phone, of the big reel rolling and the voice coming over the speaker.

I lifted my hand and pressed it against my brow. "Oh man," I said. "Oh man."

I had to stand up, to pace it off. I moved Susannah's head gently, but she opened her eyes. As I stood, she propped herself on one elbow and watched me. I walked the length of the bed, turned and returned to the head and turned again. She yawned.

"An execution, that's what it was," I said. "He was reading about an execution as we came up on the train."

"Who was?"

"Your father."

She flopped over onto her back, sighing at the ceiling.

"That's what put it in my head," I said. "That's where I got the idea for the story. The scarred man and the execution go together somehow."

Susannah sat up. She snapped at me, "Michael, if you think my father could lie to me about something like—"

"You don't understand. . . ."

"You don't understand my father if you—"

"Susie, a man came to the office today. He left a message for your father."

"I don't care."

"He said to tell him that the Turner case was over, the killer was going to be executed in ten days."

"It doesn't matter."

"You don't understand—"

She yelled at me: "*You* don't understand!"

"Susie!"

She stopped. I ran my hand up through my hair. I was afraid, but I didn't know why. Even then, my mind refused to make sense of it. All I knew was that I felt like I'd swallowed a chunk of ice.

Susannah sulked at me. I lifted my hands. "Susie," I said again, more softly now. "Susie, my parents. Turner. That was their name."

Chapter sixteen

She sat on the opposite edge of the bed awhile, her head hung down. Then she turned on her back and lay staring up at nothing. Finally she was just done in. She fell asleep without speaking to me again.

I sat beside her. I kept my hand wrapped around the pistol. I stared out into the next room at the front door.

I woke up suddenly. I got off the bed, rubbing my eyes. I wandered out into the other room. Charlie had just come home, carrying a paper bag.

"Hey there, ho there," Charlie said. "That a pistol in your pocket or you just happy to see me?"

"It's a pistol in my pocket."

"Holy shit."

I took it out.

"Aagh," said Charlie. "What the hell is that for?"

"He tried to kill us last night."

"Whodo?"

"The scarred man. With a rifle."

I followed Charlie into the kitchenette. He set the bag on the counter. "The dude you made up."

"Yeah."

"Wow." He removed a box of Ghostbusters cereal (with the marshmallow ghosts) from the bag. "So you're standing guard."

"Yeah."

"Far out. So, basically, if I'm him, you're a dead guy."

"Basically, yeah."

"Want some Ghostbusters?"

"Eagh, God, make some coffee, Charlie."

"I just made coffee."

"That was last week."

"The roach still likes it."

"The roach is fucking dead, man."

"He is? Jesus, I hope you get this guy before he kills again." Charlie grabbed the mug and rinsed the roach out. "How about you?"

I nodded, mentally checking my body for aches and pains. They were all there. I leaned against the kitchenette partition. "I'm alive. I hurt all over. I was dodging bullets."

"Are you sure this wasn't someone like . . . I don't know. That Jell-O guy?"

"That's what the cops said."

"You let the cops in here?"

"He shot at me."

"Oh man!"

"They didn't find anything. Would you make the coffee, Charlie."

Muttering, he set about cleaning the percolator. I went back into the front room, sat on the edge of his bed. I could hear him hammering, scraping, banging the pot against the side of the sink, cursing and screaming at the old grounds. I took the opportunity to tell him what had happened, what I thought.

"So what now, little butterfly?" he said.

"I figured we'd go to the library, see if we can run down the execution story and, you know, shatter our sanity with a truth too terrible to behold."

"Sounds good."

Susannah came in silently. She was still wearing my shirt. She sat on my lap, buried her face in my neck.

"I guess you can pretty well kiss the redhead good-bye," Charlie called from behind the partition. "From the sound of it, McGill is in this up to his eye sockets."

I held Susannah, kissed her. She hugged me hard.

"I'm sorry," she whispered.

"No, no."

"It's not your fault."

I kissed her hair.

"Hey, maybe you can get a raise out of it," said Charlie.

I rolled Susannah onto Charlie's bed and lay on top of her. My hand moved down between her legs. We kissed.

I heard coffee perking. I heard Charlie say: "Or maybe, you know, you can get some big scandal going, just lay it out in front of McGill, right on his desk, and leave him alone in a room with a pistol, see? Say something like, 'I know you'll do the honorable thing,' right? Then just leave the room."

Sue combed my hair back over my ears with her fingers. She said: "We have to know everything. No matter what. It's the only way."

"Blam!" said Charlie. He hummed the funeral march.

We had some breakfast, Susannah and I, and headed over to Sixth Avenue. It was a bright, windy day. The Jefferson Market branch of the library—a brown-brick church of a building with a spire-capped clock tower, stained-glass windows, concrete finials—stood poised and impressive against the racing clouds. We went up the front stairs hand in hand. We smiled at each other. Wan smiles, like we were going bravely to face the guns.

Down a spiral staircase, under the doorways of arching brick: We went to the newspaper room in the basement. We asked the librarian for the *New York Times,* the one McGill read on the way to Trent. We waited for him while he went into the back room. We kept our hands to ourselves now, folded together in front of us. We still smiled at each other. Wanly.

The librarian brought us a reel of microfilm. Susannah and I went together into the little room where the projectors were. I sat before the machine. Susannah leaned over my shoulder. I loaded the reel.

It was like that. Each movement brightly lit, each sharply delineated, like a dance under strobes. I saw my hand turning the crank of the machine, I saw the projected pages racing in a blur across the screen in front of me. I saw them slow, resolve into the pages of the *Times.* I reeled it back a little.

"There it is," I said.

I felt Susannah lean in over my shoulder. I heard her long breath shudder.

There was a short story in the "Around the Nation" column:

THE SUPREME COURT TODAY CLEARED THE
WAY FOR THE MARCH 17 EXECUTION OF
NATHAN JERSEY, CONVICTED EIGHT YEARS
AGO OF KILLING A GUARD WHILE IN INDI-
ANA STATE PRISON. THE COURT REJECTED
THE APPEAL OF JERSEY'S ATTORNEY, WHO
CLAIMED THE PRISONER IS MENTALLY RE-
TARDED.

JERSEY HAD BEEN SENTENCED TO DIE ONCE
BEFORE FOR THE KILLING, TWENTY YEARS
AGO, OF A FAMILY FOR WHICH HE WORKED
AS A HANDYMAN. THAT SENTENCE WAS
COMMUTED TO LIFE IMPRISONMENT IN
1972 WHEN THE SUPREME COURT OVER-
TURNED THE DEATH PENALTY.

I heard Susannah's breath again, the intake of it sharp this time. I rewound the microfilm.

"Twenty years back," I said.

I glanced up at her. There were tears in her eyes. I couldn't imagine why. I simply refused to make sense of it. I left her there and went to the directory. I went back twenty years and found nothing. I went back another year, and there was the name Nathan Jersey. The librarian brought me the reel. Again, I threaded it, ran it through.

Susannah said—as my hand slowed down on the crank, as the blurred whirl cleared, just before I backed it up to the right date—she said, she moaned: "Don't . . ."

But by then it was impossible to stop. The story came up before me on the screen, at the precise moment the deductions slipped into place in my head. I knew the answer to the scarred man—the obvious answer—even as I read it on the page.

It was still no more than a squib in the nationals: a minor

killing in a little Indiana town named Hickman. Details were sketchy, but it seems that on the night of November 4, an innkeeper named Robert Turner had been gunned down in the country hotel he kept there. He was found on the second-floor landing. His wife Carol was beside him. The inn's maid was at the foot of the stairs. They were dead too.

"Robert and Carol Turner," I said. "They were my parents, my father and mother."

Susannah said nothing. She just stood behind me, crying into her hands.

She wasn't crying for the Turners.

The story went on to say that two children had survived the attack on the inn. They'd hidden in a basement broom closet. A state cop had found them there. They were in shock, but otherwise unharmed.

Two children, the article said, ages five and one. A boy and a girl.

A brother and a sister.

PART THREE

A murder story

Chapter seventeen

We took a walk in Washington Square Park. Over the interweaving stone paths in the wind. Around the fountain. Under the statues. Over the paths again. I'd bought a pack of cigarettes at the little smoke shop across the street. I smoked them one after another. I wished she would stop crying.

The park was quiet. A few people were sunbathing on the grass. Someone was playing a guitar and singing. The drug dealers haunted the corners, whispering "cess," like snakes, from the shadows. In the playground, the toddlers went down the slide with little cries.

We paused beneath the arch. Susannah leaned her back against the stone, her hands folded before her, her eyes cast down. I propped my shoulder beside her, faced away from her, up Fifth Avenue toward the Empire State Building. My hand was at my belt, the smoke from the cigarette wafting up to me. I smoked the cigarette. I wished she would stop.

She struggled with it. I heard her. And after a while, she walked out beneath the center of the arch. She turned to me. I could feel her gaze, feel her studying my profile. I wished she'd stop that too.

"Do you know what I love?" she whispered.

"No. No."

"That you have blue eyes and black hair. Like a movie star. That's what Kelly and Kate said. That you looked like you could have been a movie star: sort of tough because the black hair, the contrast, makes your eyes look cold, at first. But after a while . . . You're not really so tough at all."

"No," I said. "Not so tough."

"You're a very handsome man, Michael," she said, and then she sniffled loudly. "I'll bet women just—" She couldn't go on.

I took a drag on my cigarette. "Stop crying," I said.

"I'm sorry. I can't help it."

"Goddamnit . . ." I said. And then I said: "Please. Please, Susie, try to stop."

"What difference does it make?"

I rounded on her, snapped at her. "Because I can't do a goddamned thing about it and it's breaking my fucking heart, all right?"

I had to turn away from her then. I still felt her looking at me. In another moment, she was silent. When I glanced at her again, she was dragging her palm across her cheeks—first one, then the other—to dry the tears.

"Thanks," I said.

She nodded. "Sure." She studied her shoes.

I leaned against the arch, looked up Fifth Avenue toward the Empire State.

She said to me: "Michael?"

"Yeah."

"Do you remember?"

"No."

"None of it?"

"Nothing."

"Me either. But I thought: you were older."

"I don't remember," I said.

That stopped her for a minute. Then she said: "Was it really the scarred man? Who did it?"

"I don't know."

"I mean, they're going to execute Nathan Jersey. . . ."

"I know that, Sue."

"I mean, even if he killed a guard—"

"I said I know."

She whispered: "Don't yell at me."

"Okay."

She hugged herself. She shivered. "I wish there'd been more," she said.

I had gone on in the reel of microfilm, looking for follow-up stories. The first report had been wire copy with a police dispatcher for a source. But the day after, the news was dominated by the elections. The Hickman killing vanished from the *Times* for good.

"What are we going to do?"

I dropped my cigarette to the ground, crushed it under my heel. I took out another, lit it.

"I'm going to Indiana," I said.

She nodded, blowing out a big breath. "All right."

"You can stay with Angela, if you want."

"No. I'll come with you."

"Okay."

I smoked my cigarette. I stared up Fifth Avenue. I flipped my cigarette out over the sidewalk. It spun past the curb, fell into the gutter.

Then Susannah was standing next to me. She had her hands in the pockets of her skirt. She tilted her head. The breeze pushed her hair against her cheek, strands of it curled between her lips.

"I love you," she said.

I pushed off the wall. "You can't love me. You're not allowed to love me."

"Yes I can. I'm your sister."

The words ripped into me and suddenly I grabbed the front of her dress. I dragged her to me.

She cried: "Michael, stop it, it hurts."

"What if we don't care?" I said. "What if we don't? Why should we? What is it? It's just a rule. You make a rule, I make another rule. What if we just don't care?"

I pulled her until her lips were crushed against mine. She turned her face away from me.

"Michael," she said, "stop it. It hurts too much."

I let her go. I leaned against the arch. I stared up Fifth Avenue toward the Empire State.

"Okay," I said finally. "Okay."

Chapter eighteen

We told Charlie where we were going. We swore him to secrecy. We told no one else. We rented a car—I didn't want to use McGill's. We put some clothes in two overnight bags. We put the overnight bags on the back seat. I put the pistol in the glove compartment with some maps and a flashlight. And by the time the sun went down that night, we were burning through the Lincoln Tunnel and out of town.

We drove with the radio playing. We drove with the windows down. We drove with the sound of rock 'n' roll washing over us like the wind. The night grew black around us. The air stank with Jersey. The lights of factories glowed. Then we were in the countryside, and by the time we crossed over into Pennsylvania, there was nothing but trucks and the air and the darkness.

"He always took me places," Susannah said. "Even when I was little. Baseball games and movies. Can you imagine my father sitting through those movies they make for children? We must have watched *Mary Poppins* fifteen times one summer. I mean, you know my father, you know what he's like, Mr. Tough Guy. He took me through the woods, he taught me the flowers. He made things . . . clean for me. They were always . . . everything was always so clean. He spoiled me, I guess, but it wasn't, you know, like a bad thing, it was just, he wanted everything to be nice. . . . Maybe that's why he didn't tell me."

The rising mountains were all around us, black and frowning against the sky. The road lifted steadily. I could smell her in the seat beside me, her perfume light on the rushing wind.

"Why didn't he tell *me?*" I said.

"Maybe he didn't know. About you, I mean. Maybe he didn't know about any of it."

"He knows. He's in this somehow, Susie. He did try to tell me about it over Christmas. He tried to tell me again before he left, but I wouldn't let him. He knows. It couldn't have been a coincidence, his hiring me. He knows, all right."

We went through a tunnel under a mountain. The music from the radio fizzled and died. We said nothing until we came out the other side. Then the music began again.

Susannah said: "You know, I think . . . Maybe this is something all daughters think. Still, I think I was all my father had. My mother . . . I mean, he loved her, but she was, well, it isn't fair, but . . . she was never well. You know? I mean, I remember, like, she always looked pale, so I remember asking her, one time when I was little, why she always looked like Casper the Ghost. She had heart trouble. She was always out of breath. She always had to sit down. She could never do anything, go anywhere with Daddy. So I think . . . I mean, he might have divorced her or cheated on her, but I think . . . he just had me instead, took me places, did things with me. . . . You see what I'm saying? He would have told me if he knew I was in danger."

I nodded. We crossed into West Virginia. It was after one in the morning. We saw the lights of Wheeling in the dark. We crossed the bridge into Ohio.

I said: "If I can't have you anymore, I'll die."

She started crying again.

We found a motel just off the highway: the usual series of cheesy bungalows fronting on a parking lot. We took two of them. I spent what was left of that night—that morning— staring at the wall and staring out the window. The wall was the wall between us. It was thin as paper. I could hear her shifting around on the other side. Getting undressed. Going to bed. I walked across the room and lay my hand against the wall. I could hear her, still crying.

"Damn," I whispered.

Then there was the window. The window looked out onto the dark. I stood in front of the window smoking cigarettes. I heard the trucks going by on the highway. I saw the red, then the green, glow of a nearby streetlight on the road into town. I watched the changing color of the glow.

I thought of Manhattan, of the checkerboard simplicity of its streets. The dark is not dark there, never completely. It has a kind of violet glow that is all the light from everywhere convening in the sky. There is no silence in Manhattan. You are never alone. There's always something rocking, the steady thrum underground, the new beat of the coming music. There are signs on the corners so you know where you are.

The light blinked red, then green, and in the instant of change, when the glow was gone, I saw my own reflection on the glass: a ghostly presence, full of the night, gazing into the silent passing of the hour before dawn.

Chapter nineteen

In the bright, cold, clear Ohio morning, we saw where we were for the first time. We drove toward Indiana through the hills, rolling away from us, pale green, to lines of trees stark and bare against the hazy sky. The long grass laced with highway, the decaying barns with the ads for chewing tobacco fading from their sloping roofs, the silos rising tall and somber out of the fields: all of it made us feel, after the blind night driving, that we had been thrust suddenly into another country; more like another world, or dimension; that we had gone to sleep on a planet called Manhattan and awakened in orbit around the Midwest.

We kept the windows open. Susannah kept her eyes on the view. The cold wind blew her mop of red hair all over. Her thick lips were parted. Her nose flared. Her eyes were wide, even in the rushing air. Her face seemed open and wild and receptive to everything. I had to pull my gaze from her—again and again—to focus on the road.

"It's so pretty here," she said.

We crossed into Indiana. The land did not change. The exits were few and far between. We seemed to approach Hickman by inches.

Finally, at the Rushville exit, we rolled off the interstate into the farmlands. Following the map, we went from the big green snake of the superhighway to the big red line with the state shields, then we were on the smaller red lines, and then the broad white spaces laced with thin scratches of blue. The land did not change, but now the grass and the cornfields lapped at the edge of the pavement, and sometimes the branches of the trees hung down above us.

We came into Hickman gradually. First there were houses—hardly more than nailed-down trailers—sitting on the hill. After that came the gas stations, the steak house, the bar. Then Main Street sort of grew up around us. The cluttered porches of two-story frame houses drew closer together, gave way to the gleaming white diner, the long, faceless five-and-dime, the quainter gift shops and clothing stores run, you could tell, by widows and divorcees, and the houses with the signs on them —professional buildings with lawyers and doctors and dentists inside. Things got more important then. There was the courthouse with the town police station, the library, the post office, and the church, which was the culmination of the thing, its white spire rising above the rest. Behind that the markers of a cemetery lifted on the wave of a single hill. They dropped again against a backyard fence. Behind the fence, laundry fluttered on a line over a corroded swing set and a broken bike.

As the street seemed to have risen to the church spire, it now seemed to fall away. We drove past a residential cross street and found ourselves passing a row of low-lying barracks-like offices: real estate, insurance, the town newspaper, Laundromat, army recruitment. After that came the junk shops, or antique dealers, as they were called, and then I saw the red-brick federal-style high school about a block away, with its clock stopped beneath the white dome.

We parked the car in front of the newspaper office. We got out and stood together for a moment on the sidewalk.

"Anytown, U.S.A.," I said.

"Look at the big sky," said Susannah, craning her neck. "I'll bet the stars are incredible at— What is it?"

She had lowered her eyes to me. I shrugged.

"You remember something," she said.

I made a dismissive sound. "I had a mental picture for a second."

"Tell me."

I sighed.

"Tell me," she said.

"If you want. I saw a tire swing. I don't know. I saw a tire swing out in back of a house with a porch. Water running by it, like a creek or something. A tree, some kind of spreading tree, a sugar maple, maybe. I don't know. Let's go into the newspaper office."

She glanced back over Main Street.

"None of it looks familiar to me."

"It's probably changed some in twenty years."

She shivered. I moved toward the office. She followed.

It was a little box of a place. The *Hickman Chronicle.* A glass front with the words spelled in electrical tape on the door. As we came in we saw two rows of gunmetal desks, three desks in each row. The walls were bulletin boards covered with papers. There were filing cabinets in the back near the bathroom door.

One look around gave me the layout. The people in the three desks in front of me were ads and circulation. The divorcee on the phone at the last desk in the row to our right was church notices. The fat-bellied middle-aged guy typing on the next desk down was sports. The guy at the front desk to the right, the guy with his feet up and the Indianapolis paper open on his lap and the cigarette dangling from his lips: he was the news operation, editor and reporter both most likely, with occasional help from some high school kid stringer. I told the lively housewife who greeted us that he was the guy we wanted.

His name was Ben Yardley. He was about thirty years old, tall and thin, a bullet-headed man with short sandy hair and squinty eyes set in the folds of a granite face. He looked like he'd seen things: the same things, over and over, until he'd learned not to be surprised.

I stuck out my hand and introduced myself. He did the same. I introduced Susannah, and I saw him look her over, once, shyly. She was wearing a man-size shirt, yellow with black marks, which ended where her dress ended, just above her knees. The sight of her made him pull his eyes away quickly. His pale cheeks reddened and he cleared his throat.

I wanted to deck him. I was her big brother, after all.

He leaned back again, put his feet on the desk, put his hands behind his head. He said: "I take it you want to know about Nathan Jersey."

"How'd you guess?"

"Well, Wendell Willkie's dead, and I can't think what else would bring you out of the city. What city is it, anyway?"

"New York."

"Paper there?"

"No."

He waited. I let him wait. But he was too smart. He looked at Susannah again.

"Did you say McGill?" he said.

"I work for her father, Carl McGill," I said.

He snorted. "Christ, why didn't you say so? Come on back."

He led us up the aisle between the rows of desks. He opened one of the standing file cabinets.

"You'll be interested in seeing our latest equipment," he said, and pulled open the drawer. He withdrew a manila folder, set it down on the edge of Church Notice's desk. He flipped open the cover on the first clipping.

I hissed between my teeth. Susannah let out a little cry.

There was a headline, a banner headline. It read: THREE MURDERED IN HICKMAN INN.

Under it was the by-line: Carl McGill.

Chapter twenty

"Nathan Jersey was the town idiot," Yardley said. "I don't know any other way to put it."

We were in the diner now, the three of us. The sight of McGill's by-line had hit Sue hard. She would not stay in the office. Yardley offered to buy us coffee: He said he could save us the trouble of reading the entire clip file, and fill us in on the basics of the case himself. He didn't seem to want to let us go.

We sat at a linoleum table, by a curtained window that looked out on Main Street. Our coffee cups sat before us, untouched, sending up steam, then less steam, then even less. Yardley kept a cigarette pasted in his face as he talked. It bobbed up and down, sending a shivering line of smoke toward the ceiling. Susannah watched him, her hands folded on the tabletop. She never took her eyes from his face.

"Every small town has someone like him, I guess. About twenty, twenty-five years old, did odd jobs, swept up stores, made deliveries, loaded trucks, stuff like that. Had a little room over by the railroad tracks, managed to take care of himself pretty well. That worked against him at the trial, in fact. His lawyer tried to prove he was retarded, and the prosecution kept harping on that: that he always managed to take care of himself pretty well."

He plucked the cigarette from his craw, flicked the ash to the floor and replanted the butt between his lips again.

"Well, anyway, Robert Turner was kind of an outsider around here, as I understand it. Came from a wealthy family out west somewhere, California, I think. Left all that behind, decided to live the simple life, you know the type. Ran a kind of country inn and restaurant in what we call the backlands: it's sort of a . . . a little valley surrounded by hills. Lots of forest, Jackson Lake is there, lots of little streams, you know: good hunting, fishing area, that sort of thing. So Turner did all right."

He waved his hand toward the window as if to indicate the general direction of the backlands. I thought again of the house with the tire swing. I now pictured it surrounded by woodland hills. Yardley went on.

"But the point is: Turner was what you might call a do-good type, or anyway that was his reputation. Kind of guy who'd take in all kinds of strays, and always at the town board meeting agitating for, I don't know what, better conditions at the jail or stricter dumping laws to protect the river. Not a troublemaker exactly, but you have to understand: this used to be Ku Klux Klan country, Hickman. He wasn't what you'd call a welcome guy.

"So, of course, according to anyone you ask, Turner was just as nice as you could want to Nathan Jersey, all right? I mean, the way they tell it it was like: he always had work for the guy; he overpaid him, and Jersey, man, he just followed Turner around like a dog, okay? I mean, Turner hired all kinds up there at the inn at one time or another—juvenile delinquents, ex-cons, you name it—and some of them ripped him off and took advantage of him and all that. But Jersey, as far as anyone could tell, was just devoted to him, okay? So that's the background on that part.

"Then came the rape."

I nodded, calmly as I could, trying to take it all in. I took a cigarette from Yardley's pack and lit it. Images were coming into my mind too fast for me to assemble them. They were vague. I couldn't tell what I was remembering and what I was imagining from Yardley's story. I had to struggle to concentrate.

"Now, the information on this part is kind of skimpy. You know, I've read a lot of the clippings from the time, but I never got around to reading the trial stories. You might want to look at those, there's probably a lot more detail in them. Anyway, I don't know the girl's name, but apparently she was part of one of these huge redneck clans, used to be all there was up in the backlands before the tourist trade. So, anyway, she cries rape, okay, that's all I know. Now, before long, everyone's looking for Nathan Jersey, who I guess had been seen mooning around the girl or something. The Sheriff—the county Sheriff—he wants Jersey for questioning. Every man in this girl's family wants him for hanging. Jersey knows everybody's after him, so he runs to the Turner inn for protection. Turner has the good sense to call the Sheriff. Unfortunately, the clan gets there first. They come storming up to the Turner inn like the last reel of a Frankenstein movie, okay? 'Give us the monster.' A real old-fashioned necktie party. They get right up to the door of the Turner inn and out steps Mr. Turner himself. No gun. No baseball bat. Nothing. Just walks out the door and stands in front of it. Get the picture?"

I nodded. Sat up straight.

"Now it goes from Frankenstein to a classic western. One man against the lynch mob. The way I understand it, Turner was the kind of guy who commanded respect, whether people liked him or not. He was a gentleman, you know, very quiet and refined." He put his nose in the air as he said it. "It carried a lot of weight. So, he stands there . . ." Yardley laughs. "He stands there for about ten minutes discussing the United States Constitution with fifteen guys who think it's a baseball team, all right? At which point, with a blare of bugles, up shows the Sheriff with the cavalry. Jersey is saved. Okay, now get this: the Sheriff takes Jersey in, Turner gets him a lawyer. The Sheriff questions Jersey, questions the girl, questions everybody at the inn and so on. The upshot is: Jersey's got an alibi—I can't remember—oh yeah, he was helping out, delivering chickens or something, but anyway, the point being he was out of town at the time. So he's released. This is fine with the lynch mob, right, because they're planning a private hanging anyway. Jersey—wisely—went up to stay at the Turner inn. About two days later"—he shrugged to represent the slaughter of my family—"a state patrol car is driving by, cop thinks everything looks too quiet, you know, goes to check on it, finds the bodies, and the kids, and so on."

I took a long drag of the cigarette. I glanced at Susannah. She was staring at Yardley, her lips pursed, her eyes far away.

Yardley said: "Well, when it dawned on everyone that Jersey was not among what the newspaper called 'the slain,' they brought out the dogs. It took a while, going through the backland woods, but eventually, Mr. Jersey is discovered at his new address, which I think was a cave or an overhanging rock or something. He confesses after a couple of hours, lawyer present, all perfectly legal. The rifle is proven to be his. Then he stands trial without testifying. Then he's condemned to death."

He stopped speaking suddenly. I had to yank my mind into the present. I stuttered for a second.

"Weren't there any witnesses?" I said then. "I mean, it was an inn. . . ."

"Yeah, it was an inn," Yardley said. "But it was November, early on. The good fishing and hiking and stuff were over; the gun hunting hadn't started yet. Most of the places up there are usually empty then. Anyway, Jersey confessed . . . like I said . . . lawyer present, perfectly legal. They had to try him anyway cause it was a capital case. . . ."

"Was there any corroborating evidence?"

"I don't know that. Like I said, I'm not all that up on the trial."

"All right. He gets death."

"He gets death. Which, about three years later, the Supreme Court overturns. Which, about ten seconds later, the sovereign state of Indiana repasses. Which is besides the point, because Jersey's off the hook. Except that he then is so kind as to vindicate everyone's good opinion of him by killing a guard. Beat him to death with his bare hands no less."

"Jesus."

"Back to trial, back to death row, back to the dust from which he came, all things being equal."

There were other things I wanted to ask him, but not just then. So we sat and watched each other, he and I. He squinted at me through a screen of smoke. I could almost hear him thinking.

"I've told you a lot," he said quietly after a moment. "Now

how about you tell me who you are?" My mouth was forming around the lie when he added: "Or better yet, why don't you tell me why you're here, Mr. Turner."

I looked up quickly. "You're awfully damn good," I said.

"The resemblance is there. I've seen pictures of Turner. They never released any pictures of the children, but the resemblance is there. When you said you worked for Carl McGill, I figured you were here to pick up some clippings. Then I saw your faces when you looked at his by-line. You didn't even know he covered the story, did you?"

"No."

"Why?" said Susannah suddenly. It was the first word she had spoken. "Why did he cover the story?"

Her gaze bore into Yardley. He looked down at the tabletop as if her eyes were too bright for him. "He worked here, for the *Chronicle,*" he said. "He was like twenty-five or something. Got out of the service, went to college in Richmond, worked on the *Chronicle* part-time. Before my day, but it's sort of become a newspaper legend. Even then, everyone knew he'd head east when he graduated. But actually, he stayed a whole year after that. And the murders happened, so he got some good clips. And the rest . . . is history."

"So it is," I said.

Yardley seemed grateful to be able to look at me again. "Only you didn't know it. So it made me think maybe you were here for personal reasons. And the more I looked at your face . . ." He shrugged.

I tilted my coffee cup. I swirled the black surface, examined the ripples. I was reliving that moment in the alley, the moment when the scarred man stepped out of the shadows. The moment when the gun went off. The sound of the shot seemed to reverberate in my head, echoing back into the past. If the wrong person found out where we were, I'd hear that gunshot again. It would be all I'd hear.

I felt Yardley watching me, looked up, looked in his eyes. I could almost hear his heart beating, beating hard. He was onto a big story. The Turner kid comes back. We both knew it—and I knew it was bigger still than he thought. He was good enough for it, that was certain. And good enough to be gone from this one-horse town if that's what he wanted.

"This is, like, deep off the record," I said. "I mean, deep."

He nodded.

I set the coffee cup straight. "I don't think Nathan Jersey killed my parents."

I watched it go through him. I watched the ambition flare up in him like a flame. It was a big story, all right. In this town, it was The Big Story.

He cleared his throat. "You have proof?"

"I can convince you."

"Convince me."

"I need help. I won't know who to call, where to go. . . ."

"Yeah, yeah, yeah."

"We need someplace to stay. Someplace safe."

"My house. I live alone, outside of town. It's secluded. No one comes there. No one will know."

"That's the other thing," I said. "No one knows. We're deep off until it's over. Then it's all yours."

He hesitated over that one, chewing on his cigarette. But he finally went for it. "Right," he said.

He leaned toward me. He wanted the rest. He wanted it now. But my head was still crowded with images, memories, sounds. It was like being in the subway at rush hour. I needed to get out, I needed some air.

I said: "Tell me how to get to your place. I'll explain the rest this evening."

He wrote out the directions for me on a napkin. I took it, slipped it into the breast pocket of my shirt. We stood up. He was still staring at me. So was Susannah now. She seemed concerned.

We shook hands all around. We walked out onto the sidewalk. Yardley went back to the office. Sue and I headed for the car. I went around to the passenger side to open the door for her. But I didn't. I stood there, staring up Main Street at the rising white steeple of the church. Susannah stood beside me. When she spoke, it seemed to come both from far away and from inside my head.

She said—she just stated it in that way she had: "You remember."

And without thinking, I answered her: "Yes. I remember everything."

Chapter twenty-one

They were buried in the churchyard. I took her to the grave. We climbed the little hill and stood before it, side by side. One plain rounded marker with the name Turner in large letters, then my parents' names beneath and the date of their death. There was no other inscription.

The sinking afternoon sun had edged the shadow of the church spire over the ground on which we stood. The chill air made me shiver. The housewife next door had banged out through her rear screen door and was gathering the laundry from the line. The traffic on Main Street was whispering by. I heard a sparrow singing. I felt the calm, steady sweetness of an unwavering rage.

"It was after midnight," I said. "We had a cuckoo clock out

in the hall. I think it must've awakened me. Then I lay in my bed, in the dark. I was scared. I don't know if I heard him downstairs. Maybe I did. Maybe I was just scared the way you get scared in your bed in the dark when you're a kid. The way you lie there in a sweat, listening to the house settle, figuring it's some monster or killer come to get you. Talking yourself out of it, but not quite relaxed. Still listening, still clutching the covers. Then the house creaks again, and you're sure. Whatever it is, it's coming to get you.

"And this time, it was."

I was staring at the grave. I had almost forgotten Susannah was beside me.

"It happened so fast. So fast. Whispered voices. I remember. I still wasn't sure. The wind seemed to be whispering at the window. Footsteps—there were footsteps in the hall, but I couldn't tell, I was so scared by then. I couldn't tell if it was the house or . . . I got out of bed. My parents' room was right next door. But I didn't want to wake them up. I wanted to be a big boy. I crept out into the hall. I crept toward the top of the stairs. I thought I'd take a look—you know the way you tell yourself you'll take a look and then you'll be sure it's nothing and you'll be able to sleep. I thought I'd take a look and then I'd be sure.

"I remember—I remember reaching out, reaching out toward the banister, and I just . . . my ears, my head seemed full of whispers, the creaks of the house seemed to be inside me. . . . I turned the corner of the stairs, and just at that moment, down below me, down in the front hall, there was a scream, God, a woman's scream, and I saw—I saw Laura, the maid, trying . . . She was trying to run up the stairs, and the stairway light went on. She might have hit it. Maybe he did. He was standing below her with the gun, the rifle. She screamed, and at the same moment, the gun went off, and Laura was thrown against the wall. I remember. Pinned against the wall, and her eyes wide and horrified for a moment. Then wide and blank. And she slid down slowly, forever, it took forever, and it seemed like her hair was rising up the wall behind her, but it was the trail of blood she left as she slid down. And at the same time, it seemed like the same time, I saw him, standing below me. I looked right into his eyes. I wasn't . . . It didn't even . . . surprise me. I knew who it was. I'd been waiting for him since midnight. It was the bogeyman, raising the rifle at me, smiling that little smile, the scarred man, raising . . . And then I was pulled out of the way. I thought: Just like Laura, the way the gunshot threw me to one side. But it wasn't the gunshot. It was my father's hand on my shoulder, pulling me back, pulling me off the stairs. But he'd put himself in the line of fire, and I heard the gun again, and I heard my mother scream, and I screamed, too, because she was running to him, running to him at the top of the stairs as he tumbled backward, and then there was the gun again and again, and they were both lying there. They were both lying there."

I let out a sharp breath. Blinked up toward the spire with the sun gleaming behind it.

"They were both lying there," I said.

Susannah put a hand on my arm. I looked around, half surprised to see her.

I said: "He started coming up the stairs."

She closed her eyes. She leaned against me. The smell of her hair was lush and clean. I looked down at the grave markers.

"He started coming up the stairs. He knew I'd seen him. We'd looked right into each other's eyes as he was raising the gun. He knew I'd seen him and he was coming up the stairs. I ran into my room. There was a tree outside my window. No one could get down that tree as fast I could. But the window . . . we'd put the storm windows up, my father and I. I kept fighting with it, and he was coming closer and closer, I could hear him, I was tearing at those little tabs they have, you have to lift them up to get it to move. And I heard his footsteps on the landing. And it opened. The window. It opened. I went out. I went down the tree. I scrambled down the tree and I ran. I ran and ran and ran into the dark. I knew the forest, see. I knew he couldn't find me there. I knew . . . But then . . . But then . . ."

Susannah pressed against my side. "Then you came back for me."

"You were so little," I said. "I heard you crying. You started crying when the first shot went off. You had a room downstairs. I heard you crying in your crib. You were screaming. Mommy. I didn't even realize I'd heard it until I was running into the woods. Then it came to me, and I thought of you, pictured you, down there, all alone, crying, while he came back down the steps, while he came down the hall to your room. . . . And I came back for you."

I turned my head a little until my cheek touched hers. I breathed the scent of her deeply.

"Let's get away from this place," she whispered, leaning against me, staring at the grave. "Let's get away from everywhere."

"The window to your room was closed," I said. I pursed my lips against her hair. "I could see it as I came running back. I had to go in through the door, the front door. The front door was open. I came in and the stairs were in front of me. I saw his legs as he came down. They stopped. He saw me. I ran, to my left, through the kitchen, down the long hall. I heard him coming after me. He was taking long strides, walking quickly, but he didn't know the way. I came into your room. You were standing up, your hands were holding the top of the crib railing. You'd stopped crying for a minute. You were looking out into the dark. I remember your voice. You said something. You said my name. You said Michael. I picked you up. I told you to be quiet. I heard him coming down the hall now. There was no time to open the window, to get the storm window up. So I went to it, I went to the window, and I opened it. I opened it up. And then I ran back and stood behind the door. And he came in. He came through the door. I saw him pass by like a shadow on the sun. The scarred man came in, and he headed straight toward the window, across the room. And I ran out the door behind him, holding you in my arms."

I heard myself let out one dull laugh. I felt a little better about him outsmarting me in the alleyway. I'd outsmarted him when I was five years old.

"I went down the hall. I thought: I better keep to the parts of the house he hasn't been in before. I couldn't run too fast carrying you. I couldn't have made it back to the door. So I went to the cellar. There were lots of places to hide in the cellar. I didn't think he'd even be able to find the lights down there. So I took you into the broom closet. I had such a hard time keeping you quiet. I kept trying to get you to fall asleep. I don't . . . He was out there. I don't remember anymore. He was out there, he was calling us. . . ."

"My dream . . ." Susannah said.

"Yes. I don't . . . He got closer. I wet myself. I was crying, too, and trying to keep quiet. And you kept talking. And he was right on the stairs above us, calling, 'Come here, children. I promise not to hurt you. Come here.' "

Susannah let out a strangled noise. "All real. It was all real," she said.

I shook my head. A moment ago the images had been running through it like a movie. Now they all seemed to have collided and blended together. It was all a jumble. I couldn't think about it anymore.

I moved away from her a little. I moved among the graves. I moved until I saw the sun come out from behind the steeple. The sun seemed pale in the cool blue sky. We were on the ridge of the hill. Below us, the woman on the other side of the fence had finished bringing in her laundry.

Susannah still stood in front of the graves. Her head was bowed like a mourner's.

She said: "We'll go where they don't know us."

I said: "What do you think they were like?"

"What?"

"That story Yardley told about . . . about our father . . . about Dad . . . him standing out in front of the mob like that . . ."

"I don't remember," she said. "I don't remember either of them."

"No. Me either. Still. He must have been something."

She didn't answer.

"Don't you think so?" I said. "I'll bet he was. I'll bet they both were. Hell, the way she ran to him on the stairs, I'll bet—"

Susannah raised her face to me. I saw weariness in her eyes, and sadness.

"Yes," she said gently. "They must've been something."

"Sure," I said. "Sure they were. Do you really think so?"

"I'm sure of it."

"Sure," I said. "Sure."

I came back to her. She leaned her arm on my shoulder. We stood in front of the grave. We stood a long time. We were silent a long time.

Then I said: "I'm going to kill him."

And Susannah said: "I know."

PART FOUR

A love story

Chapter twenty-two

In the evening, we drove to Yardley's place. We went one more block on Main until it intersected with Grand. To our left, we saw gas stations and a supermarket, a little mall. Beyond that, there were small, gloomy two-story houses. One porch after another, one lawn after another.

As we stopped at the intersection, we could see a train crossing down past those houses. We could see the red lights flashing and the guards lowering. We could hear the warning bells and the whistle of a freight.

On the other side of the tracks, the wrong side, box elder and elm trees crowded the curb, blocked out the light with overhanging branches. But even so, I had a sense of the dismal places hidden in the shadows. I could imagine the white paint chipping off the sides of two- and three-family dwellings; the old woman's face in the window of the apartment above the grocery; the yellow stare of a man on a porch rocker during working hours. I thought of Yardley saying, "You have to understand: this used to be Ku Klux Klan country." I realized—with a small shock—that Nathan Jersey was a black man.

And the freight barreled by, by and by without end, blocking the view.

We turned away, onto Grand Street. The old, white houses here were not luxurious, but they were well kept. Some had signs in front advertising candy stores or antique shops inside. The lawns grew wider, greener as we drove along. The houses grew larger, older. We passed a stretch of turn-of-the-century homes with rising turrets and shingled walls. Then, at the end of Grand Street, there was a traffic circle surrounded by antebellum manses, their white porticoes upheld by stately columns. At the center of the circle, on an island of grass, a bronze union soldier stood atop a pedestal on which were carved the names of Hickman's Civil War dead.

We followed Route 312 out of the circle. It wound beneath the budding branches of maples, willows, and white oaks: proud old trees stretching from powerful trunks. They guarded the iron gates of long driveways that ran toward the colonnades of the finest old mansions. We passed these on a road that had become a two-lane highway. It carried us on past an old stone church, then past a couple of stark, ugly modern churches, and then through the center of a cemetery that vanished over the crests of gentle hills on either side of us. And then we were in the farmlands.

The evening sun was sinking now. The sky was a metallic blue. To our right, the east, where they caught the sun, the houses, barns, and silos gleamed. To our left, they sank into shadow, and the hills melded with the horizon.

Susannah kept her eyes to the window. She watched the scenery with intent interest. More than that. She stared at the changing colors of the clouds. Turned to catch the subtleties of light on distant hills. Shielded her eyes to see the hawks fly. Breathed all of it in deeply, as if she wanted it inside her.

I stole glances at her from the driver's seat. I remembered how I'd found her in the mist outside her dormitory three days ago. I thought of her wild and weary eyes then. Of the dream haunting them.

I thought of her laughing in the snow outside her father's house.

Susannah gazed out the window, hungry for the rolling hills and the wide sky. She belonged here, or someplace like it. She was born here, after all.

The dirt road appeared suddenly to our left. I hit the brake, but it was a hard turn. The tires bounced, spitting rocks at the muffler as we left the blacktop.

The road ran into the rolling hills. It ran past a post fence and past a gate in the fence that led to a farmhouse. Then it lifted to a crest of land where a row of hickories stood. The car bounced through the trees. A small valley opened below us. Susannah drew in her breath with a sharp hiss. It was lovely. There were hills on every side. A little stream ran through it. The water caught the scarlet of the sinking sun. Thin young elms stood here and there, their light green buds fading into the twilight. To our right, nestled among sycamores, was Yardley's place: a two-story cottage. A little shabby, actually, but sort of quaint all the same. There was a battered white Chevy in the drive out front. Slowly, we bounced toward it down the dirt road.

Yardley met us in the doorway. Yardley and his cats. Two orange ones and a calico with cute names that ended in *y*.

Susannah said, "It's so beautiful here!"

For the first time, Yardley looked directly at her. He seemed surprised she'd noticed. Then he glanced toward the western hills where the sun was setting. "That it is," he said.

Toting our baggage, we went inside. It was drab in there. Everything was threadbare and shoddy. It smelled of age. We came into the kitchen first, where the yellow linoleum was peeling up from the black foundation beneath. We went down a hall lined with ancient wallpaper and into a living room where torn curtains dangled over dirty windows and colorless furniture shed its stuffing through tears and burst seams. The stairs groaned as we went up. I saw Susannah run her finger over the railing, leaving a trail in the dust. Yardley directed us to two bedrooms. Mine had a four-poster in it, draped with fading lace. It had a rocker with a wickerwork seat ripped to pieces. It smelled musty. I thought of an old woman propped up in bed, peering through the fading light at life.

Yardley took Susannah to her room while I unpacked.

When I came downstairs, they were in the kitchen. I heard Yardley say: "I'm not very good at this." I heard Susannah laugh.

I walked in. They were standing next to each other, making ham and cheese sandwiches on a rickety wooden table.

Yardley glanced up at me. "I was just telling Susannah: I haven't had time to fix this place up since my mother died."

"She only died two months ago," Susannah said.

I said I was sorry.

"No, no, she was sick a long time," said Yardley. "God, forever." He said this without bitterness. "But the thing is, she couldn't keep up the house and we couldn't afford much help. It was everything I could do to pay off the property taxes to keep the place together. Anyway, that's why it's sort of in disrepair. Like, falling down around your ears."

"It's fine," Susannah said. "And the land . . . it was worth keeping."

He smiled at her. Laid a last slice of ham on a piece of white bread and said: "I give up." She laughed again. He sat down at the table. She continued to stand over him, slicing cheese. He slapped a cigarette in his mouth and lit it. I did the same.

I said: "I guess we ought to talk about—"

"Let's not." Susannah had stopped working at the table. She looked up at me, then at him. "Just for a little while," she said softly. "Let's not."

I shrugged. "Okay. How about them Buckeyes?"

We ate at the kitchen table. Yardley talked. He talked a lot. He was smart and he was funny, and he probably didn't have too many people to talk to. He seemed to want to tell us everything, fast, the way lonely people do, like they're afraid you'll stop them. He talked about Hickman's politics, and the county's. He made Susannah laugh with stories about the clowns on the town board. And he had some good crime stories with an eerie rural quality to them. Every now and again he'd stop and say to me, "I guess that's nothing compared to some of the stuff you've covered." But I didn't tell any stories.

After dinner we had drinks. We took them outside. Yardley put out some beach chairs. We held off the deepening chill with the liquor and looked at the stars.

"I've always liked this time of year," Yardley said. "It's easy to find the zodiac early in the evening. It cuts right across the middle of the sky." He gestured at the night with his cigarette.

"Oh, I can never find anything," said Susannah. "Show me where."

He showed her the lion, and the crab and the twins. He showed her where Orion battles the bull and told her about the scorpion who chases the hunter through the year. I drank silently.

It was just after ten when Susannah got up to go inside. We hadn't slept much in the past few days. She looked exhausted. Yardley rose from his seat and offered to show her to her room. She laughed: a pretty laugh that made him look bashfully at his shoes. She went indoors alone. In a few moments we saw her light go on behind a curtain on the second story.

Yardley snorted, embarrassed. He hid his face behind the blaze of a match and the smoke of still another cigarette. As he sat back in his chair, a cat jumped onto his lap. He stroked it. It purred.

He cleared his throat. "She's very nice," he said.

"Yes."

"Are you, uh, are you guys . . ."

"No," I said. Then I took a breath. Then I said: "She's my sister."

"What?"

I told him. Not everything, but enough. I told him what I had remembered that afternoon, and I told him about getting shot at in the alleyway. I didn't tell him about my story or her dream —or anything that might hint that we had been lovers. I did tell him about the scarred man. When I was done, he glanced up at Susannah's window.

"Sounds tough," he said.

I didn't answer him. I listened to the peepers and the cicadas and all the whirring sounds of the night.

He said: "I've always sort of wondered about her: the sister, I mean. She wasn't in any of the clips. She was mentioned in the first story, maybe the first few, but after that . . ."

Still I said nothing.

"Why do you think that is?" Yardley asked.

After a while I said: "I'd like to know."

My voice sounded harsh, even to me. It seemed to bring

Yardley out of a reverie. "Okay. Okay," he said. "How do you want to do this?"

We talked it over. We needed to know more about the rape: who was in the lynch mob, who might have been angry enough to kill my father because he'd protected Jersey, who might have been smart enough to set up a frame. I left that job to Yardley. For myself, I wanted to talk to Jersey's lawyer.

"I don't want this poor bastard to fry while we play the Hardy Boys," I said.

But Yardley's gaze had drifted around to the house again, to the window. The light up there went out.

"What's his name?"

"What?" said Yardley.

"Jersey's attorney. What's his name?"

"Oh. Uh. Wait a minute. Marks, his name is. Howard Marks."

Chapter twenty-three

I did not spend a pleasant night. I lay on the bed in the dark fully dressed. The old bed squeaked. The old room smelled. The dark was full of images.

I saw them die again, my parents; heard the gunshots, saw them fall. Some of it came to me in flashes of crystal clarity: Laura sinking down the wall, the trail of her blood seeming to rise from her hair; the moment my mother went down; the moment I ran; the moment I turned back. Other scenes were dreamlike and uncertain, as if they were taking place underwater. They were no less frightening for that. More so, if anything. It seemed to take them out of my control, as if they might appear, shimmering in the dark before me, without warning, at any minute. I saw the scarred man turn to me and smile and raise his gun like that. I saw the dark of the broom closet like that as I waited for him, listened to his voice beckoning us, calling us to come out.

I saw other things, too. Things that kept me turning on the bed, awake. That made me reach for the cigarette pack repeatedly, promising myself that each time was the last. That made me, sometimes, sit up on the edge of the mattress and lay my head in my hands. It was one of those nights when I felt very close to things as they should be, and very distant from things as they are.

I didn't wake up until nearly eight-thirty. Susannah and Yardley were already in the kitchen. I found them standing together before the big old stove. They were making eggs and toast.

"You overslept, doof," said Susannah.

I didn't answer her. I sat at the table. She brought me coffee and I saw Yardley steal a quick glance over his shoulder to watch her move. I drank the coffee in silence.

The two of them carried the food to the table. They sat down with me and we began to eat.

"Hey, you wield a mean spatula," Yardley said.

Susannah laughed and he laughed. Then she turned and saw me staring at her. Their laughter faded away.

After a few minutes, Yardley said: "I better . . . I have to go to work."

When he went out, Susannah and I sat together without speaking. We heard his car revving up in the drive. We heard the dirt crunch under the tires as it pulled away.

Susannah moved her hand out to me on the table. "Michael," she said.

I threw my fork down on the plate. It clattered noisily.

"Let's go," I said.

Slowly, she raised her eyes to me. I got up and went outside without her.

The little Honda we'd rented sat alone in the drive. I went to it, opened the door. I stood still for a moment in the chill morning mist. I scanned the pale blue sky, the clouds scudding over the surrounding hills. I heard the cottage door bang shut.

"I need some time alone," she said. She was standing beside me.

I turned to her. I lifted my hand to touch her lips. She caught my hand in hers. Her eyes were very wide, very blue. I kissed her hand. I got in the car.

Howard Marks kept an office on Main Street. It was a modest place, a converted house hidden among the antique stores near the school. He had the second floor, but stairs led to it through a private entrance. I went up, gave my name to the receptionist.

When Marks peeked out of his office, he seemed at first not to remember me. He studied me with a blank smile, his damp eyes peering over half-lens reading glasses. Then the smile faded. He remembered me, and he knew my business. He came forward, extending his hand.

"We met on Monday," I said.

"At Carl McGill's office in Manhattan. I remember. Come in, please."

I followed him into his office. He sat in a swivel chair behind an enormous wooden desk, gestured me to the seat in front of it. The room provided the perfect backdrop for a country lawyer. There was a shelf with books and mementos to my left, a window on Main Street to my right. There were plaques and diplomas on the wall. There were pictures on the desk: two freckle-faced towheaded boys and a blond girl, the youngest; a slim, elegant woman with a bright, nervous smile. There were loose sheets of paper everywhere.

Marks spoke first: "Have you reached him?" He still spoke in his slow, porch-swing drawl, but the urgency was unmistakable. His client had a week to live.

"No," I said. "But I may be able to help you."

He removed the glasses, sat back, waited.

"My name is Michael Turner," I said.

Marks's lips parted. He stared at me. Slowly, he nodded. "You are, aren't you," he said. He shook his head. He made a clicking sound in his teeth, a purely rural sound. "Do you know why I came to see Carl McGill the other day, young man?"

"No. No, I don't."

"Grasping at straws." He shook his head again, bemused. "I was grasping at straws like a man going down for the third time. I guess I was doing that, too, wasn't I? Going down for the third time." He sniffed. "Listen to me. Lawyers love to talk that way. High-blown. Dramatic. Makes people think they got something at stake 'sides a fee. Which they don't. When it's all over, when the jailing's done, or the hanging, lawyer, he's right back in his office where he started from, talking high-blown while his client takes the ten paces from one wall of his cell to the other, or walks to the gallows." The wrinkles of his face lifted in a sad smile. "Sorry," he said. "I guess I'm a little beat. What I mean to say is: I came to New York looking for you."

"Is that right?"

"Yup. Came . . . See, the thing is, young man, after the trial the children, you and Susannah, you were in shock. Pure shock. Staring at the walls. The doctors, they said there was no chance you'd remember anything. Now, o' course, Susannah, she was such a little thing, cute little thing, she could hardly talk to begin with. So she was out of it right off. Then, when we tried to question you, well, it was pretty clear the doc was right and, of course, no one wanted to . . . well, make things worse for you, you see. Anyway, the children were sent away . . . separately, as I recall. . . . Boy, I hated to see you two split up, you were awfully fond of each other. . . . Anyway, what was I . . . ? Oh yeah, well, I lost track of you over the years, and after the Supreme Court threw out the death penalty, why, I figured that was as good as we could hope for. Good as we could hope for," he said wistfully. He stared into space for a moment, then blinked, coming out of it. "Then this unfortunate thing occurred. Sadistic guard. Pushed Nathan . . . Nathan's a . . . a simple man. The guard pushed him past his limits and he lashed out, that's all. He lashed out. What happened to your parents has nothing to do with this case, I know, but, well, McGill always took a special interest in the kids, right from the beginning, he took a special interest. I figured he might know where you were, and I thought, maybe, if I could find you, if you would come forward and plead with the governor for mercy, maybe . . ."

"Mr. Marks," I said. "What if I can show that Nathan Jersey is innocent?"

It was a moment before the attorney said: "Innocent of what?"

"He didn't kill my parents."

Marks began to speak, then stopped. He gazed off thoughtfully, twisting his lower lip between thumb and index finger. He smiled to himself. Then he looked up at me.

"Mr. Turner, my client did kill your parents. I know it. He knows it. He confessed to it. He was a poor man in a tough town, a black man in a white town, he was a retarded man in a town filled with ignorance and bigotry. You might say, well, why would a fella like that strike out at the one man who was kind to him. But the fact is, it happens all the time. Human nature. Happens all the time. I've claimed that he was mistreated, and he was. I've claimed that he was not competent, and he wasn't. But in all these years, dearly as I would've liked to, I've never claimed he was innocent."

I leaned forward in my chair, one hand holding the other before me. "You can start now," I said.

I gave him the rundown, again glossing over my relationship with Susannah. I told him she and I seemed to share a subconscious memory of a scarred man—and that we had seen him in the mist one night. I told him how he had shot at us in the alley. I told him I had now recalled some of the events of the night of the murder. I thought that was enough.

Marks sighed. He put his hand out in front of him. He pointed at one of his long fingers.

"I always seem to be doing this," he said. "Counting on my fingers the reasons why something won't work. Probably sixty percent of a lawyer's job. So: The scarred man is nothing. Forget the scarred man. A subconscious memory won't even get us a hearing."

"We saw him, Sue and I both."

"In the night. In the mist."

"He shot at us."

"Didja see him that time?"

I didn't answer.

He counted it off. "You didn't see him. People out here think shooting goes on in New York every day. Anyway, if you work for Carl McGill, you must have enough enemies to fill a phone book. Am I wrong?" I didn't answer. He counted it off. "I'm not wrong. I'm running out of fingers here."

"They can't execute him if I remember he didn't kill my parents."

"They're not executing him for killing your parents, they're executing him for killing a vicious, sadistic prison guard who got exactly what he deserved." He had raised his voice. He put his hand on his forehead. "Sorry. Sorry."

"Forget it."

"Seven days is not very much time."

"But if I can prove he shouldn't have been in jail in the first place—"

"If you can *prove* it, sure."

I sat back, letting out a held breath. "That night," I said. "I ran away from the killer. I kept outrunning him. Because he didn't know the way and I did. If Nathan Jersey worked there all the time, why didn't he know the way?" Marks was about to count on his fingers again. I said: "What if I can find the scarred man. He must've been in the lynch mob. He must have known that girl. He must be somewhere."

"You've got seven days," Marks said.

My eyes moved over his desk again. To the pictures of the kids again. In one shot, one of the boys had a protective arm flung over the girl's shoulders. The girl was giggling happily into her hand.

I spoke more fiercely than I meant to. "I want to talk to Jersey."

Marks lifted his eyebrows a little. "What's that?"

"Can you arrange it? I have to talk to him."

"Can I . . . ?" He shook his head slowly. "Believe me, son. It's useless."

"Maybe. Maybe it is. I want to try."

He sat slumped in his chair now, his chin on his chest. His silver-white hair hung limp. His friendly wrinkles sagged. He studied me sadly. When he leaned forward—slowly, wearily—I could almost feel the weight of the case on him, the years of attempts and failures.

"All right," he said then.

"You'll do it."

"Yes. Hell, it can't hurt. Is Susannah here too?"

I hesitated a moment, then nodded. "Yes."

"How can I reach you?"

I looked over my shoulder toward the office door.

"Forget that, forget that," said Marks. "Arlene can't hear you."

"Still," I said. "I have a man hunting me with a rifle. No one knows where I am. Let's keep it that way. I'll call you."

"Okay. Call me tonight. Here's my number at home. I'll set up an appointment for you and Susannah."

"Yes."

"And you'll . . . you'll talk to the governor?"

"Sure."

I stood up. I shook his hand. "I'm sorry this had to come back into your life," he said.

"I don't suppose it ever left."

He smiled at me. His eyes were sad. His client had seven days to live.

Chapter twenty-four

After lunch I went out to the backlands. I went out to see the inn. It was on the side of town opposite Yardley's place. I took the highway, then turned off, and off again, onto smaller and smaller roads. The trees seemed to accumulate at the edge of the pavement until the land around me was forest. There were wooden signs with burned letters pointing the way to Jackson Lake. I followed them. Soon I saw the water gleaming through the trees. I parked the car on a dirt shoulder, got out and followed a footpath into the woods.

The forest was cool and quiet, streaked with the early afternoon sun. I heard loons laughing on the lake below me. When I reached the edge of the water, I could see them gliding on the surface of still water, making the reflection of the trees and the misty sky shimmer beneath them. It was a large lake, running out of sight around bends to my right and left. There were one or two boats sailing out there, far away. There was an island of trees at the center, a rising hill of trees on the opposite shore. Yardley had told me the inn was there, on that shore, but I couldn't make it out. I went back up the path to my car.

I drove around the lake, trying to keep close to it, losing it sometimes behind the trees. Finally the hill was directly to my right. I watched for the inn. I still didn't see it.

Then I spotted the driveway. Or what was left of the driveway. The macadam was crumbling. Vines and shoots and grass pushed through the holes, covering the chunks and pebbles. Trees had stretched their branches out over it. Deadwood had fallen across. The forest's uncontrolled growth cast a shadow over the entrance; the presence of decay cast a pall. I wrestled the car through the debris and began to make my way.

The drive climbed the hill for about half a mile. It was half a mile of hard going. Logs blocked the path, broken stones rattled the tires, sudden pits made the steering wheel jump in my hand.

Slowly, I came around a bend. The inn was there.

It was set back in the trees, and the trees had folded in around it. It seemed weighed down by the naked branches that bent over its roof and clustered around its walls. Those branches streaked the place with shadows—shadows that reached and wavered in the breeze—and their movement made a steady whisper, a nearly human murmur of complaint.

The inn itself was a broad-faced old Victorian, two stories and a large front porch with gingerbread trim. It was all in ruins: sagging weatherboard and shattered windows. It had the hapless stare of the dead. Shrubbery, grass, trees, and wildflowers: everything was rotting around it. It brooded in a field of gray.

In the dead yard behind was the little stream I had remembered. The maple tree too, though the swing was gone. I stood there for a long time, looking. I didn't move forward. I didn't want to.

I just wanted to stand there. I just wanted to have been standing there all those years. I wanted things to be the way they should have been, instead of the way they had been. I wanted to talk to him. I wanted to talk to my father.

I wanted to tell him I was sorry about Susannah. I hadn't known, I would have done anything to have known, to have kept it from happening the way it had. I wanted to explain to him that it had happened because I loved her so much and I hadn't known. I wanted to tell him that I could not live without her; that her hands were always busy with things but her eyes were steady and spoke her mind; that her smile made her face lopsided. I wanted to tell him what a great team the Mets would have this year, and ask him if he'd ever read Herodotus and wasn't he fine. I wanted to tell him that I was going to nail the scarred man, and that Nathan Jersey would not die and that I knew how to make a stand, too, and even Scarangello couldn't push me around.

"He's a gangster in New York," I whispered.

I heard a noise behind me: a footstep on the forest bed.

I turned slowly, naturally, as if I hadn't heard anything at all. I swept the woods with my eyes. Many of the trees up here were new growth with slender trunks. But there was one big red oak on the edge of the driveway, a few yards down the hill. A man could have hidden behind that one.

I started down the drive at an easy pace. I reached the oak and made my move. I feinted to the left, then came around the right side of the trunk fast. I had one hand extended, the other cocked at my shoulder, ready to go for his eyes. He broke toward me, and I had him. I grabbed him by the throat, brought up my knee and struck with my clawed fingers. Nearly killed him before I realized he was eight years old.

"Aw, Jesus, kid," I said.

I dumped him on the ground. We spent the next few seconds trembling in unison. When I finally looked at him, I saw a red-haired kid with a pug's face: a tough guy in jeans and a plaid shirt. I helped him to his feet. He dusted himself off.

"The place is haunted," he blurted out. His face was pale beneath his freckles.

"Yeah, by you. What do you want?"

"I just wanted to see who was coming up here. My dad owns the Lake Motel nearby. I saw your car. No one ever comes up here."

"Because it's haunted."

"Yeah. So I wanted to see." He waited, belligerent, his hands hooked in his pockets. "Well?" he said.

"Well, what?"

"Well, so what're you doing?"

"Oh. I was thinking of buying it."

"Oh, heck, mister, you can't buy it. It's haunted. I just told you."

"Yeah? How's it haunted?"

"Just is. There was a murder there. Long time ago. Before I was born. Three people shot dead just like that. Guy's gonna fry for it next week too. My brother told me."

"Yeah? So? What do they do, these ghosts? Come back and chant or something?"

"I don't know. All I ever seen 'em do was just moving around."

"You've seen that."

"Me and Freddy both. Saw them pacing around up on the second story. Middle of the night. Could hear them too."

"When was this?"

"Anytime. Saw it a couple of times."

His eyes were wide. He hung toward me, eager for me to believe him. I didn't believe him.

"Well, thanks for the tip," I said. "And be careful next time."

"Okay. I sure will. 'Bye."

He started to run off into the woods. I called after him: "Hey!"

He stopped, turned.

"What's it like?" I asked. "Growing up around here?"

He considered it for a few seconds. Then he shrugged. "It's regular," he said. "It's just regular."

I nodded. "Okay. Thanks."

He disappeared among the trees.

Chapter twenty-five

I stopped off at the courthouse on my way back to Yardley's. I asked for a transcript of Nathan Jersey's trial. The court clerk told me he'd have one ready by Monday. I left him some cash for costs.

It was late afternoon before I came down the dirt road, through the bank of hickories and into the valley again. The sun was still bright. The mist had burned away. The little stream that wove among the elms had the blue sky in it. Yardley's cottage did not seem as shabby as it had at twilight.

The Chevy was not in the drive. I parked beside the cottage door and went in. At first I could not tell what was different about the place. Then I saw how clean it was. The rust and stains were gone from the kitchen, the torn curtains gone from the living room. The sun poured through the window and there was no dust floating in it. Upstairs, new sheets had been put on the bed.

I heard a car pull up outside. I looked out the window and saw them get out of the Chevy. They were carrying bags of groceries. They were laughing.

I heard them come into the kitchen. I started down the hall and heard their voices.

Yardley was telling a story about an elephant that had thrashed his trainer during a two-bit traveling circus. Susannah was flushed and laughing. The peals of it tailed off as I came in. She looked down at the floor. Yardley ran a hand up through his hair shyly.

"So anyway," he said.

I grinned. I chuckled.

We had drinks outside in the fading light.

Susannah said: "It looks like . . . I don't know. It looks the way things look when you remember them."

I watched her gaze run over the twilight valley. Her eyes were soft, wistful.

"I went out to the inn today," I said. I told them about it and about my meeting with Marks.

As I spoke, Susannah stared at her drink. Yardley was silent. He smoked his cigarette. He watched her, his eyes narrowed, through the haze of smoke. Even when I finished speaking, he went on, studying each feature of her face while the silence dragged on and on. Finally, she lifted her face to him. He smiled and she smiled back slightly. He cleared his throat, glanced at me, started talking.

He'd found out about the rape, he said. The Sheriff—the old Sheriff, now retired—had remembered. The victim had been a woman named Louisa Campbell. Her father, Fred, ran a tavern near the Turner inn. Louisa waited tables there sometimes, and sometimes she did other things, and sometimes nobody knew what she did. She had been nineteen or so.

The night of the rape, she came in drunk. Her hair was messed, her clothes disheveled but not torn. She said, "I've been raped by that retard nigger: Jersey." She said it angrily, throwing her purse down on the bar. Fred and his son Marvin got up the lynch mob.

The old Sheriff had his theories about the case. He told Yardley he'd seen rape victims before, and Louisa wasn't one of them, not by his lights. He said he wasn't sure Jersey hadn't had sex with her, but she was the sort of woman who might have done that on a bet. Maybe she was ashamed afterward or just afraid it would get around, maybe she was ticked off about something, or maybe it was her idea of fun. In any case, the Sheriff said, there was something wrong with the girl, something mean about her. Guilty or not, he said, if Nathan Jersey burned next week, Louisa Campbell would be the one who pulled the switch.

"Is she still around?" I asked.

Yardley polished off one cigarette and lit another. The butts and matches were piling up in the patch of dead grass between his feet. He shook his head. "Moved away. Years ago. Sheriff didn't know where."

"Are any of them still around?"

"Marvin, the brother. The father died of a stroke quite a while back. Marvin runs an RV camp out where the tavern used to be." He went on with a smirk. "Interesting fellow, this Marvin. He was sixteen at the time he led the good people of Hickman on a lynching raid. Not long after that he joined a motorcycle gang. He spent two years in prison for assault with a deadly weapon, said weapon being a tire iron, said assault being on a motorist who had accidentally run said Marvin's bike off the road. While in the slammer, he discovered Jesus—

who was doing time, I think, on a traffic offense. When he returned to his native soil, he turned his back on his pappy's sinful gin mill and set up the first Church of God, which answered the musical question: What if they gave a religion and nobody came? Anyway, pappy Fred died soon after that, so Marvin closed down the tavern and opened the RV place. He apparently still holds Sunday services for the faithful out of a trailer set up for the purpose." He held his cigarette out before him. He turned it this way and that, watching it glow in the growing dark. "Something else you ought to know about old Marvin too," he said.

"All right."

"He has a scar."

"Everybody has a scar."

"On his cheek, from a prison knife fight."

"Then he wouldn't have had it at the time of the killing."

The dusk was deep now, but I could see Yardley's shrug. "Just thought you ought to know," he said.

Susannah made dinner that night. She worked on it a long time and it was very good. Afterward, I called Marks at home. He told me he had to go to Indianapolis for the weekend to plead Jersey's case. He said he and Susannah and I could visit Jersey in prison on Monday.

I hung up. I meant to rejoin Sue and Yardley outside, but I paused on the threshold. Their voices drifted to me on the still night air. They were speaking quietly, about the stars probably. I saw the glowing tip of his cigarette pointing them out to her, like he was drawing pictures on the sky.

I didn't go out. I started upstairs to my bedroom. On the way I stopped by the phone again. I called American Express and left another message for McGill at the Lima office:

Now I know. Who is the scarred man?

Chapter twenty-six

Marvin Campbell was a very bad man, and he looked like what he was. His face was a huge, shapeless wad of putty. It had the looming dimension of a storm cloud blowing toward you over the top of a hill. Sunk in the mass of it were two flat, cold, and colorless eyes. They looked like the instant before a snakebite, and that was when he smiled. He had a scar, all right: an ugly red crescent on his right cheek just above his jaw. It lifted in a sort of miniature grimace as he squinted at me, studied me.

We were in his trailer. It served as the office for the place. His living area was on one side: a kitchen, a sofa, a TV, and a john. On the other side there was a little desk piled high with pamphlets, fundamentalist religious literature. Campbell was in front of the desk, leaning against a wooden rack with travel brochures on it. He looked down at me. I shifted from foot to foot.

The trailer was small. Campbell was immense. He was six-four, six-five. He had to weigh at least three hundred pounds. He was wearing a denim jacket with cutoff sleeves. His bare arms hung down like sides of beef in a freezer. His torso looked like the freezer.

Those colorless eyes glinted at me.

"You want to talk about my sister?" he said.

"In a few days a man named Nathan Jersey is going to die in the electric chair."

He raised and lowered his enormous head. "Praise Jesus." He had a voice like a landslide.

"Mr. Campbell, he may be innocent."

He snorted. Walked over to the refrigerator. In the narrow trailer he had to go through me to get there. He did. I smelled beer on him as he passed. He opened the refrigerator door and pulled out a bottle of the stuff. He came stomping back. He stood in front of me while he ripped off the bottle cap. He tilted the bottle back and let half of the beer burble down his throat. He surfaced, belching.

"You a lawyer or something?"

"A reporter."

"Same thing. Worse. Sinners in the sight of God. Straw for the fire. No respect for anything."

He stopped. I could hear children laughing. I glanced out the window and saw the rows of vans and campers parked in the dusty lot. The children were playing in the first really mild day of spring. They seemed very far away somehow.

"Mr. Campbell, what I'd like to know—"

That was as far as I got. "What you want to know is shit," he opined. "Shit you can write in your paper or lie about on TV or what the fuck, whatever. I know. Making a hell on earth for the Antichrist to live in. You want to say, Oh feel sorry for the rapist nigger, the mean people made him do what he done, kill a guard." His voice rose to the level of a limited nuclear engagement. "Killed a guard, for chrissake, got you no respect at all?"

"So you've followed the case," I said.

"Fucking A, man. It's a sign of the times. Sign of the fucking times, fucking A, you hear me."

"I take it you think Nathan Jersey is guilty."

"He killed a fucking guard, man. You got no fucking respect for authority?"

"But maybe he shouldn't have been in prison to begin with."

He had started to drink again but now he waved the bottle dismissively instead. "Would've hung the little retard twenty years ago, anyway."

"Because he raped your sister."

"Nah." He waved the bottle again. "My sister's a whore. She was a whore then, she's a whore now. Now at least she makes some money at it. Let me ask you something," he went on, leaning toward me. "You think God don't know?"

He breathed into my face, waiting for an answer. I couldn't untangle the syntax of the question.

"Uh . . . yes," I said.

"God knows. God sees her out there in Hollywood or what the fuck, wherever the fuck she is. God looks down on her and he says to the angels and the archangels, he says, 'Write that one down right there. That one's a pussy peddler.' "

My imagination failed me.

"God sees the fall of a fucking sparrow," Campbell said. "You think he don't see Louisa peddling her twat? It's all right there in the Bible. Look what he did to Turner."

"And Jersey?"

"God. That was God's hand moving on the face of the water, my friend, believe you me."

I nodded.

"Killed him fucking stone dead for the pimp he was, and his wife and that whore he pimped for too."

"Saved you the trouble."

"You got that right, fucking A. I'd'a been happy to do the job."

He swilled more beer. I said: "And you'd have hung Nathan Jersey?"

He gasped out of the bottle. Thumped the empty down on top of the TV. A line of foam ran from the corner of his mouth to the tip of his chin. Some expression was beginning to mold the paste of his face. Something misty and faraway, almost sweet.

"Yeah," he said, with feeling. "Yeah, I'd'a hung him. Fucking A."

"Even though he didn't rape your sister."

He shrugged, his gaze distant. "He was a nigger. And he touched her, didn't he? Drooling over her. Louisa was just fooling with him, getting him on for laughs. Shit, she was never no nigger lover. Not then, anyhow. Now . . ." He shivered. "I don't know. But Jersey . . . Jersey got carried away. Figured to touch a white woman. She told him to stop. Had to slap him before he would. Left a mark on her arm."

He touched his massive shoulder dreamily.

There was a long silence. I realized I was holding my breath.

"That's a lynching offense, is it?" I said.

He blinked. He nodded. "To me it was."

I swallowed hard. "So you went after him."

"Oh yeah. Oh yeah."

"So what happened?"

He stared over my head. The memory had hold of him now.

I could see it moving in his eyes like the swirl inside a marble. "The pimp," he said dully. "Yeah. The pimp. Turner. The pimp for the redheaded whore, he comes out, he starts talking like some kinda, some kinda . . . I don't know. Sheeyet." Half of his mouth lifted. "Me, shit, I didn't care. I'd'a hung him anyway. Turner too. I said, 'Daddy, shit, he ain't even got no gun.' 'Cept . . ." His voice trailed off.

"Except the mob backed out on you," I said.

"Fucking cowards. Fucking pimp Turner talking them into cowards."

"And your father too."

"Shit. My sister, man. You know what I'm saying? Wasn't their sister, not even Daddy's. You know what I'm fucking saying?"

He stared over my head. The putty of his face was tinged with pink. The memory was still there. It still had the power to make him mad.

I swallowed hard again. "Mr. Campbell, did anyone who was with you that night—anyone you can remember at all—have a scar down the middle of his face? Like this?" I traced it on my own face with a finger.

Vaguely, he shook his head no.

And I heard myself ask him suddenly: "Where were you the night Robert Turner died?"

He was silent. His beady eyes kept swirling with the memory. With that, and more than that. With the dream, too, of how he thought it should've turned out. Slowly, one corner of his mouth lifted in a faraway smile. Then he punched me in the face.

I went stumbling backward across the room. The edge of the desk hit me in the spine. I gasped as the wind went out of me. My knees would not lock anymore. I collapsed in a heap on the floor. I sat there for a while and watched the stars swirling in front of me. I saw constellations and galaxies. My mouth hung open and I drooled.

Marvin Campbell picked up his beer bottle. Vaguely, I thought: He's going to kill me. He didn't. He poured what was left of the beer over me and tossed the empty onto the sofa. He towered over me. He laughed.

"I was in jail for D and D that night," he rumbled. "You can check on it."

He bent down and grabbed me by the belt buckle and the shirt front. He lifted me into the air. He carried me across the trailer. He set me down against the wall while he opened the door. Then he pushed me. I fell down two steps and hit the dirt below. I lay there with Marvin Campbell standing in the doorway like a titan.

"Pray to God for forgiveness for your wicked thoughts," he said.

He shut the door.

I lay in the dust, staring up at the sky. The sky, it seemed, stared back. The kids who had been playing had gathered around me. They gazed down at me curiously.

"You all right, mister?" one little boy asked.

I mumbled something. I heard the door snap open again above me. The children's faces vanished. Marvin Campbell's face loomed over me instead.

He smiled at me. I thought about the pistol in the glove compartment of the car. It seemed a million miles away. I thought: Oh God.

"I ever hear you said anything against me," he said, "I'll come for you. You remember that. Will you remember that?"

I nodded eagerly. "Yes," I said.

He leaned down and grabbed me by the shirt front again. "Now get out of here."

He hauled me to my feet. I jammed my fingers into his eye.

He cried out and his head snapped back. I hit him in the throat with the web of my hand. He gagged and let go of me. I kneed him in the groin. He gasped and bent double. I hit him on the back of the neck with my clasped hands. He dropped to his knees. I kicked him in the face. He toppled over into the dust with a loud thud. I kicked him in the temple. He lost consciousness.

I began to walk away. I have a rule about that. I never hit a man when he's unconscious. It's a point of honor with me. I started for the car.

"Oh, fuck it," I said. I went back and kicked him again. Then I left him lying there.

Chapter twenty-seven

I drove back to Yardley's cottage. It wasn't easy. My vision was blurred. My mind was foggy. My stomach rolled. I had to stop the car three times. Three times I pulled over and fell out the door to vomit in the dust by the roadside. The last time it was the smell of the vomit itself that made me sick. My face was swelling. My head hurt. My mouth bled.

When I finally coasted down the dirt road into the valley, I knew I was losing it. I parked next to the Chevy. I stumbled out, dropping to my knees, dragging myself to my feet by the car handle. I stumbled toward the door. It was open. I went in. With every step I felt like I was going down. Then I took another step. I crossed the kitchen. I tried to call out: "Susannah." The effort made me ill.

Another step brought me to the threshold of the living room. I leaned against the jamb.

They were standing close together in the center of the room. The afternoon light spilled, misty, through the window, fell in a pool around them. The rest of the room hung back in the shadows as if it had withdrawn discreetly from the scene. They were facing each other, and his hand was on her shoulder. He was staring down at her, dazed and ravenous, like he'd die if he didn't kiss her soon. Her eyes were filled with tears and very blue and she had to make up her mind in a moment. She had to decide whether to tilt her chin up imperceptibly and make the offer or turn away and let it die in the talk that followed.

I saved her the trouble by peeling off the threshold and taking the long, long journey into the dark.

She was sitting on the edge of the bed when I came to. She was changing the ice in a compress with new cubes from a basin beside her. She turned to look at me. She looked sad at first. Then she saw my eyes were open. She smiled.

"What's the other guy look like?" she asked.

"Big," I told her. "Big and muscular."

Her smile widened, skewing her face. "He really gave you a working over."

"He hit me once."

"Wo."

I shut my eyes. My whole head hurt and my whole body seemed to be inside my head.

Susannah lay the compress against the bruise, held it there.

"It's all right," she whispered.

I wanted to open my eyes fast to catch the look that went with the sound of her voice. I couldn't manage it.

I said: "Susannah, Susannah."

"Ssh."

I finally looked, but she was expressionless by then.

"I asked him where he was on the night our parents died," I said.

"Oh please be quiet, Michael," she whispered with a breath. "Be quiet and lie still."

I reached up and took her wrist. I pried her hand and the compress away. She closed her eyes as if she were in pain.

"They were your parents too," I said.

She shook her head at me. Her gaze was gentle. "They weren't," she said. "I'm sorry. I never knew them. I had a family of my own that raised me and I loved them and I'm sorry you didn't, Michael, believe me, I'm so sorry for you, but I just . . . I just want to be all right again."

I let her go. My hand fell to my side. I rolled my head to evade her goddamned kindness.

"I hope you find out what happened," I heard her say. "I hope you do. I know you will. I know that Nathan Jersey won't die because you will. But I don't care about the rest. I don't care . . . Michael . . . brother . . . I just want to be all right again. Everything has been so awful ever since . . ."

"Ever since you met me," I said.

"Ever since you told that story. Even before that. The nightmares. I'm glad it's out now. I'm glad I know what it is. Maybe I never would have if I hadn't met you. And if it would bring our parents back to life, I'd want to know more, I'd want to know everything. Like you do. But I think it would be fine with them . . . I really think it would be fine with them if I were just . . . all right again. I really do."

I started to speak. I thought better of it. I took a breath instead. She stood up.

"Listen," she said.

"Yeah."

"I think you should eat. Do you think you can eat?"

"Oh, jeez. No."

"I'll get you something."

"Thanks."

She moved to the doorway.

"Are you sorry?" I asked her.

"Never," she said.

Chapter twenty-eight

*I*t was a long weekend. Saturday I lay upstairs in bed. Sometimes she came and sat with me. Sometimes, she sat downstairs. I could hear their voices, but not what they said. I had dizzy spells whenever I tried to stand. I didn't sleep most of the night. I lay awake, listening intently to the silence of the house.

On Sunday I came downstairs and sat in the living room a while. I told Yardley what had happened between me and Marvin Campbell. Yardley listened with a cigarette stuck in his mouth. The smoke rose and veiled his granite face, and his eyes squinted through the smoke. Now and then he plucked the filter from his lips: like pulling the drain from the tub; I half expected the smoke to swirl away into his mouth like water.

Now and then he'd ask me to repeat myself, and his finger would lay against the side of his jaw and his eyes would close and he'd listen. When I finished telling it, he was quiet for a long time. I excused myself. I went to the bathroom and was sick. Susannah came and stood in the doorway while I knelt by the toilet.

"Get out," I told her.

She went back to the living room.

It was a long weekend.

When Monday came, I lay in bed until I heard Yardley's Chevy drive away. Then I got up gingerly. I felt better. My head felt smaller. I was hungry. I dressed and went downstairs.

Susannah gave me coffee and eggs and toast. I ate it all. She sat and watched me with her hands folded on the kitchen table in front of her. The morning sun was shooting in through the window over the sink. It made her red hair glow. I finished my coffee and set the empty mug down with a thud. She reached out and put her hand on mine. I stared at it. After a moment, I stood up.

"Well," I said. "See you."

She smiled.

I went to see Nathan Jersey.

Chapter twenty-nine

I sat at a long white table in a long white room, waiting. I stared at my fingers raveling and unraveling on the Formica in front of me. Now and then my gaze lifted to Howard Marks. He was leaning back in his chair with his hands laced on his stomach. He looked slender and frail in the billowing sweater he wore. His face looked drawn, weary.

The attorney had been disappointed when I arrived without Susannah. I told him she was ill. He nodded silently. I couldn't see how her presence could have made much difference. But I could see how everything mattered to him now.

When he saw me looking at him, he smiled a little. I smiled back. We were in Indiana State Prison, waiting for Jersey to be brought from his cell.

When the door opened, I stood. Nathan Jersey came in. I caught a glimpse of the guard as he closed the door behind him.

Jersey was a shambling black man, six feet tall or so. He was massive and substantial, with long heavy arms and a broad solid chest behind his khaki prison uniform. His skin was a thick, dark brown. It seemed to have an almost liquid texture. He was about forty-five, no more than that, but the skin sagged on his face as if he were dragging it down with his fingers. It made his eyes seem blurry and bloodshot. It made it seem as if he were melting.

Marks stood up. He and Jersey shook hands. Then Marks said:

"Nathan, this is Michael Turner."

I waited for him to react. He turned to me heavily. He nodded heavily. He shook my hand. His hand was hard and callused, but his grip was lax.

"Pleased to meetcha," he said. "I don't get to meet too many people nowadays. I really am pleased to meet you."

His voice was mellow, flowing. It made me think of a man sitting on a hill, smoking a pipe, watching the clouds. He smiled as if he were thinking of the same thing. But it seemed an effort to lift that sagging skin, and the smile dropped away.

We all sat down at the table. Jersey was at the head. Marks and I were on either side of him. I leaned forward with my hands clasped to begin speaking.

But Jersey said: "You like . . . ? Excuse me, but—do you like the baseball games?"

"Uh . . . what?" I said. "Well—yeah, sure. Sure I do."

He nodded. "I like the baseball games. You ever see a real baseball game? Live?"

"Well . . . yeah."

"You did?"

"Sure."

"What that like?"

"Uh . . ." I looked to Marks for help. Marks looked down at the table. "Uh . . . it's very . . . nice," I said.

His eyes glistened. "Yeah. Yeah, I think about that. I think about that." He kept nodding at the middle distance. He said: "You ever see Charlie Hustle?"

Slowly, I nodded too. "Yeah," I said. "Yeah, I've seen Rose."

"Seen him hit?"

"Yeah, sure, he was great, great."

"George Foster, he was there, too, used to be."

"Yeah, sure. The big red machine. Georgie was there."

"And it's nice out there? At the stadium?"

"Yeah," I said. "It's special, all right."

"Special." He rolled the word on his tongue. I wished I'd given him a better one, but he stuck with it: "Special."

Finally Marks broke in with a quiet drawl: "Now, Nathan . . . Nathan, uh, Mr. Turner here, he . . . he didn't come to talk about baseball. . . ."

Jersey chuckled like a naughty child. "Mr. Marks, he don't like baseball."

"Well, it's not that," said Marks. "It's just . . . he's come to talk about your case."

I saw that work its way in behind Jersey's eyes. "Mr. Marks," Jersey said to me slowly, "Mr. Marks, he's trying to work it so they let me see the games again this year. I like to see the games, even on the TV. Not like live, but I like to see 'em. Except they want to electrocute me for what I done to that guard. Mr. Marks gonna tell 'em I didn't mean to hurt that boy. I forgive him for what he be doing to me all the time. It was a sin, but I forgive him so the Lord forgive me. I don't even know what come over me. He just done that to my mouse I had, Davy. I caught that little mouse, trained him up just like you would a dog. Now, I never put up a fuss against what that boy done to me, not ever, sin though it was. But Davy didn't do him no harm. Davy never hurt anyone. When I saw the way he be hurting Davy, and torturing him . . . I guess I just lost my mind . . . I guess I just went right out of myself. But Mr. Marks, he's gonna tell 'em I didn't mean to kill no one, never. I just went out of my head about Davy, that's all. Then they gonna let me watch the games again this year."

Marks looked down at the table. "I'm gonna do the best I can, Nathan. I promise you," he said quietly.

"That's all, that's all," said Nathan Jersey. "I ain't afraid or nothing. I just don't like missing the games, that's all."

I sighed. I said: "Mr. Jersey, do you remember Robert Turner?"

He considered it a minute. "I remember they said I killed him," he said sadly.

"Did you? Can you think back?"

"Well, I don't remember it exactly. But I don't remember killing the guard boy either. I just seem to come right out of myself."

"Mr. Jersey . . ." Without thinking I leaned toward him, put my hand on his arm. "Mr. Jersey, do you remember a man with a scar? Can you think of anytime you ever saw a man who had a scar like this?" I reached up and traced the line of it with a finger down the center of my face.

Nathan Jersey watched the finger move. Then he shook his head. He smiled a little. "You know, the people come to me. They ask me these questions. Seems like lifting a shovelful of mud to think about them. I try to look back—I don't see nothing back there. Nothing but mud and fog." He paused. His smile broadened. "Except the games sometimes. Sometimes, I look back—I see the games as clear as day. I see Pete up there, he's like a fist flashing open into a hand in front of your eyes.

Little white ball up the middle like a casting line, plunking down in the water. Old Pete at first again." He tilted his head to one side and chuckled. "Yeah. That's the only thing sometimes. Sometimes, I remember the games."

Chapter thirty

The prison grew small in the rear window: a small block of fenced-in concrete in the vast empty fields of grass around it. The inside of Marks's Lincoln was quiet. The ride was soft. Before us the pale white clouds floated in the pale blue sky. The air was mild. I faced front and watched the road. I felt the prison following us, creeping up behind us. I turned and it was gone, lost in the Indiana plain.

I slumped back against the passenger seat. I lit a cigarette. I watched the smoke trail out the window. Marks drove silently.

"He's got the IQ of a seven-year-old," I blurted out finally.

Marks said: "Yup. Just about."

"Isn't there some kind of law against killing a man like that?"

"There are plenty of laws. I just can't seem to convince anyone that they apply to Nathan."

I didn't answer him. Marks smiled gently as he drove.

"Well," he drawled. "Go on."

"I didn't say anything."

"No. But you're thinking it, all right: Maybe it's me." I still didn't answer. "Well, maybe it is." He let out a long breath, shaking his head at the windshield. "I've thought a hundred times about turning this over to someone else. Give 'em a chance to try the incompetent counsel plea."

"Isn't that what they usually do?"

"Yeah. Yeah, it is. Never works, of course, but it is what they usually do, yeah."

I leaned my head back. My temple had begun to throb again. Every toke of the cigarette ruined me. I tossed it out the window, watched it in the passenger sideview as it bounced, sparking, back over the pavement.

"I'm sure you've done your best, Howard," I said.

"Yeah, well . . . I guess I have."

For a long moment he was quiet. I closed my eyes and felt the car hoisting and dropping and speeding along. My stomach began to churn again.

Howard Marks said: "Ya know, I don't take criminal cases anymore."

I tried to concentrate on my breathing to keep the nausea down.

"Haven't taken a criminal case for nearly a dozen years. Real estate mostly. Sales, zoning appeals, that sort of thing."

There was another pause. I licked my lips and put my hand on my stomach.

"But I keep on this one. I keep on this one and I can't let it go. Know why?"

I said nothing.

"Because," Marks said, "because I know it's right. I guess that's a pretty stupid reason but . . . The thing is . . . The thing is, you know, everything just . . . everything just gets so fuzzy after a while. Like the print on a newspaper page. It used to be clear as a bell to me. Now it's just a mass of dark gray spread out on a mass of light gray. Right and wrong, the same thing. Used to be easy for me to tell one from another. Now, they just sort of . . . blur over the borders, right into wrong, wrong into right. I took on the Nathan Jersey case twenty years ago because it seemed right to me, the right thing to do, seemed that clear, as clear as you could ask for. And after all these years, with everything else blurring and running together, it still seems that way. And I guess I feel sometimes if I let go . . . if I let go of it, turn it over to someone else, I'll just sort of become a blur myself, like everything else is. Because the best of me believed in this case. And if I let it go, I'm scared the best of me will be gone."

I opened my eyes. I rolled my head on the seat until I could see him. He peered mildly through the windshield. He frowned with the corner of his mouth. He said: "Maybe Nathan Jersey is going to die on Thursday morning because I didn't have the grit to let a better man defend him. Because I didn't have the sand to look at life the way it is."

I didn't answer. I didn't have an answer. I turned my head away from him. I stared out the window. I breathed in deeply against the rising nausea.

He drove me back to his office. I had parked outside. We stood in the driveway together beside his car. We shook hands. His damp eyes moved away from me; his lips tightened.

"We're not gonna make it, are we?" he said.

My hands in my pockets, I lifted my shoulders.

"It's a shame. Well . . ." Howard Marks took a breath and smiled a little. "You'll call me then. About the governor, meeting with the governor."

"I'll call you."

"The three of us'll go to the capital. Say tomorrow evening."

"Sure."

He took a card from his billfold and handed it to me. Now he looked me directly in the eye. "And listen. I know you have to keep where you're staying secret and all that. I understand that. But you may find that you need a friend some of these days. I'm an old fella, and I may have made a mess of things."

I slipped the card into my pocket. "You'll be the first person I call."

He smiled. Slouching in his billowing sweater, he looked old and frail. I walked to my car. I did not look back at him. I could feel him standing there behind me. I could picture him with his hands half in his pockets and his sad eyes watching me go. I slid behind the wheel. I raised my hand and waved. But still I did not look back.

I drove the two blocks to the courthouse. I picked up my copy of Jersey's trial transcript and carried it to the newspaper office. Yardley wasn't there, so I headed for the diner. I ordered a BLT and a cup of coffee, then went into the phone booth in the back. I called home, collect.

Charlie answered. "Die a thousand deaths."

"Uh, would you accept a collect call from Mr. North?" the operator asked him.

There was a pause. "Yeah. Yeah, okay," he said.

"Sorry to wake you up, Charlie."

"Hey, is that you, camarado? Where are you, man?"

"Still in Indiana."

"Oh wow, you need me to change some money for you or something?"

"Yeah, maybe. How's Metropolis?"

"Big time, big time. Oh, hey, listen, I got some things to tell you."

"Okay."

"McGill has been trying to reach you."

"Really?"

"He kept asking me where you were. So I didn't tell him, like you said."

"Okay."

"Did I do good? Huh? Huh? Did I?"

I laughed. "Fuck you, Rose."

"He told me to tell you he doesn't know who the scarred man is."

"Bullshit."

"He says you should call him in Lima."

"Okay," I said.

Charlie gave me the number.

"Okay. So, like, you still don't want anyone to know where you are?"

"Someone shot at me, man, I'm not gonna give—"

"Oh yeah, that reminds me, I also saw that scar guy."

"What?"

"God, he looks real."

"Where was he? When was this? Did you talk to him?"

"Oh stop, stop, please, I can hardly think."

"Rose!"

"He was coming out of our building last night just as I was coming home."

"Damn."

"So I followed him."

"Are you joking?"

"I have no sense of humor."

"Charlie, the guy's a fucking killer."

"Hey, I know no fear."

"You can't even sit through The Wizard of frigging Oz, Charlie."

"Oh, sure, but that's Margaret Hamilton, man. Who the hell is this guy?"

"All right. So where'd he go?"

"He went to Astor Place."

"Yeah?"

"Then he got in a cab and drove away."

"You couldn't keep after him?"

"My legs gave out."

I sighed as audibly as I could. "He didn't see you, did he?"

"Maybe when I grabbed him and screamed, 'My friend North says you're meat.' Other than that, I was stealth itselth."

"Swell. How's Angela?"

"Great. How's Sue?"

I opened my mouth. Then I closed it. "Better," I said. "She's getting better."

I hung up and went to my table. The BLT was waiting. The waitress brought me coffee when I sat down.

The trial transcript sat before me in a cardboard box. I opened the box and removed about fifty pages. I passed over the jury selection and found the prosecutor's opening statement. I lifted my sandwich and ate, reading. I read about a page. I put the sandwich down and picked up my coffee. I read another page. That was all I read.

There are fissures in the past. I really do believe that. There are little openings that run through time, this way and that. Sometimes it's just a slit, and you have to pry it apart, sometimes it's a gaping hole and you can walk right into it. But once it opens for you, once you look inside it, not only the past, but the future, too, becomes clear for you.

One of those fissures opened then.

My hand jerked violently as I read the page before me. The coffee spilled on my wrist. I cursed and set down the cup, spilling more of the scalding coffee on my fingers. I wiped my hand with a napkin. I turned back to the page, afraid the fissure had closed, was no longer there.

It was still there.

I called to the waitress as I shoveled the transcript back into the box. I paid her as I fumbled with the box top, pushed it down over the pages, catching corners of them. I didn't wait for change.

I walked to the door quickly. I walked to the car. I felt my legs moving under me. I felt the pavement shooting under my feet. I stared ahead at the car. I saw it coming closer.

I slid behind the steering wheel. For a moment I could not remember what I was supposed to do. Then I had the car started, and again I sat still, staring. Then I was moving down Main Street, heading for the highway, forcing myself to pay attention to the road until attention to the road became a routine that carried me along.

I drove slowly, though. I went down the highway slowly. Other cars ripped by me. Trucks ripped by me. I just pushed on. I turned onto the dirt road. I went over the dirt road slowly. Slowly, I went up the last hill into the bank of hickories. Then the car poked through and the valley stretched away beneath me.

The light white clouds above the hills weren't moving. The high grass was still. The cottage was also quiet, with the dangling branches of the sycamores motionless all around.

And Susannah was there. She sat alone in the grass beside the stream. The light of the late afternoon sun caught her. It set her aglow while the grass and the stream sank into shadow.

My car came down the road. She didn't turn at first. I watched her every minute and she didn't turn. She was staring down at the water of the stream. She was twirling a blade of grass idly in one hand, leaning on the other, and watching the water run by. I pulled the car up in the empty drive before the cottage. She didn't turn.

I shut off the car. I ran my fingers through my hair. I got out. I closed the door. I could still see her over the little rise before me. I could see her head, her hair glowing. She didn't turn.

I began walking toward her. The grass grew higher around me. Soon it was up to my knees. She didn't turn.

I could see the water now. I could see it run beside her. It burbled white over the rocks. It dipped between them and caught the fiery sun. Still, only she seemed to glow in the light of it. Still, she didn't turn.

I was no more than a few steps from her when she faced me. She swung around in surprise. I stopped. Her lips parted and her eyes grew wide. She climbed to her feet, watching me. Stood with her hands on her elbows, her chin sunken down in the collar of her blouse, as if she were trying to grow smaller, to escape me. She was shaking her head. She kept shaking it back and forth: No, no, no.

It was too late. It was too late. She kept shaking her head and I kept repeating silently: It's too damned late.

I spread my hands.

"You're not my sister," I said.

Her lips parted even farther. "Oh!" she said. She reached for me.

I took hold of her arm and pulled her to me. We went down together into the grass.

PART FIVE
The whole story

Chapter thirty-one

I know a jazzman down in St. Mark's Place. His name is Moe. He plays the saxophone. He's also an alcoholic. I didn't know that when we met because he was on the wagon. Then one night he started drinking.

I was with him at the time; me and Charlie Rose. And we watched him, me and Charlie. We watched the way he drank. He sipped at the surface of the amber scotch at first, just as he was getting started. Then, slowly, he delved into it. Finally he tilted the glass and drained it in a long, even flow. Charlie and I saw it. We saw the focus of his mind contracting. We saw all his purposes fall away but one. Fall away so that the long, even amber flow was soon continuous, so that all his mind was bent on making it that way, making it never end.

Charlie and I could barely carry each other home when we left Moe in Ingmar's. We left him there with his elbow bent and his wrist tilted and his mind at one with the long, even flow that still was not finished, that has not finished since. I have to admit I almost admired him. I wondered: How can you want anything so much? What can be so fine that it ignites the attentive center of your soul like that and brings it into perfect alignment with the object of your desire?

Now I saw her lying next to me and I knew.

We had come inside finally. We were in my bed upstairs. It was just twilight. Her red hair was splayed on the pillow like the rays of the sun. We were lying on top of the covers.

"I have to get under," she whispered.

"No, don't."

"I'm cold."

I wouldn't let her. I ran my hands over the length of her. I kissed her. I couldn't stop.

She was Laura's child, the maid's. Once I had read it in the prosecutor's opening statement, it seemed that I'd always known. I remembered the image of Laura dying, of her sliding, gunshot, down the staircase wall. I remembered her hair seemed to extend over the wall as she fell. Because her hair was red. Like the blood. Like Susannah's. That was why she was downstairs with Laura when the rest of us were on the inn's second story. That was why a lot of things. The fissure was open now. Not only the past, but the future, too, was clamoring to be seen. But for now I could only run my hands over the length of her. I kissed her. I couldn't stop.

The next time I looked at the window, it was full dark.

She was on her side. Her head was resting on her hands. I was behind her. I was running my finger down over her back.

"I must have been illegitimate," she said. It was opening for her too.

I said: "My father must have taken her in. Laura, I mean. That Campbell guy kept calling him a pimp. That must be why. She was pregnant, unwed."

She rolled around to me, grabbed me, kissed me fiercely.

"Oh North, North, has anyone ever loved you this much?"

"My mama," I whispered. "But she died."

She kissed me.

"Are you really going to kill the scarred man?"

"Yes."

"I think you're sexy."

I tilted back from her. "Because I'm going to kill him?"

"Yes. Or if you don't."

"I like your attitude."

"Doesn't it seem to you . . ."

"Yes."

"What? Tell me."

"That nothing matters."

"Yes," she said.

"Except us."

"Even all of it. None of it. Except us."

I kissed her, held her. I hardly knew anything but how white her skin was and how pink it was in places.

She pulled back from me a little. "Lights," she said. Her throat was taut. I lay my lips against it. "Lights," she whispered. "North, he's home."

I looked up. I saw them for an instant too. I saw their glow against the wall. I heard the Chevy's motor. Then the room was dark again. The motor died. I heard the car door open and shut.

Susannah had rolled away from me. She turned on the lamp on the bedside table. She was sitting on the edge of the bed now, looking back at me over her naked shoulder.

I got up. My pants lay sprawled on the floor. I grabbed them, started pulling them on.

"North . . ." she said.

I found my shirt draped across a corner of the bed. I yanked on one sleeve, the other. Then I was dressed and heading for the door.

She stood up, holding the bedsheet in front of her. "He was very nice to me," she said.

"We belong to each other. We always have."

I went out to meet him.

He was inside and calling out to her when I came to the top of the stairs. He was swinging around to mount, his hand on the newel post. He looked up and saw me. I started down toward him.

He began to smile when he saw me, but he stopped. He waited. I came off the last step and stood in front of him. He glanced up and then at me again. He was not surprised.

He turned his back on me and took a few steps into the living room. He flicked on a lamp.

"You were too smart from the beginning, Ben," I said. "Too smart by half. You had all the papers, the documents."

He swung around, his eyes blazing.

"You knew," I said. "You had to know."

His lips were tight in that granite face. His voice snapped out at me, a whisper, though, a hiss: "There would have been someone else for you."

"What were you gonna do, keep her here?"

"I didn't have to keep her here."

"She'd have found out."

"I would've played for time."

My fists were clenched at my sides. "There isn't enough time."

For a moment I thought he would try to hit me. I was hoping

he would try to hit me. But he hesitated. Then he turned away, shaking his head.

"No," he said. "I guess there isn't. I guess I never thought there was." He breathed sharply once through his nose. He glanced back at me. "Consider it a loan."

"How did you find out?"

"Oh, hell, I had it from the beginning. The minute you told me the story, with her downstairs, and the maid's hair and everything . . ."

"Jesus." He was awfully damned good. "Did she tell you? About us?"

He laughed bitterly. "I could smell the wood burning, North, she didn't have to tell me. I could sit for hours with her and watch her burn. And you."

"Jesus," I whispered. "You had all of it. You held on to all of it."

"They were only suspicions. Technically, anyway. You can suspect a long time before you know."

I nodded. "Yeah." My fists weren't clenched anymore.

"I only got all of it this evening." One corner of his mouth lifted. He dug into his pocket and hauled out a cigarette. Slapped it into his face. Leaned into the flare of the match. "I'd have ducked it if I could," he said, breathing out the smoke.

"Gimme," I said. He tossed me the pack, the matches. I lit one. He watched me.

"How did she take it?" he said finally. "The part about McGill, I mean."

I had been waving my hand to kill the match. I stopped, my hand hanging in the air, the dead match smoking in it.

Slowly, Yardley smiled.

"You don't know," he said.

"What about McGill?"

"You don't know." He spoke proudly now.

I acknowledged it. "All right. I don't know. What about McGill?"

"He's her father."

We heard it hit her where she stood. We heard her gasp. We both turned to see her at the top of the stairs.

Chapter thirty-two

The three of us stood a long time without speaking. Stood still, with the lamplight pinning our shadows to the floor. Susannah was at the window now, her arms folded, her reflection staring back at her. I was sitting on the stairs, tracing shapes with my finger on my jeans.

Yardley sat in the easy chair, his legs crossed at the knee, a cigarette moving to and from his lips. As if he were enjoying a relaxed smoke at the end of the day. But though his stony face remained impassive, his eyes went deep. I could see the longing in them, the loss and the regret. Or maybe I only imagined I saw them, knowing they were there, knowing how they felt.

We went a few minutes more without a word, and then

Susannah broke it. She didn't turn from the window. She just whispered, "I want to see her."

Yardley and I both lifted our faces to her. Now she did glance back at us.

"Laura. My mother. I want to see a picture of her. Do you think at the *Chronicle* . . . ?"

Yardley put his cigarette out in an ashtray on the lampstand beside him. He pushed wearily out of the big old chair. Wearily, he moved toward the door to the kitchen. Just beside it, there was a rickety old phone table. A manila envelope lay atop it. He picked it up, seemed to weigh it in his hand. Then he brought it across the room, held it out to Susannah.

She did not reach for it right away. She looked up at the man.

"Old clips," Yardley said. "I brought them home to read."

"Yeah," I said, "and would you have shown them to us?"

He didn't answer. Just stood there, holding out the envelope. Susannah lowered her eyes to it finally. She took it from him with a trembling hand.

His shoulders slumped, Yardley moved back to the chair. He sank into it. He looked at me.

"I only brought them tonight," he said. "After McGill called."

My lips parted. "McGill. He called?"

"That's how I knew about him and Laura. That's how I got it solid anyway. He got the message you sent. When he couldn't reach you at home, he figured you were in Hickman. And figured you'd have stopped in at the paper. He reached me when he called." He smiled sadly. "Not bad for an old man."

"No," I said. "Not bad. What did he say?"

Before Yardley could answer, there was a sound from the window. I turned in time to see the manilla envelope slip to the floor. Susannah stood holding a yellowed newspaper clipping in her hand. Her eyes were fixed on it. The dim light glistened in her tears.

She stared a second more and then stepped back—almost stumbled back—until she was propped against the windowsill. The brittle old newspaper page rattled as her hand shook.

I got up, went to her. Took the page from her hand. She kept staring at the place where it had been.

"Jesus," I said. "That's . . ." My voice trailed off.

"Uncanny," Yardley said softly.

"The eyes. The look in the eyes. The lips."

"Bee-stung lips. That's what McGill called them."

As Yardley spoke, Susannah's fingers rose to touch her own lips. Bee-stung lips—a good description.

She shook her head forcefully. Her hair whipped back and forth, a few tears flew free. Pressing her lips together now, she took the page from me, looked at it again, hard.

"What else?" she asked hoarsely, not looking up. "What else did he say?"

Yardley took a deep breath. He leaned his head back in the chair, fixed his eyes on the ceiling.

"It was tough," he said. "I didn't want to tell him where you were without your say-so. He didn't much like that. I finally got him to agree to call back after I'd had a chance to talk to you. After that, we started fencing, back and forth. I'd let him know I was onto something, he'd confirm it and give me a little more, I'd make a deduction from that and so on."

He lowered his head. Looked at Susannah. I looked at her. Leaning against the windowsill, she continued to stare at the photograph of her mother.

"After a while, though," Yardley went on, "he gave me the whole story . . ."

∎ ∎ ∎

Carl McGill [Yardley told us] liked to play down and dirty, but he was, in fact, from the upper crust of Indiana, which is about as upper crust as you can get. He married Patricia Blake when they were both nineteen, and entered the Army under an officer's training program. When he got out, he went to college and began working on the Hickman *Chronicle*. His wife came with him.

McGill liked the newspaper business. It suited him. It was smart and tough, and so was he. He found the idea of working on the college rag distasteful, beneath him, so he drove an hour each way, every other day, to put in some time at the *Chronicle*. The minute he graduated, he was planning to take his clips and head east. He had hot contacts in Philadelphia.

It was all planned. And then he met Laura. His wife was ill, and he'd taken his laundry to Hickman so he could dump it in the Laundromat while he worked. He met her there. Saw her sitting before a machine, her legs crossed, a magazine opened on her knee. She had red hair and blue eyes. And those bee-stung lips. They made her face look lopsided and goofy whenever she smiled.

She was a reserved young woman, even shy, with a soft voice and a southern accent—she'd grown up in New Orleans. She wasn't rich. She wasn't smart particularly. She was just a waitress. But she was sweet and very gentle and had an innocent quality that made McGill crazy. The first time they talked seriously, she told him she'd left the south after a bad love affair. It turned out that, at twenty-three, she was still a virgin and had headed north when boyfriend Stan turned out to be "not so nice" as he'd seemed. "Not so nice." McGill loved that. That was how it started between them.

McGill had married young and, up to that point, he thought he loved his wife. Where he came from, she was the sort of girl you married. She knew how to say the right things and do the right things and impress the right people, and how to stand by her man. She knew how to prove herself by scrimping and saving until the trust fund clicked in. That was how it was done. Anyway, she was strong and loyal and stiff and prim and wan, and McGill had thought he loved her. He still did, but he was drunk on Laura now, and not all the guilt in the world could sober him up.

As for the baby: that was dumb. McGill and Patricia had been trying to have one. When they didn't, McGill assumed he was sterile. But the fact was, Patricia was sickly. She always had been, and he might have guessed that the problem lay with her. Maybe he did. Maybe he knew. Maybe there are no accidents, anyway.

So Laura got pregnant. McGill wanted to marry her. Laura refused him. She wanted his baby but she wouldn't break up his home. They kissed, they wept. But Laura stood fast. She went into the backlands, to my father's inn, to have the child. McGill stayed with his wife. His heart was broken.

Two years later McGill enters his senior year. He's not the man he was. Something is sour in him. His wife, hurt, is even colder than before. Sometimes, he still works at the *Chronicle,* but a lot of his time there is spent staring out the window, checking out the passersby.

Coming out of the Army, McGill had entered school halfway through the year. Now, two years after he lost Laura, he was ready to graduate. It was November. He was ready to go home for Thanksgiving, then collect his clips and head for Philly. It was all planned.

Then, just before the holiday, someone killed her. Killed Laura and my parents. And Sue and I alone survived to tell the tale. The way McGill told it, he suddenly changed all his plans. To the amazement of his family and friends, he started working at the *Chronicle* full-time. He was the best they had—he was the best there was—and he took the job on one condition: he got to cover the murder. He said clips on a really big story like that would secure his reputation. But naturally that wasn't it. And it wasn't revenge, either, not according to McGill. He didn't come to the paper to make sure justice was done for Laura's murder. He didn't give a damn about justice for Laura. She was dead.

He came back for Susannah.

The police had mistakenly identified her as my sister—that's how it got in the paper. After that there were the elections, the news marched on, and no one cared who she was but the *Chronicle*. McGill just let it ride. Very quickly, he stopped mentioning her in the stories altogether. He must have known that wouldn't work once the trial got started, but he didn't plan to hang around that long. Anyway, he wasn't trying to keep Hickman from finding out about her. In a town that size the townspeople already knew. He was trying to keep his wife from finding out about her. And he was trying to adopt her.

He pulled strings. With his family background, he had plenty to pull. Laura had some family down south, but they were dirt poor and completely uninterested in feeding the bastard of a woman they barely remembered. Within three months he had it set up. He convinced his wife to adopt, and then he convinced her to adopt Susannah. He quit the *Chronicle,* and he quit Hickman. Patricia never found out the truth, or if she did, she never let on.

As for me, McGill told Yardley, he figured I'd be all right with my rich relations. But he kept track of me. And when he tracked me to that Poughkeepsie rag, he came to find me. He said he felt he owed me that.

■ ■ ■

"That's why he never told me," Susannah said. She was the first to speak when Yardley finished. She was sitting on the floor now, her back against the wall. She had the newspaper clip on her raised knees. She was still looking at it. "He didn't want mother to know."

I nodded, then hung my head. Maybe that was it. But Patricia McGill had been dead for quite some time, and Carl had finally told the truth only now, when it seemed to him I might already know. He'd had plenty of time in the interim to invent noble motives for himself. Like his motive for finding me. It may have just been curiosity, after all. Or maybe he wanted to keep an eye on me.

Still, Susannah seemed satisfied. In fact, she seemed now, sitting there, to have slipped off somewhere far away. And as she gazed into her mother's face from that distance, a slight smile—a smile of understanding—slowly appeared on her lips.

"It doesn't help us much in the end," said Yardley.

I pulled my eyes from Susannah.

"This is Monday night," he said. "Thursday at dawn, all things being equal, Nathan Jersey dies. Two days away, and we're no closer to getting him off the hook now than we were before."

"Further if it comes to that," I said. "We're at a dead end."

He nodded. "The motive."

"Right." I ran a hand up through my hair. Let out a long breath. "Unless there's something about Louisa Campbell's rape, something we're missing."

"Or the lynch mob." Yardley's voice was tired, heavy, as if it were an effort for him to work the thing over anymore. "Maybe if we went back to Marvin Campbell."

"Not unless you have an elephant gun."

"Maybe if we could track down Louisa."

"We might. He said she was out west . . ."

"Oh hell." Yardley sat forward, his elbows on his knees, his hands dangling down. "I mean, it's not like a motive is missing or anything. It's just that we have so many. A guy like Turner— like your father—a guy who took in strays, blacks, unwed mothers, he'd have so many enemies in a town like this . . . I mean, once you get rid of Jersey, that only leaves everyone else."

I tapped my fist once against my knee. "Still," I said. "Still. It happened so soon after the thing with the lynch mob. It had to be connected. Someone must've killed my father for . . ."

"Don't you see . . ."

Her voice startled us, stopped us. We both turned to her where she sat against the wall. That same half smile still played on her lips, but the tears had spilled over now and were running down her cheeks. She did not look at us, but kept studying the picture of her mother, kept smiling into that picture, as if she had not been talking to us at all.

She swallowed hard. "Don't either of you see?" she went on hoarsely. And now at last, she looked at me, her eyes swimming. "Whoever it was—he didn't come to kill your father, Michael."

She choked back tears. It was a moment before she could continue. In that moment, Yardley squinted at her hard, disbelieving. And I felt my own face go blank with the sudden understanding of what she was trying to say.

"He came to kill my mother," she said finally. "Your father just got in the way."

Chapter thirty-three

So we started searching for Laura. Trying to find her past, trying to find some reason someone would want her dead. We started with the trial transcripts and the clips we had out at Yardley's. We read them into the night, until an hour before dawn. By eight A.M., we were at the *Chronicle*, going through the old bound editions of the paper. But there wasn't much there. Even at the time, Laura had not been considered a central figure in the case. It just seemed to be a possibility overlooked by everyone.

When the county offices opened, Yardley went over there to snoop around. He came back with some ancient tax records showing Laura had worked at a diner in town before going to work for my father at the inn. Susannah and I, meanwhile, had tracked down some numbers for people who'd testified at the trial. Yardley and I left Susannah at the phones, climbed into his Chevy and went out in search of the diner.

We found it—or what was left of it. An old shell of a train car on a back road near the Hickman railroad station. Jagged edges of glass in the windows. An interior picked clean by scavengers. But Yardley had gotten the name of the diner's owner too. We drove off together in search of him.

We found his widow. An ancient mass of putty-like flesh rooted to her sofa. The sofa was in the living room of a small, two-story house. The house was near the freight tracks, just this side of them. We sat with her in her living room with her TV on. We smoked our cigarettes and watched her intently. She watched the TV, never took her eyes off it. The trinkets on the mantelpiece rattled when the train went through.

"Never said much about herself," the old woman said, mashing her gums together. "Never one to say much, Laura. I 'member her well enough though. Harvey hired her soon as he saw her 'count of her being pretty, bringing the people in and so on. And she'd had some experience down south where she came from."

"New Orleans," said Yardley. He tried not to sound too eager.

"New Orleans, yeah," said the old woman. "That was it."

When we got back to the *Chronicle,* Susannah was still on the phones. We joined her, going through the list she'd made.

We went all the way through it. Slowly. It was past noon by the time we ran out of names. Yardley threw his phone down into its cradle with a clatter.

"Damn it!" he said. "Nothing!"

I murmured a good-bye into my own phone and set it down. After a minute or two, Susannah did the same. We sat there silently.

Yardley was in his seat at the front of the room. Susannah was at the sports guy's desk behind him. I was across from them in the church notices desk. I'd usurped the divorcee. She'd left in a huff.

The air was smoky. Yardley and I had been going at the cigarettes hard. I peered through the smoke at the storefront window. Out through the glass at the elms on Main. The buds on their branches were fiercely bright in the midday sun. Their shadows gathered at their trunks in dark little pools.

"Twenty years," said Yardley.

I nodded.

"There's nothing left of her," he said.

"There is." This was Susannah. "There's got to be something. Something somewhere."

She reached for the phone again. Yardley and I watched her wearily. She started dialing, searching for another person or agency or establishment that might have come in contact with her mother all those years ago. Her fingers hit the phone hard, her lips stayed pressed together. When she leaned back in her chair, listening to the ring, her eyes were focused sharply on the wall across from her.

She'd been like that since the night before: focused, sharp. Ever since she'd guessed it had been Laura who'd been the primary target of the scarred man. It seemed to galvanize her. To make her want to know more. To make her want to know everything.

As Yardley and I watched, she turned to her desk: hunched over, the phone to her ear, a pen in her hand. She murmured briefly, scribbled on a pad. Hung up after a moment. We watched her. Brushing a red curl off her forehead, she pushed out a breath. Then she picked up the phone again. Looking for Laura. Looking for the scarred man who had come to the Turner inn to murder her.

That was the way it had happened. The moment she said it, all three of us knew it was true. It made sense of all my memories, anyway. The sequence of those awful old events had fallen into place as Sue gazed at her mother. I had gotten out of bed, gone to the top of the stairs because I'd heard whispering. There had been a lot of whispering before the shooting started. Laura must have been talking to the killer, he must have been someone she knew. She had started running up the stairs because she realized, finally, that he meant to kill her. And only when my father stepped out to protect me did the killer determine he would have to take us all.

If there was a motive for the killings, it lay with Laura. We felt sure of it.

Yardley and I watched Susannah dialing again.

"Who're you calling now?" Yardley said at last. "We've practically gone through all of Hickman."

"New Orleans," Susannah answered quietly. "I'm going through New Orleans now."

Yardley and I sighed in unison. We took our phones up too.

Susannah hit the government offices: tax departments, motor vehicles bureaus, anyone who might keep a record. Yardley went at the cops and the D.A., looking for anything he could. I went after diners, restaurants, neighbors, family; I was practically calling through the area at random.

I got lucky around four o'clock.

I had phoned a restaurant, The St. James Pancake House. One of maybe two dozen names I'd gotten from information. A waitress answered at this one, a whiskey-throated woman with a thick, slow-moving drawl. Her name was Jeannie.

"Is this some kind of a joke?" she asked me.

"No, ma'am," I said. I pinched the bridge of my nose with my fingers, closed my eyes, resigned to another dead end. "It's very important."

"Yeah, that's what t'other one said."

I opened my eyes. "Pardon me."

"Well, you're the second man who's asked me about her, honey. After all these years, too."

I was tilted back in my chair, one hand wrapped around a coffee cup, my feet up on the desk. Now, though, I straightened in my chair. I lowered my feet to the floor.

"The second . . ." I cleared my throat. "The second man."

"Yeah. Fellow came by here just t'other day. Said he was a private de-tective. Asking me about Laura, just like you. Asking me what I knew about her."

"A private detective."

"You hear all right, fellah?" she asked me. "That's what I said, you don't have to tell me. A private detective by the name of Johnson. Sandy-haired fellah with a mean-looking scar right down the middle of his face."

Susannah and Yardley turned in their chairs as my coffee cup spilled over the edge of the desk. One look, and they hung up their phones, left their chairs, came to me where I sat.

"I told him the same thing I'm gonna tell you," Jeannie went on. "I wrote to Laura once or twice a long while back. But I ain't seen hide nor hair of Laura for over a quarter of a century."

There was a long pause. I couldn't speak. I swallowed hard.

The woman said: "Not since Stan Harris killed that debutante."

Yardley called the police again, and then the FBI. It took a little while, but they dug up the records for us. It was that easy in the end. If anyone had thought to ask, they'd have done it twenty years ago. No one had thought to ask.

By the time the street outside went dim with sunset, Yardley had everything he needed. He hung up and told us about it as dusk gathered at the window, as the office grew dark.

I had an odd feeling, as we sat there, as we listened. I had an odd feeling that it was Christmas again. That we were trading ghost stories again and that it was Yardley's turn to tell the one about the scarred man.

Only this time, it was the real story. The one that had taken place in New Orleans twenty-five years ago. The one that had taken place when the killer's name had been Stan Harris.

It was Mardi Gras. The streets of the French Quarter were packed with people. There were the solemn shuttered facades and the wild places with neon lights and the wrought-iron railings that looked down on green mermaid fountains in the courtyards, and jazz, jazz everywhere: in little smoke-filled halls like caves, where old men jammed while the beatniks nodded and snapped and yeahed; and in big nightclubs, too, where fat guys with name tags would take off their green ties and dance on the tables, swinging the ties around their heads; and in the streets, which were packed with people.

One of the people was Stan Harris. He was about twenty, a scholarship student at Tulane University. He was very smart. He would have had to be. There are towns in the south that are mostly dirt and hunger. There are places where the sun beats down on the tin roofs of the shacks and the roofs glare back at the sun and nothing much else happens except sometimes there's a new baby and it cries and sometimes someone passes away and sometimes, if the driver's lost, a car goes by. That last kicks the dust up, but it settles again soon. Stan Harris was from a town like that, but he was very smart, and he had made it to Tulane.

His scholarship didn't take him far. He still had to pinch

pennies. But he couldn't resist taking the Desire streetcar into town that long-ago February night to see the Mardi Gras. His first Mardi Gras.

He pushed through the people—or he tried for a while—but soon he saw there was no pushing against them, there were just too many. He let them carry him along instead, and they carried him through the quarter on a tight, smelly, steady flow of bellies and shoulders and sweat and beer and coarse laughter. Openmouthed as the hayseed he was, he saw the light and he heard the jazz. He watched the parades in the street where the people dressed up as gods and the women in short dresses threw necklaces of plastic beads to the crowds. He had never seen women who looked like that before. He reached out for the plastic beads. Some of the women waved at him.

The crowd carried him into the heart of the quarter, and there he saw the people swell and eddy under an iron balcony on the third floor of a pale yellow town house. He looked up. Debutantes stood on the balcony. They were dressed in shiny lamé gowns that flowed down to their Cinderella slippers. They were fresh from their coming-out balls of the night before. They, too, were throwing plastic beads down into the crowd. Hands reached up at them, each one stretching to get higher than the hand beside it, to grab the beads tumbling down from the balcony.

Harris just stood there, just stood there looking up. The crowd jostled him like the ocean jostles you if you stand in it. He swayed back and forth in the waves, but he did not move. He would not be carried on. There was a woman up there in the balcony, a woman in gold lamé with a tiara in her hair. Her hair was golden. She was plump and had a round, sweet face. She was throwing beads to the crowd, and when she saw him staring at her—it seemed to him—she threw one necklace down to him directly, dropped it right above him so he couldn't miss it. He didn't even reach up. It fell on his shoulder and slid down into his cupped hands as the others grabbed for it. He stood, jostled by the waves of the crowd, and he stared at her.

Stan Harris didn't have many friends. There was his roommate, who was a nice enough guy, and a pretty waitress at the university coffee shop who would listen to him talk. He told them about the girl in the gold lamé. They listened to him and kidded him, but he didn't think it was funny. He went back to the pale yellow town house to find her. He fought the crowds. He stayed there. He waited for her through a night and a day. Finally, he saw her. She was coming into the house with a man on her arm. It was night. She was dressed in a midnight blue gown that showed off her ample cleavage. Her golden hair was shining in the light from the streetlamps. The young man was decked out in a tuxedo.

Stan Harris didn't care about the young man. He approached her. He told her who he was, how he had been standing under the balcony when she threw the beads down. She was flattered. She saw how things were and she tried to be nice. The young man with her tried to be nice, too, but Stan wouldn't back off. Finally the young man took the girl by the arm and began to guide her into the big house. Stan grabbed the young man's shoulder. The young man knew how to box. He hurled javelin on his college track team too. He didn't want to hurt Stan but he swung around and dusted him back a little. Dazed, Stan stood shaking his head while the young man and the girl who had worn gold lamé went inside. She looked back at him as if she felt sorry for him.

Stan went home then, but he came back later and killed her. It took him a week. First he had to find them. It turned out the big house was not a house but a hotel where the girl had been staying. She lived out in the suburbs, not far from the school, in fact. But it took Stan quite a while to find that out. When he did, he went there and waited. He was good at waiting, Stan was. He waited until she was at home alone, and then he broke into the house. He had apparently decided to give her another chance, but she screamed and scratched him, and he took his hunting knife and cut her throat. Then he stabbed her several times in the chest and stomach. Then he left.

It didn't take long for the police to get on to Stan. They interviewed the young man in the tuxedo and he, of course, remembered the confrontation outside the hotel. It took him a while to remember everything Stan had said but he got it eventually. Then the police knew.

It's possible this took Stan by surprise. As the cops found out later, he hadn't had much trouble with the police the last time he'd killed someone. It had been an argument over a dog, and all he'd had to do was bury the man's body in a shallow grave and forget about it. But then, that was back in his home-town. He hadn't figured on the big-city publicity and the big-city police.

In any case, Stan got away just an hour before the police arrived at his dorm room to arrest him. Somehow, he just decided that he wasn't waiting around. He was spotted once on a streetcar, and then again down by the Mississippi where the freight trains go. And then he was seen no more.

But the case was a sensational one. It was all over the papers and the television. The mayor and therefore the chief of police and therefore the police themselves were not about to give up easily. They went after Stan, and once or twice they almost got him. In fact, they had Stan cornered just north of Shreveport, but that was as close as they ever came.

What happened next was important, however. It was right about then that a vagrant was found dead and buried by the train tracks. No one could ever identify that vagrant. He was a man without a name. But Agent Frederick Sample of the Federal Bureau of Investigation strongly believed that Stan Harris had killed him. The marks of the knife seemed the same as those in the murder in New Orleans. And there was more. After Harris got away outside of Shreveport, the law never came close to him again. He vanished without a trace. Agent Sample stayed on the case, off and on, for the ten years until his retirement, but he never found a single clue to Harris's whereabouts. He eventually developed a theory. He believed that Harris had sat and talked with the vagrant before he murdered him. Maybe the vagrant wasn't even the first one Harris had talked to. Maybe he had talked to several and taken the best of the lot. Anyway, Sample believed Harris had found out the man's name and his history, and then killed him—and then taken over his identity. He believed that's how he had evaded the law so completely: he had literally become someone else.

And that was all we knew about Stan Harris.

That, and that the waitress in the university coffee shop had been our Laura. She must have liked Stan before she found out he was "not so nice."

Chapter thirty-four

For another hour, we sat in the newspaper office and talked. Yardley sat with his feet on Susannah's desk, his chair tilted full back. His head rested on his laced hands, and the cigarette in his mouth pointed straight up at the ceiling. Susannah sat behind the desk. She was enveloped in a huge purple sweater. One of her hands was lost in the folds of it. The other held a cup of coffee. She sipped at it and shivered. I had climbed up on top of the desk and was now seated at the center of a pile of paper and debris. My back was against the wall, my knees were bent in front of me, my hands were resting on them.

"Is it enough?" said Susannah.

I shook my head. Yardley stared upward.

"I mean, if we tell," she said, "they can't just kill him."

I glanced at the clock. It was six-thirty. Jersey had about thirty-six hours left.

"We oughta call Marks," said Yardley. "Tell him anyway."

I nodded. "There's a lot though . . ."

"A lot we don't know," he said. "But we should tell him. Anyway."

I drummed a grim little riff on my knees. "It doesn't make sense. What the hell happened to him? It doesn't . . ."

"Michael," Susannah said, "we'll never know every . . ."

"Yeah, but look: he killed a man in his hometown. Then he went to college in New Orleans. He killed a woman there. Then he's on the run and he kills a vagrant. Then he vanishes. For the next five years there's not a trace of him and all that time the FBI guy, Sample, is on his trail." I paused.

"Yeah?" said Yardley around his cigarette. "So?"

"So where are all the other killings? I mean, the man's a murderer. That's what he does. He kills people. Where are all the other killings over the next five years? And over the next twenty years?"

Yardley shrugged. "So he got away with them. Lot of these guys, they kill hundreds of people before anyone catches up with them.

Susannah cocked her head at me, one eye closed. "Or maybe he stopped," she said.

I looked down at her. "Yeah?"

"Maybe when he became this other guy? Maybe he, like, *became* this other guy."

I started drumming my knees again, rocking with the rhythm, staring into space. "Yeah. He kills the vagrant and takes his identity. Harris becomes Johnson."

"He sure had a way with names," Yardley said.

"And it takes," said Susannah.

"Yeah," I said. "It takes. I mean, Harris is smart. Comes out of nowhere, gets a scholarship, makes a new life when nobody ever gave him a damned thing . . . So what if he does it again."

"Takes on a whole new life."

Yardley glanced at the clock. "We oughta call Marks," he said.

"And Johnson starts winning through, making good for himself." I drummed faster, rocking faster. "Burns his past behind him like a conquered town. Comes to Hickman to make a fresh start—and . . ."

I stopped. Susannah pursed her lips. Yardley lowered his chin to his chest.

"And there's Laura?" he asked. "Just waiting for him?"

"All right," I said. "All right, he's hunting her, then. She's the one link between him and the New Orleans murder."

"The one link. There are plenty of links. The debutante's boyfriend, he's a link."

"Shit." I stopped drumming, slapped my legs.

Again, for a long moment, we sat, we stared, we didn't speak. The night pressed at the window outside. The smoke pressed back against the glass from within.

Then Yardley said: "He must've . . ."

"Followed her," I said.

"Loved her," said Susannah.

"Not loved her exactly."

"No," she said.

"Wanted . . ."

"A friend."

"Yes," I said. "He must've followed her to find . . ."

"His only woman friend," said Susannah.

"Yes."

Yardley's chair squeaked as he shifted in it. "And she must

have moved here because she was afraid. She was too poor to just take off for no reason. She must have been afraid of Harris and moved here. Maybe to see family."

"Maybe at random," I said.

"And he followed her," said Susannah. "And she turned him away. Like the debutante."

"Plus she could expose him," said Yardley.

"Right," I said. "Take away his new life."

"And then the Louisa Campbell incident came along and Nathan Jersey became ripe for a set up. Johnson was smart enough for that."

I nodded. Susannah nodded. Yardley nodded.

"So why's he in New Orleans now?" he said. "Asking questions, stirring things up."

I started to answer—but I had no answer. I glanced at Yardley and he looked back, his mouth half open, like mine.

"I think I know," said Susannah quietly.

We turned to her. She raised her blue eyes to me.

"I think he's looking for us."

I shook my head. "No, that doesn't . . ."

"Sure," she said, her voice still soft. "He thinks we know more than we do. He thinks we went to New Orleans to put a case together against him."

The words hung in the air with the smoke, with the shadows.

"I think he's looking for us," Susannah said again.

Yardley was out of his chair. "Shit."

"She's right," I said.

"Would you call Marks? Would you call him?"

"Okay, okay. He's probably in Indianapolis trying . . ."

"Would you call him, North?"

I reached down over my legs and picked up the phone. I took Marks's Hickman number from my wallet and read it off to Susannah as she dialed. The bell rang twice, then Marks picked up.

"Michael. Michael. I'm glad you called." Exhaustion made his voice thick, hoarse. "The governor says he's willing to talk to you, but there isn't much time."

"All right," I said. "Listen to this."

I told him. I tried to take it easy, tried to make it sound rational.

"Laura was just the maid, no one even thought of her," I said. "But she was the one, see. She was the one this Harris guy was after."

The pause that followed was long. Slowly, it grew longer. Yardley, his fists pressed into the desk top, hovered over me. Susannah, in her chair, stared up.

"Michael," Marks said very slowly. "You can't see me, but I'm counting on my fingers . . ."

"No. No. This is it. I'm telling you. We don't have it all. We're guessing a lot but it makes sense . . ."

"I don't *need* sense!" It was the first time I'd heard him raise his voice. He stopped at once. I could hear him breathing on the line, fighting for control. "I need proof."

"But this . . ."

"I need proof and we don't have time. You've got to come with me to Indianapolis, you and Susannah. You've got to come tonight. You've got to, I can't . . ." It trailed off into a low half groan, then nothing. "You've got to," he said again.

The sound of him killed the protest on my lips. I sagged, the breath coming out of me. "All right."

"All right?"

"All right," I said.

I gestured my surrender to the others. Yardley turned away. Susannah leaned back in her chair.

Marks's tone was apologetic now. "Michael. Michael, I swear

to God, if there were . . . some way. If we could . . . if we could even go out and search the inn again, but the time . . . not even a day and a half . . . you have to, have to understand . . ."

I nodded. I started to say "all right." But I didn't say it. I said: "Search the inn for what?"

"What?"

I began to climb off the desk. "For . . . what did you search the inn for? You said search it again, what did you . . . ?"

"I was grasping at straws."

"You've been out there. You went looking for something."

"A long time ago. We've got to . . ."

"Howard," I said. I came into the aisle. I paced, the phone held tight against my ear. "What. What were you looking for? You've got to tell me."

I stood still, aware of nothing but the silence on the wire. The dark distance and the silence between him and me. And then Marks sighed. And then he said: "No one ever found your father's account books. I went back a couple of times to look for them but, like I said, I always figured Jersey was guilty . . ."

"His account books."

"Yeah. Yeah, well . . . those and . . ."

He stopped. I opened my mouth. No sound came out. I licked my lips. "And what else?" I said.

"And Laura's letters."

I wrote to Laura once or twice a long while back.

"I never really took much time looking for them, I . . ."

I wrote to Laura . . . That's what Jeannie said.

". . . but when you mentioned Laura, I thought . . ."

My palm was wet and slick against the phone's black plastic. "The ghosts," I said.

"Michael."

"A little boy, out by the inn, he told me there were ghosts. Haunting the place. Rummaging through the place."

"Well, I haven't been back there in . . ."

"Not you. Not you."

He tried one more time: "Michael, the governor will . . ."

"I'm going out there."

"It's too late. It's too long ago. Twenty years. The governor . . ."

"I'm going out there. Just for an hour. Two or three hours. I'll meet you at your house afterward. I just have to . . ."

"Michael."

"I just have to," I said. And quietly, I lay the phone in its cradle.

"Let's go," I said.

"We'll take both cars," said Yardley. "You two can drive to Marks's from there."

We grabbed our jackets, headed toward the door. Only as Yardley was pushing it open did we pause, the two of us, and look back at Susannah.

She was standing in the aisle now. Standing there with her arms wrapped around herself, trembling. She watched us with wide eyes.

"Go on," I said to Yardley.

He didn't move. He could not take his eyes off her.

"Go on," I said.

He glanced at me once. Then he pushed through the door and was gone.

I went to her. She took my shoulders. I pulled her close, kissed her neck, put my hand down the back of her jeans to her warm skin.

"When will it be over?" she said.

When I have my hands on him, I thought. *When I have my hands on him and I feel him stop breathing.*

"Soon," I whispered gently. "Soon."

The phone rang. Susannah groaned against my chest. I held her in one arm, reached for the phone with the other.

"What?" I said.

"North. This is Carl McGill."

I let Susannah go. Stepped away from her, turned my back to her, struggling to keep the rage from sounding in my voice. "Where are you?"

"Lima," Mcgill said. "Listen—"

"No. No, the line's too clear. You sound like you're around the corner. Where are you?"

"I'm in Lima, damn it. Shut up and listen."

"Who's the scarred man, Carl?"

"Carl?" said Susannah.

"I don't know," McGill growled. "Would you listen?"

"You were there, Carl. Who's the scarred man?"

"I'm telling you, goddamn it, I don't know."

I felt Susannah's eyes on my back. I felt my heart beating hard.

"I'm sorry," McGill said then. "I am. What the hell else do you want me to say? I should have told you. All right? I should have told her. That's why I brought you two together finally, on Christmas. I figured it was gonna be over for Jersey after all these years. I figured I could tell you and we could put an end to it. I wanted to tell you. I tried. Damn it, you know I did."

"Is that what I know?" I said. "How come when we were on the train—when you were reading that article about Jersey's execution—how come you tried to hide it from me, Carl? You didn't want me to see it. That's what I know. I know that."

The silence was longer this time. Then: "Yeah. Well. I haven't got an answer, Michael. Old habits die hard, I guess. I guess I'd kept it from her mother for so long. I guess I'd worked so hard to make Susannah's life all right—to make it perfect. I mean, I wanted her to know and I didn't, okay? Hell, she was a little girl, Mike. My little girl. It didn't seem to hurt anyone. And you—the way you were—I got the feeling you didn't even *want* to know, anyway. Or maybe I was hoping you'd just remember on your own and save me the grief. Anyway, I couldn't tell you. That's the story. I tried, but I couldn't. That covers the whole thing." Both of us breathed into the pause. "I'm sorry your life jumped out at you like that," he said.

I frowned. I didn't answer.

"North?"

"I'm here."

"I'm on my way back. A few days. I've got good stuff for the book."

I nodded. "You want to talk to Susannah?"

He took a deep breath. "Yeah."

I held the receiver out toward her. She hesitated only a moment, her eyes growing damp. Then she took the instrument from me with both hands. She held it to her ear. Her lips parted, then pressed together trembling.

"Daddy?" she said.

I went out and waited for her in the car.

Chapter thirty-five

A wind had risen in the dark: a March wind blowing clouds across the moon. The moon was full. The clouds turned iridescent as they passed. Sometimes, in the seat beside me, Susannah pressed her face to the window and watched them. Sometimes she sat with her head pressed back against the seat. She hummed quietly to herself and sang. "Adeste Fideles." The sound of it made me ache inside.

We sped along the highway, going past the town, toward the backlands on the other side. At either window, the moonlight was shining on the face of the fields. And the wind was moving there, rippling through the high grass or the corn.

Susannah watched them, the moon and the wind and the fields. Or she leaned back and sang softly in her sweet, clear voice. Before we left the office just after she had gotten off the phone with McGill, she was crying. Crying and smiling at once. I had held her a long time.

"I'm all right," she kept telling me. "I'm all right."

And so she seemed to be. She seemed to be just fine.

As for me, I kept silent. I did not want to go back to the house.

Now, as I had once before, I turned off the highway onto a smaller road, and then a smaller. The forest seemed to creep up on me this time, the trees seemed to shuttle to the edge of the road in the dark until they formed a long, long wall of looming silhouettes shouldering out the moon.

Susannah had her window rolled down though she had to huddle in her sweater. She took deep breaths of the green forest air.

The sparkling line of the moon on the water flashed out at us through the breaks in the trees: We had reached Jackson Lake. I kept an eye on it, following its edge toward the hill again.

I went past the driveway a few yards before I realized I had seen it. I brought the car to a stop.

Susannah stopped humming and looked at me.

"That was it," I said.

She glanced over her shoulder as I backed up.

The driveway, overgrown as it was and littered with forest debris, looked threatening in the dark: the sort of dead end that swallows your footsteps, covers your traces, sucks you in. The clouds, I think, had covered up the moon. I guess that's what it was.

As the car bounced over the growth and the ruin, as it pushed up the forest hill toward the inn, the headlights fought against the forest blackness all around us. We could see the broken branch or the tangled vine or the pit just in front of us, but everything else was obscure and shadowy, vague shapes sunken away in the wood.

We came around the bend and saw the inn. Gray and shrouded in branches. Yardley's Chevy was parked outside. I pulled up next to it and killed the engine. Then I killed the lights.

The dark fluttered down over us like a blanket. We could hear the wind whirling around the car. We sat there, staring at the house in the dark.

At first it was just a presence, a tenebrous mask over the face of the forest. Then, as our eyes adjusted, it became a shape, a wedge of black louring against the racing clouds. The wind kept blowing, and the clouds ran by, and the moon reappeared. The house seemed almost to step out of itself and into the silver light. Its broken windows stared at us. Its weatherboard gleamed, dull gray. All the dead branches and grass and vines around it drew their shadows back and forth across the facade, shadows that melded with the ornate tracery of the porch overhang, shadows that answered, with their movement, the movement of the wind.

Susannah shivered. She glanced at me and laughed nervously.

"It's so quiet," she said softly. "It's so dark. Where's Ben?"

"I don't know. He must be in there, nosing around."

She turned her eyes to the second-story windows. The windows stared back at her.

"It's so dark," she said.

I popped open the glove compartment. The light went on in there. I took hold of the small plastic flashlight we'd brought along. I hesitated a moment, my hand hovering over the pistol I'd also brought. Susannah touched my arm. I looked at her, at her lips. I managed a smile. I left the pistol alone and slapped the glove compartment closed. I shoved open the door and slid out into the night.

The wind made motion everywhere. Motion and noise. The branches moved and whispered, and the leaves scuttled and scratched across the earth and lifted into the air and whirled around. The clouds moved, and the moonlight lived and died as they went by as if the moon were breathing in and out. I shut the car door and walked to the passenger side quickly. Susannah already had her door open. The car's dome light gleamed yellow. She stepped out beside me. Her eyes remained fixed on the house. I shut the door. The dome light went out and, at the same moment, the moonlight was extinguished all around us. The house slipped back into the shadows.

I turned on the flashlight. A dull beam flickered and flitted about the trees, illuminating nothing.

I took Susannah's arm. She stared at the house.

"It's just a house," I said. "Don't think about it."

I give great advice.

Following the beam, we moved together to the porch steps. I kept hold of Susannah's arm at the elbow. We ascended side by side. When we stepped onto the porch, the wind dropped. And, as if the wind had been keeping the dark at bay, the blackness closed in on us, even thicker than before. The flashlight's sallow circle played over the front of the house. It picked out the front door and we shuffled toward it carefully. The door hung loose on its hinges. We could hear it shiver and creak against the jamb.

I pushed the door. It opened easily, and we passed into the house.

At once, the whisper of the wind grew to a roar as the air burst through the broken windows and skittered over the walls like poltergeist. For a second Susannah and I stood motionless, my fingers touching her arm. I felt my stomach churning as I passed the flashlight's beam in front of me with a shaking hand. The beam waxed and waned, glowed and died amid the cobwebs and empty corners of a ruined foyer. It picked out the gilt frame of a mirror on the wall, all the glass shattered; a cupboard, covered with dust, stripped of drawers; the cabinet of a grandfather clock, its face ripped away.

I followed the beam with my eyes awhile, and then my eyes wandered. I stared at nothing. I was finding it hard all of a sudden to catch my breath. The place smelled old and sour. The air was thick with dust. I felt dizzy, sick, closed-in, as if the house were tightening around me, trying to work its way inside me. Then, for an instant, my whole body was racked by a violent shudder. I felt like that house, that old inn, my father's inn, and I were locked in combat. It pulled at something in me and, against my will, that something rose up to meet it. Something like a wave rose up, crashed out of me, filled the darkness all around. It was a shapeless something, but it was filled with a million shapes, a million faces. They swirled around me on the currents of air, each of them babbling with its own voice, all of them babbling with one voice. Some of them would come clear for a second. A bleeding face, a pleading eye, a dying hand would rise up before me with sudden violence. I could not place any of them, but I knew them all.

Susannah made a small noise beside me. I clutched her elbow.

"It's all right," I said—I croaked.

"It's dreadful," she whispered.

"You're right. It's awful. Jesus."

"Where's Ben, where's Ben?"

"I don't know."

"Can we go? Can we just go?"

In fact, I had completely forgotten why we'd come.

"Uh . . ." I said.

Just then a noise rose out of the wind. A human voice that mingled with its howl. Soft, but keening and terrible.

Susannah gasped. "Oh, what's that?"

"Jesus."

"Is it Ben? It must be Ben."

I shouted. "Ben!"

My shout fell away into the sound of the wind. The noise had ceased but the silence still seemed to shimmer with it.

"It was coming from upstairs," said Susannah.

"Where? Where are the stairs?"

"I don't know."

"They should be right in front of us," I said.

I swung the flash this way and that, too violently to really get a view of anything. I fought to steady my arm. Then the beam settled on a newel post, lowered to a stairway. Susannah took my hand. Our fingers twisted together. We edged forward to the first step.

The noise began again.

"Yardley!" I shouted.

"Ben?" Susannah called.

We went up together.

It was a long climb. What made it long was the dark. Not the dark around us. The flashlight cut through that a little. It was the dark waiting for us up there beyond the stairs. The light made no dent at all in that. In that endless darkness, the shapes and faces were swirling still. Now, too, there were sounds, wrenching sounds, mingling with the mingled voices: sudden gunshots, sudden cries, sudden groans that seemed torn from a wild desperation. And then that noise again, the real one, a sustained note of anguish, coming from upstairs, coming from the darkness waiting for us up there. The darkness grew closer and closer as we ascended. Tighter and tighter all around me. It was a long, long climb.

We came onto the landing.

"Ben?" I said.

There was no answer.

I passed the flash around. I saw the vague shapes of the upstairs corridor. A two-legged table, stretched on its side. Jagged holes gaping from the wall plaster with thick webs shivering over them. Floorboards twisting through the threads of what had been a carpet. And doorways. Doorways, here and there, illuminated ever so faintly by the window light from inside the rooms beyond them.

The human voice we'd heard was gone. The wind had died down. But the demons all around me, their cries, their faces, the sounds of their lives and deaths, they kept on.

This was where I'd stood. Right here, this landing.

"Michael?"

"What? What?"

"Are you all right?" she asked me.

"Yeah, yeah."

"I hate this place."

"Yeah, yeah," I said. "I'm fine."

We moved to our left slowly. We moved to the doorway from which the sound had come. It was my doorway, the doorway to my bedroom. To the left of it was the room where my parents had slept: I moved with Susannah toward my bedroom door. She was about to go through when I hesitated at the threshold, held her back.

I had lain awake in there, afraid of monsters.

I took a breath. We stepped into the room.

There was nothing. Nothing but blackness. The flashlight cut into it only weakly, casting a faint glow over clusters of debris. I saw boards lying in a pile in one corner. In another I saw a clot of bedclothes that had decayed almost to humus. And then, against the wall to my left, the light picked out a grimy mattress, torn open in the middle for the rats to nest in. I stared at it, hurting for it, for the big old bed it had been and the warmth of the big old bed and the cool sheets under me and the kiss good-night sweetheart good-night good-night. The stink of rat dung drifted to me. I moved the flash away.

I found a window on the far wall. It was opened on the night. The pane was broken and my beam traced the jagged shape of the remaining glass. Just beyond it, I could see the faint shimmer of the moon behind the passing clouds. Then the wind rose. It rushed through the window. We heard again that soft, almost human sigh of pain. I felt Susannah relax beside me.

She said: "It was just . . ."

The clouds rushed by. Moonlight pierced the window like a spear. The torn, bloody face of Ben Yardley stared up at us from the floor. And the chaos of voices gibbering in my brain tightened like a fist into a single sound: Susannah screaming.

Her hands were at her mouth. "Oh, God, God, God!"

I took a step forward. I knelt down beside the body. The mutilated flesh that had been Ben's features shone black and silver.

"Dead," I rasped. "Like all of them." I hardly knew what I was saying.

Susannah began to whimper.

The moonlight dimmed again.

Ben Yardley reached up and grabbed me.

I cried out. His hand curled around my shirt front. He pulled me down to him. That tangle of blood and matter that was his face seemed to open as if to devour me. His breath was hot and rancid. It stank of the grave.

". . . out," he whispered—gasped. ". . . out . . . the scarred . . . the scarred man . . . the scarred . . ."

His hand fell away. Then I heard him die.

It was just a little noise, lost in all the other noise around me, within me. It was just a little breath, so small it rattled in his throat. But it was a white-hot breath with all the life of him in it, and somehow, amid everything, I heard it go.

I turned away from Ben's body and I stood.

Susannah was fighting for control. I saw her hug herself and shiver.

I went to her, put my arms around her. She pressed against my chest, trembling. I could feel her tears through my shirt.

"Ssh, my love, my love," I whispered. "Hush, my love, my love."

Slowly, she raised her face to me.

She said: "He's here, isn't he?"

I saw the tears gleaming on her cheeks in the last dim moonlight.

"Yes," I said. "Yes. He's here."

And now we could hear him, coming up the stairs.

Chapter thirty-six

I killed the flashlight. The moonlight at the window faded completely. We were in the dark again.

He was coming up the stairs methodically. Unhurried. Step by step.

He was almost to the landing.

"He knows we're here." Susannah's body was rigid in my arms.

He crested the stairs. We heard the floor creak outside the room. He was heading for the door. Methodical. Unhurried. Step by step.

"Stand by the wall," I hissed. "There." I figured I had about thirty seconds.

Susannah did not argue. She moved to the wall next to the

door. She pressed herself against it. Her body disappeared in the shadows.

I stepped over Ben's body and went to the window.

It was the same window. The old oak tree was still out there. Its branches waved crazily in the wind, swaying this way and that like a ballerina's arms. That was the tree I had climbed down the last time he had come for me, scrambling to the earth as he came through the door with his gun.

He was almost at the door now. Maybe five steps away.

I braced my hands against the windowsill. The moaning wind battered me through the broken panes. I shoved—and the casters screamed as the window flew open.

In three swift and silent steps I was at the door again, at the wall beside the door, pressed hard against it as if I would push myself through. My shoulder was brushing Susannah.

The scarred man came in. He was cradling a rifle in his arms.

I could've touched him easily. He was maybe a foot away. But I couldn't see him, not really. He was just a huge shadow looming in the doorway; crossing the threshold then with a long stride. He was standing right beside me where I was clinging to the wall. I was afraid to breathe lest he feel it on his cheek. He had to remember. I kept saying that to myself. He had to remember how I went out the window last time. How he hunted me. How I got away . . .

He paused. I sensed the motion of his head toward the window. He saw that it was open. He crossed over to it.

I grabbed Susannah by the arm and we bolted out the door behind him.

The black corridor tipped and yawed as we stumbled through it, racing for the stairs. Half blind, we fought the walls off with our shoulders, with our splayed hands. The landing opened before us. We were at the stairway.

But it was too dark, it was just too dark. My hip slammed into the newel post. I was spun halfway around. The flashlight flew out of my hand as I shouted in pain.

"Shit!"

"Michael!" She reached for me.

"Go down, baby!"

She started down in a mad clatter of footsteps. I swiveled back and forth, searching desperately for the flash. The faint light of the bedroom doorway was behind me. Then, as I turned, I saw that light blotted out.

I grabbed the newel, whipped myself around it. Tumbled after Susannah, my feet barely touching the stairs. I was one step behind her. My head was thrumming with the sound of my own breathing. I could not hear him following, but his footsteps seemed to pound inside my brain. I knew he was after us. I could feel him moving to the top of the stairway. I could feel him lifting the rifle. I could feel the black bore of it centered on my back.

I was at the second stair from the bottom. Susannah was ahead of me. I had it in my mind—the leap—I could see myself hurtling after her out the front door.

Then she fell. She miscalculated that last step, and tumbled down. She spilled sideways and out of my sight.

I came off the stairs and stooped to the side to grab her. The house seemed to erupt around me. The air seemed to swell and explode as if we were inside a balloon. He'd fired at us— he'd fired just at the moment I'd dodged to the side. I heard the front door splinter as the slug slammed into it.

I grabbed Susannah. She clutched at my shirt, gasping, as she scrambled to her feet. If we broke for the door, he would gun us down for certain. We took off—into nothing, into the blackness.

I felt her hands on me. We ran. I heard her breath, her panting cries. We were in a narrow hall, running. We slammed and rocketed off the walls. We grunted and cursed and the sounds seemed to echo around us. We ran, we just kept running. At the end of the hallway there was a small square of gray light. I watched it bounce and shimmer and grow larger as we neared it. Behind us, where the corridor began, there was another patch of gray. I looked behind me, watching for him; running.

We spilled out into a larger room. I couldn't really see it, but I knew it had been the kitchen once. I tried to pause, to get my bearings. There had to be a way out.

"Michael!"

Susannah's scream tore through me. I saw his shadow at the corridor's end. He was coming at us. I saw him raise the gun.

She screamed my name once more. "Michael!" And I threw myself against her as the scarred man fired again.

The event played itself out slowly, every second of it a small eternity. I saw a gout of fire from the hallway. I felt my body slamming into Susannah's. I felt us both tumbling toward the wall and had time to think with some satisfaction that when we hit it, it would probably be me who wound up in the line of fire. I imagined the slug hurtling at me. I waited for it to hit my chest.

And then we were falling and falling through empty space. At first that's all there was. Then there was noise and pain everywhere. I was reaching out for purchase. I was being battered. I saw stars. I was tangled up with Susannah and I kept on falling. I thought I'd been hit. I thought *This is dying.* In another moment I realized: I had shoved Susannah through an open doorway and followed after. We were both tumbling down a flight of stairs.

We hit bottom. For a second, or maybe for an hour, I didn't think about anything. I lay flat on my back on a floor that seemed to be half concrete and half dirt. I watched a dozen little lights of different colors dancing above me on the face of the dark. I liked them. They were pretty.

But Susannah kept hissing at me. She kept hissing my name. She was tugging at my arm, cursing at me, straining to drag me to one side. I wanted her to leave me alone. My head was spinning like a gyroscope. It wasn't pleasant. All the same, I fought to my knees and tried to follow her. I tried—but I went over and knocked her down instead. She tugged at me still. I could hear her sobbing with the effort. I got to my knees. I crawled as she tugged at me. After a few moments, we collapsed again. Susannah leaned back against a pillar. She helped me prop myself against her. She had her arm around me. Dazed, I drew in breath, felt the loamy, cool air of the cellar come into me. I turned my head a little, swept my eyes over the vast and shadowy expanse around me. I could see why Susannah had taken so much trouble to get us away from the bottom of the stairs. He could've come to the door, aimed down, and popped us like targets. Now, he would have to come and get us.

In another instant his shadow snuffed the dim light in the cellar doorway above.

I struggled to sit up. I struggled to think. He'd be down here in seconds. I had to clear my head, remember the layout of the place. It was one room, divided only by the iron supports here and there. But there were niches; crevices and corners: a huge boiler somewhere in the far reaches, a forest of pipes and boxes and cylinders; a washing machine; a broom closet. I couldn't know how much of it remained, but I had to find a spot for us to hide, a way to outmaneuver him.

I was still trying to figure it out when the door at the top of the stairway closed, very gently. We heard him bolt it from the other side. We heard his footsteps receding.

Susannah's breath was harsh in my ear. She whispered: "What's he doing?"

"I don't know. Going away, it sounds like."

"What's he—"

"I don't know. Be quiet. Listen."

His footsteps faded. They were gone.

I started to get to my feet. My knees buckled. I dropped to the floor like dead weight. Dirt and pebbles bit into my palms.

I heard Susannah's sudden whisper behind me. "What're you doing?"

"Help me up," I mumbled.

"You're hurt."

"Hell, I know I'm hurt. Help me up." I pushed off the floor again. Again I fell. The shock of it went up my spine. I stared ahead stupidly.

Susannah grabbed me under the arm. I reached out and braced my hand against the pillar. She hoisted me, grunting. My feet sought a place to stand, found it. I straightened. A wave of nausea passed over me. When it receded, I was standing at Susannah's side. Her hands were on my face, her fingers running over it in the dark.

"Don't go," she said. "Where are you going? Don't go."

"I want to try the door. There's got to be windows too. A way out."

"This is the cellar, isn't it?" Her voice was strained.

"Yeah," I said. I stumbled forward a step. "Yeah."

"This is the cellar. Where we hid. Where we hid together. Where you held me in the little room. This is the cellar."

I paused, looked at her. I could only make out the violet outline of her in the darkness.

"Sue?" I said.

"This is where he comes, where he always comes, this is

where you hold me, waiting for him, where he . . . this is the cellar."

"Susannah."

"This is the place, the place, I remember, I dreamed, this is . . ." Her voice was rising—slowly, steadily, louder, higher. I could hear the hysteria expanding under it. I could sense she was about to break.

I took her by the shoulders.

"Susannah."

"Oh, Michael. Oh, Michael, he's going to kill us. He's waited all this time, he's waited for us here, it was always here, and now he's going to kill us . . ."

"No, no, no," I said, as calmly as I could. "Wrong movie, angel. We kill him. He dies."

"No, don't you see, don't you see who he is, what he is . . . he's been waiting, and he called us, in the stories, in the dreams, when he was ready . . . he waited and then he—"

I shook her. I didn't mean to but I lost control and I did. I shook her hard.

"Damn it, damn it," I hissed. "He's a man, that's all. He's a man with a gun and a twisted mind. We take him, we take him out, that's all, angel, it's in the Big Book, remember?"

I said something like that. I don't know what it was. I didn't know at the time. I just shook her and kept talking. It seemed to calm her down. She slumped in my hands. Her head came forward.

"Oh God," she whispered. But the hysteria was gone.

I took a breath. I felt her slender shoulders in my hand. I drew her to me and laid my cheek against her hair. Her soft hair. Her red hair. It did not smell of shampoo now. I smelled the sweat in it and the dirt. I smelled the blood. But I pressed against its softness and closed my eyes and I could see, almost see, for a second, the figure of her in bright sunlight as it moved ahead of me up a rising slope of snow.

"Susannah," I said.

She gasped and jolted and jerked away. "Oh please!" she sobbed.

"Susannah, what is it?"

"He's come back."

Chapter thirty-seven

I heard him then, too, moving upstairs. Right above us, in the kitchen. His step was not slow and methodical the way it had been before. He seemed to be sliding swiftly from spot to spot now, pausing, moving again.

"He's not coming down," Susannah whispered.

"No."

I stood still and listened. My mind came clear as I focused on the sound.

Susannah's hair brushed my face as she cocked her head. "He's doing something," she said. "What's he doing?"

"Ssh."

I moved forward a step, away from her. She came up beside

me quickly, put her hand on my arm. We moved together toward the stairs, reaching out in the darkness, groping.

I touched the banister. I drew myself to the bottom of the stairway. I peered up. I could hear him plainly: his footsteps and other sounds, sounds that were at once metallic and liquid. It sounded as if he were washing something.

I lifted my foot and placed it tentatively on the stair. The stair groaned under the weight of it.

"Don't," Susannah whispered.

I tried the stair again. It groaned again. It was old and rotten. If I tried to climb—if I tried to take him by surprise before he finished whatever it was he was doing—I'd get about halfway. Then the door would fly open, his silhouette and the silhouette of the gun would rise out of the dark above me. There'd be a flash, maybe a sense of falling . . .

I came off the stairs and Susannah gripped my arm. I hated to just stand there waiting for him to make his move.

But I didn't have long to wait.

There was another second of silence. And then there was a second in which I smelled the gasoline and understood. I pulled my arm free from Susannah's hold and bolted up the stairs.

Then he torched the place.

It wasn't violent. The gas did not explode. It simply crawled up and all over everything like a nightmare of spiders. Some of the gas had seeped beneath the door, and the top steps went up at once. The flames sprung up out of the dark, blinding me with sudden light. I raised my arm before my eyes. I tried to push forward to the door. But the fire grabbed hold of the ancient stairway wood and began to devour it. The white light lifted higher and higher. It danced down the stairs, closer and closer to me. The first heat of it stung my face. I staggered back a step; another. And I felt the entire stairway giving way beneath my feet.

Everything was roaring. The flames were. The stairs were as they crumbled underneath me. And I roared as I leapt and tumbled, blind, into the pit of blackness beneath the flames.

I couldn't time my fall to catch the shock. I just hit and crumbled as the stairs caved in. Sparks showered over me. Smoke billowed up around me.

Susannah shouted. I shouted back. She was there, grabbing at my shoulders, trying to lift me. I grabbed back at her and pulled myself to my feet. With my arms around her, I stumbled from the burning rubble.

We fell against the far wall. We sank to the floor together. I heaved at the air there and swallowed tendrils of the drifting smoke along with it. I hacked and spit. Moaning, I turned to Susannah.

I could see her face by the firelight. Her cheeks were streaked with soot and tears. Her blue eyes reflected the orange glow as she watched the stairway burn.

Above us, the door caught. It went like paper. It was a rectangular silhouette bordered by flame. Then it was flame only, roaring and rising.

I sat up against the wall, choking, feeling the heat parch my skin, sear the sweat off me.

"Help me," I said.

We stood together. We stood side by side, watching the flaming door where it seemed to float and grow in the surrounding smoke. I watched it, and I understood.

I hung my head, coughing.

Susannah's voice was suddenly quiet, calm. "What is it?"

I waved her off.

"You know a way out," she said.

I nodded. "The window. I didn't remember."

"And now he's waiting there."

"That must be it."

"With the gun."

"Yes."

I looked at her, saw her with her face raised, her lips parted. She looked like someone staring at a vision. She stared up at the burning door.

"I don't want to burn," she said.

"No," I said. "Neither do I."

The window was directly above my head. I could see it now by the firelight. The glass was broken clear out of it. It was a small space, but I judged it large enough for us to get through. I would give her a boost, then drag myself over. A slow process. Plenty of time for him to take aim and pull the trigger. Nice and easy.

"Damn it!" I ran my fingers through my hair.

"It's all right," she said softly.

"Damn it, damn it."

"I'm not afraid," she said. "Really."

"I should've beat him."

She wrapped her arms around me.

"I should've had him beat."

"Next time," she said.

There was a loud tearing sound. The flaming door ripped from its hinges. It spiraled through the air above us, swirling and blazing. It hit the ground with a crash, fell into the pile of embers that had been the stairs. The embers flew up around us. I felt pieces of them bite at my arms and my face. Susannah and I both pressed back against the wall with our arms raised in front of us. The heat battered at my palms, my cheeks, my brow. The smoke washed over me, stripped my throat raw. When I looked again, the rubble was ablaze, the flames curling toward the ceiling.

I turned away from it, to the window.

And what happened next was a gift.

Across the small rectangle of darkness in the wall above us, I caught the sweep of headlights. I was amazed. I half expected them to go by. They didn't. They grew brighter. They peeled off.

Someone had just pulled into the drive.

I was afraid to move. I was afraid to believe it. I said: "Susannah?" The two of us just stood there, unable to move or believe.

The headlights went out. I thought: Marks. He was the only one who knew we were here.

And as I thought it, I heard the scarred man's rifle go off in the near distance. I moved.

"Go," I said.

I grabbed her by the arm, pushed her toward the wall. I stooped, made a brace of my hands, and she stepped into it. I hoisted her and she was at the window. I drove her up and over the sill, and she was gone.

I leapt. Caught hold of the rim. I pulled, my feet scrabbling for purchase on the concrete wall. The heat seemed to eat into me, weaken me, drag me back. My vision dimmed and faded with smoke. I stuck my head through. I sucked at the air and got nothing but ash. I gagged. My hands shot forward. My fingernails dug into the cool earth.

And Susannah had me under the arms and was yanking at me. I was through, I was outside. Still coughing, I stood and wheeled, looking for the way to go.

Flames. I hadn't known there would be so much fire. The house was blazing away into the sky. The roar of it was overwhelming. The windows spit flame, the plasterboard buckled and the flames shot out; parts of the roof had collapsed and released the fire within. The place was a single rage of red light and thunder, and the heat was washing out from it, wave after wave, driving me away.

I stumbled back. Everything was blotted from my sight by the blaze. Susannah cried out, and I turned to find that she had fallen.

I reached for her, pulled her to her feet.

"It's going to come down," I said. I couldn't hear myself. I shouted: "Run. For the car."

She ran. We were at the side of the house. The driveway and the car were directly before us. She ran and I went after, my eyes drawn back over my shoulder, mesmerized by the old house as it torched the night and burned the stars to nothing.

Susannah reached the car, grabbed the passenger door. I ran toward her. I saw Yardley's old Chevy pulled up on the grass to my right. To my left, just in front of the porch, I saw another car—a big one, American made—that had not been there before.

I saw Susannah pull the car door open. I ran past her, past the front of the car, toward the driver's side. My hand went out, clawing for the door handle. The door came open and I turned to get in.

I saw Susannah turn. I saw her turn, with her eyes wide and her hand lifted to her mouth. I shouted at her, screamed at her to get into the car, but she didn't move. She was paralyzed with fear.

The scarred man rose up in front of her, his face red with the flames.

His mouth hung slack. His eyes danced crazily in the crazy light. The gash that split his face in half seemed to be burning with reflected fire. He gripped the rifle in his right hand.

I had no time to get to her. No time. And she was motionless before him as he came toward her.

He never reached her, though. Howard Marks was there to

stop him. He stepped up behind the scarred man, wrapped his arm around his throat and yanked him back, away from Susannah. I ran around the car again, back to her.

I saw the silhouettes of Marks and the scarred man, the rifle gripped between them as they struggled for it. I saw them staggering toward the burning house. The scarred man was lean and wiry, but so was Marks, and I was surprised by the lawyer's sinewy strength.

I turned, bent into the car. Slapped my hand against the glove-compartment door. It opened and the pistol fell out into my hand.

I swiveled. I raised the gun. My finger tightened on the trigger. My sight found the scarred man. I followed him as he battled with Marks.

I had a bead on him. I had him nailed. I had him right in my sight.

But I could not fire.

I could not. I was no longer there.

Somewhere, far away, I heard Susannah screaming. Somewhere, some other place, the fire burned. But I was far away now, far away and long ago. I was crushed into a dark room, shivering. I was drenched in my little boy's urine and cold with my little boy's fear. I was trying not to scream don't scream only don't scream he'll hear you if you scream don't scream for mommy and daddy because they're dead heck they're all dead anyway I seen em didn't I and man they were all they were all my mommy and daddy they were all dead you know what dead is like Buck the setter like they're not in their bodies anymore mommy mommy don't scream don't let me scream.

I was there, I was there again. I was there in that little so-dark place, clutching the little girl I'd tried to save, and they were gone my parents and I was all alone and he—oh, he was out there, coming for us, out there, calling to us, pretending to be nice, but he's not nice, he's not nice at all he made my mommy and daddy dead he's mean he's just pretending to be nice calling to us like that getting closer and closer and closer step by step by step . . .

But it seemed to take forever before he finally came. Or did he come, the scarred man? I remembered. I remembered he found us. The broom-closet door flying open. That horrible nightmare of a face pushing in at us. Oh yes, oh yes, he found us all right.

But if he found us . . .

If he found us, why are we still alive?

The silhouettes of Marks and the scarred man wrestled before me against a wall of flames. Before me, and yet far, far away in the netherworld of the present where I was no longer. The house had begun to crumble inward, the fire to strive upward from it till even the clouds seemed to be burning. All around me the wild, blowing trees were etched in the red light. And yet I—I alone remained at the dark center of things. I could not feel my hand upon the gun. I could not feel my finger on the trigger.

He had found us. But it was later, somehow. It was later and he was coming again, coming again, oh God, don't scream. What did I do? Where am I? Did I fall asleep? I must have. I must have. Oh God and now he's coming. How could I fall asleep, but he just kept coming for us, coming for us, out there in the cellar looking for us, getting closer, closer, and then . . .

I remembered. I remembered now. The footsteps and the voice of him getting closer as I clutched Susannah in my arms, as I clutched her and whimpered and pissed and cried. But after a while they began to recede, that's right, they grew softer, he's going away, up the stairs I could hear and there was silence, there was silence for ever so long and I waited, afraid to move, don't move, afraid, I waited, every muscle tense, my eyes wide, and then slowly, slowly relaxing, bit by bit . . .

I fell asleep in there, I must have. Fell asleep or fainted. And then I was awake again, suddenly. Suddenly he was coming again, he was calling us again oh god mommy daddy daddy. And then he was there, there at the door, at the broom closet door, and while I watched wide-eyed, unsure if I was awake or asleep, the doorknob turned, the door flew open. The closet door flew open . . .

And he was there. At last. The bogeyman come to get us. The scarred man, with his face twisted and torn down the center. With his hands reaching for us, grabbing us, as I screamed and screamed and screamed and he shouted:

"It's all right. It's over now. I'm here now. I'm a police officer. A policeman. I'm here, I'm here."

I remembered. I remembered how I came to the top of the stairs. How I saw him gun down Susannah's mother. How he turned to me—not the scarred man, not the scarred man at all, but the other—he turned to me as I looked down. He turned to me from Laura's murdered body and I saw his face, and he knew I'd seen it. And he looked at me then with an expression of calm and musing. As if I were a puzzle. That's all. A puzzle he would have to solve.

But he couldn't. Not quite. Not then.

Not now.

Because now, two things happened at once. First, I came back to myself, back to the present. It felt as if my soul had run out from me to the limit of an elastic distance, as if that distance had suddenly snapped and I now came hurtling back into myself through a roaring vortex of wind. The fiery house was there, right before me. The porch was collapsing in a blinding red flash that made me squint. The scarred man and Marks were there. They were maybe ten yards away. Fighting for that gun. Their screams and cries and curses rising in counterpoint to the roar of the flames.

And then, at the same moment, the same moment I returned to myself, just then, one of the struggling men let out a guttural shout. It was the scarred man. He fell backward, away from Marks. He stumbled, dropped to the ground. Marks stood over him, gripping the rifle. He leveled it at the scarred man.

I shifted my arm and the pistol swung from one of them to the other.

My voice seemed to be torn from my throat.

I shouted: "Marks!"

He wheeled toward me and fired.

I saw him. I saw all of it. I saw him spinning around through stopped time, the rifle in his hand. I saw the spout of flame erupt from the barrel as the flames erupted upward from the roof behind him and the old Turner inn came tumbling down. I heard the sound—the muffled thunder—of the shell exploding. And I saw him: Marks. I saw his thin, lined, sweet, almost angelic face wild and gleeful, terrible and twisted in the red flamelight. I saw his face as I had seen it all those years ago. I saw the face of the man who had murdered my people. And I watched it as he took his best shot at me.

I watched it calmly. I wasn't afraid. He couldn't kill me. I knew that. He could fire and fire till damnation came and the bullets would whistle by me forever. It had been ordained in the soul of revenge from the beginning. Etched in my child's heart with a hatred too awful even to know. Oh yes. He could fire. But I would never die—not until I'd done what I had come for. That was written. It had been in the Big Book all along.

So Howard Marks turned to me with the house alive with

burning behind him. He turned to me and lowered the black bore of the rifle at my chest. He turned to me and the bore exploded with death and flame.

And then I squeezed off a single shot and killed him.

PART SIX

The end of the story

Chapter thirty-eight

The shell from Marks's gun nearly ripped my arm off. I understand the best medical minds and hands at Fayette County General Hospital labored for hours to keep me in one piece. I understand I made it hard for them. At one point, I'm told, I came rocketing out of the anesthesia and nearly sat up on the operating table. I grabbed a nurse by her starched white shirtfront, dragged her to me and whispered: "You see. He never had a chance." Then I dropped back onto the table like a stone.

In any case, despite my efforts, I was preserved intact for future generations to wonder at and admire. I plan to charge a nickel a pop.

After the shooting, a week went by. As far as I'm concerned, that's all it did. I lay in my hospital bed drifting in and out of sleep, in and out of pain, in and out of a drugged fog. Faces passed before me. I remember Susannah's eyes—those blue eyes—staring down at me hour after hour. I remember voices, but I don't remember words. I remember talking, but not what I said. The time just passed and I just lay there. A week went by.

What brought me out of it, finally, was the sight of him standing in the doorway. Somehow, in my confused state, I was still certain it was he I had killed. . . . Or rather, that in killing Marks, I had killed him as well, as if the scarred man were a symbol and not a person, and I had laid it to rest.

But he was no symbol. There he was, standing rather awkwardly in the doorway, a slender man in his early forties. Short sandy hair and gray-blue eyes in a thin face. A cheap suit. A thin tie. A jagged scar down the center of his face. I saw him with ambling vision, alternately fading and focusing at the center, blurred at the edges. I wondered if I was dreaming. My heart sped up a little when he came in. But he only walked to my bedside and lay a gift-wrapped book on the table there.

"It's about the Yorkshire Ripper," he said. "I hear you like true crime."

He had a soft voice with a hint of gravel in it. His thin lips barely moved as he spoke. His eyes looked me over. I remember thinking: he's a man used to listening and watching, not talking. Then I tuned out again for a while.

It was all very weird. It never came fully clear. He stayed and he talked to me and I listened to him as best I could. But I felt like a car radio on a cloudy night taking in distant stations: getting snatches of talk and jazz and news, all of it somehow jumbled together in a solution of static, all of it at once exotic and mundane, some snatches of it clearer than others. He talked for a long time and I suspect he told me things he'd never told anyone. To this day I believe I'm the only one who ever heard it all.

His name was Zachary Johnson. He had been a state highway patrolman when Laura and my parents were murdered. He had been the first to find me and Susannah and, clearly, the sight of him had so terrified us, we had come to associate him with the killer. During the early seventies he quit the force. Some kind of identity crisis. I didn't get the whole thing. The upshot of it was he moved out to San Francisco. He worked as a bartender there and he fell in love with one of the girls who worked the place. She liked fancy clothes and he bought them for her. She liked drugs, and he bought those too. She liked it when they took drugs together. When he was broke, she left him. He was hooked, by then, on heroin. I think it was heroin.

So he kicked around for a while. There was more to it than that, but I can't remember all of it. Basically, he kicked around for a while and it was tough and the drugs were bad. He got clean, though, eventually. He got clean the hard way: cold, in a jail cell, while the guards laughed. But it stuck. He made it stick. He got clean and he got free, and started an investigation agency. I remember he said he had to pull a lot of strings to get the license, call in a lot of favors.

Anyway, he went private, and he made ends meet, but it wasn't pleasant. Keyhole jobs, mostly. Then, one day, he read about Nathan Jersey, about him getting the death sentence. It got to him, nagged at him, stuck in his mind.

He'd never really been happy with the case. He'd followed it because it was sensational and he'd been involved, and something about it had always bothered him. The pieces just didn't fit together. Of course, that's not the sort of impulse a person acts on, not in real life. And Zachary Johnson wouldn't have acted on it either, except he had no real life left.

It seemed to him—when he read about Jersey being sentenced to die—that that moment, the moment when he'd found Susannah and me, had been the best moment of his life. And as that thought occurred to him, it also occurred to him that a private investigation into the Jersey case was called for and that he was the perfect man for the job.

He began it casually, almost as a hobby. And he began it by tracking down Susannah and me. Being there on the west coast, it was easy for him to find the family that adopted me. It took him a lot longer to find me, however. By the time he did, he was caught up in it. It had become more to him than he understood. It was, by then, a way to justify himself to himself, a path to vindication, and he wanted desperately to follow that path to its end.

What he needed was money. What he needed was a client.

So he went to the attorney representing Nathan Jersey. He went to Howard Marks.

I can't say what Marks was thinking. He'd apparently never worried about us before; I don't know why he should have wanted to track us down now. Maybe, having kept control of the case this long, having shepherded Nathan Jersey right up to the death house, he was beginning to get a little nervous. Or maybe, more likely, he didn't want Johnson acting independently. Yes, that must've been it. If Johnson was going to reopen the case, Marks wanted to keep an eye on him, wanted to be in control, as he always had been. Whatever the reason, he hired Johnson to find us under one condition: that he would operate in the strictest secrecy so as not to upset our young lives unnecessarily.

So Johnson tracked us down. He found me, and then McGill, and then Susannah. . . . Her he found on the very night I came to visit her at Marysvale. But he was pledged to secrecy: When I saw him, he ran.

The McGill connection baffled him—until it occurred to him

that McGill and Laura might have been what he called romantically involved. As we would later, he began to wonder whether Laura might have been the prime target—and he began to theorize that McGill had killed her in a fit of passion, that McGill was watching us to make sure we did not remember. Excited, he phoned Marks to report his findings. Marks, realizing Johnson was closing in on the truth, forbade him to act. Johnson argued. Marks fired him . . . then, on second thought, asked him to wait until he arrived in New York, where they could discuss it.

Johnson was pissed, and figured Marks could stew. He headed for Louisiana to see what he could find out about Laura. Marks, meanwhile, must have been alarmed to learn that Susannah and I had been reunited. He arrived in New York with the plan of killing Johnson, Susannah, and me in one blow. But Johnson was in New Orleans by then, and Marks had to settle for me and Sue. He came to McGill's office first to make sure he had the right man; he tested me with the remarks about the Turner case to make sure I hadn't remembered and talked already. Then, that night, he called, pretending to be Johnson, hoping to tangle the scarred man in our deaths. That was the second time in our lives Susannah and I escaped him.

Johnson, moving in secret among his Louisiana colleagues, soon knew the Harris story. But it took him quite a while to find the photograph that showed him that Stan Harris and Howard Marks were the same man. The police no longer had one. The papers didn't; neither did Tulane. Johnson finally lucked out and tracked down one of Harris's former classmates, who had caught the killer in a candid all those years ago.

With that, Johnson came rushing back to Hickman, hoping he could get his story told. He was on his way to the Sheriff when he saw Susannah and me drive by. He followed us, lost us

—and then guessed where we had gone. It was a good guess. A timely guess. He drove to the Turner inn.

Marks had drawn us there. When I phoned him with the Harris story, he made up that crap about Laura's letters and I went right for it. He hadn't wanted to kill me alone and risk Susannah going to the cops. Out at the house, with me and Susannah together, he figured he could finally finish off the Turner killings with no loose ends. Unfortunately, Yardley got there first.

"And that's it," said the scarred man. "When I drove up, he fired on me. I swung the car at him. He fell back. I scrambled out, got on top of him, got the rifle. Then I saw you . . . Well, you were there for the rest."

He shrugged and looked away from me. Even in my clouded state, I realized he wanted me to say something: something resonant and profound that would give the case the meaning it had obviously taken on for him. I tried to. I really did. I tried to think of something. But the painkiller was wearing off and the throb in my arm was returning and the tranquilizer was still kicked in and my head was swimming and I was tired. I was just too tired.

"Listen," I said groggily. "Thanks. Thanks a lot."

He shrugged again. "I'll let you get some sleep," he said. He turned, his hands in his pockets. He walked to the door.

"Hey," I tried to say. I mumbled it. He didn't hear me. "Hey," I said again. He turned. "Where'd you get the scar?"

"Oh." He smiled. He touched the gash sadly. "When I was a kid. It's a long story. Not very interesting."

I nodded. My eyelids drooped. The next time I woke, he was gone.

Chapter thirty-nine

I was unwell all summer. My arm got infected and I needed another operation. I had to lie around a lot, in the hospital first, and then at home. It gave me a lot of time to read. I read the news. I read about Nathan Jersey.

He got to see the games that year. The Reds went nowhere, but he got to see the games. It was a close call for him there, but once the story hit the papers, the governor had to act. The execution was stopped with about five hours to spare. After that the headlines started. It was a quiet news season otherwise, that summer, and Jersey's case had become a minor cause célèbre. The papers had a good time with the old murder angle, and the story of how the victims' children had come home to see justice done. It made me sad to see Yardley's big story torn to pieces by the competing vultures. But Yardley was dead. Jersey was alive. And for Jersey, all in all, it worked out well. The law-and-order types stood against him for a while. He had killed a guard, after all, they said. But in the end no one could really hold that line. Jersey was paroled. He wound up in one of those halfway houses for the retarded. I saw a picture of the place in the paper. It looked okay.

So that kept my interest while the arm healed, and then there were the Mets and Charlie Rose. And, of course, Susannah.

She had to take six weeks of summer courses to get her degree, but she came down to visit every weekend. We studied together. I studied her eyes and the places on her neck that her hair covered and all the rest of her, and she studied me. We made love a lot in the dead heat of the summer days. Then, slippery with sweat, we lay tangled together and talked the fading weekend evenings into dawn, into the cooler hours when we could make love again.

At first we talked about what we had come to refer to as It: our story, the story of the scarred man. Suddenly I found I had a mindful of memories that had not been there before. As if the old neglected closet door had opened, and all the junk that had been stuffed inside it had come tumbling out. I wanted to share it with her, that junk. I wanted to show her every piece of it: the broken toys, and the pictures in the shattered frame, and the boxes that held old smells in them, and the ones that somehow held old voices. I wanted to tell her about my mother in the kitchen in the afternoon when the light hit the ringlet of hair that curled under her ear. I wanted to tell her about the smell of my father's pipe on the porch in autumn. I wanted to tell her about the strangers who raised me and how they were cruel and sometimes kind.

Susannah listened. The way she listened made me love her,

want her; even the fact that she listened. I talked so much that summer that sometimes even I couldn't listen to it anymore. Then, finally, I'd shut up, and she would talk, and she would tell me about her dreams. She would tell me about her childhood—not the Connecticut woodland idyll, although that was also part of it, but about the fear—the gnawing anxiety that had been with her, in one shape or another, her whole life long. She had tried to tell me about it—a little—that first time we walked together through the woods of her childhood. She had told me about the invisible bogeyman who followed her, so she thought, down the forest paths, who hid from her behind trees and rocks, who waited for her while she lay in bed at night. She had been trying to tell me that she was afraid. That deep in the wordless interior of her mind, she had always been afraid.

I hadn't wanted to hear it then. I had believed—I had wanted to believe—that she had a mind like crystal, untouched by fear. That she had never even had a nightmare.

But she had. She'd had plenty of them. Even as a little girl she'd had them. The perfect little rich girl McGill had raised was tormented by them constantly. And though the dreams faded by breakfast time each morning, they became a part of her after a while, they were her little secret, they were the thing about the perfect little rich girl that no one knew.

And now they were gone.

"I almost miss them," she told me one night. "I feel empty inside where the dread used to be."

All that summer I could actually see the fear fading, packing up its home behind her eyes and moving on. Something new moved in after a while. I don't know what to call it, but it seemed to me to finish her up, to make her complete somehow. I hadn't missed it before it appeared, this new thing, but now that it was there, in her eyes, in her smile, I was glad to see it. It made me crazy with love for her.

Anyway, by October I was back at my job. McGill had almost finished the drug book and was planning another one on murder for hire. I hesitated for a while before agreeing to work on it. There were still things between me and him that were not settled.

One night we went out to Truffles together to talk. We drank. We talked. We pointed cigarettes at each other's chests. We screamed.

"Moral cowardice," I shouted.

"Fuck you," he yelled.

"You knew."

"You're seven years old, what the fuck do you know about moral cowardice?"

"I know plenty," I said, draining my scotch.

"You know diddly shit," he said, draining his scotch.

We ordered two more scotches.

"You wanted to keep her all sweet and sheltered," I said.

"So did you, my young friend."

"You couldn't face the truth."

"Neither could you. So what? Life's tough."

"Yeah, yeah."

"Moral cowardice. Jesus! If you weren't an invalid, I'd ask you to step outside."

"If you weren't an old man, I'd go."

We drank some more. He sang a medley of Johnny Mercer hits under his breath. I rested my head on the table.

"And another thing," I said.

"What? I can't hear you like that. Pick your head up."

I raised my head. "Another thing . . . I wanna know about Laura."

McGill straightened a little. His gnarled fingers tightened on his glass. "Well," he said softly, "it's like this, North: go fuck yourself."

"Did she ever—"

"And the horse you rode in on."

"Did she ever tell you about Harris?"

"Oh hell." He hunkered over his drink. "Hell, no." He laughed. "Only that he was 'not so nice.' "

I laughed. He looked at me. I stopped laughing. "Why'd she come to Hickman?" I asked.

"Born there."

"What?"

"Sure, she lived there till she was, like, three or something, then her father got a job down south."

"So she probably told Marks that—Harris—whoever the hell he was—you know—probably told him about it when they talked back in Louisiana. That's how he knew where to find her."

"Swell. You're a genius."

"Or maybe he just remembered the name and came there and was surprised to hear about her when the lynching thing happened."

"Swell. You're a genius."

"Or maybe . . ."

"Swell, already. You're a fucking genius."

"I mean, it's almost like he had to screw it up," I said. "He was home free and he couldn't stop . . . being who he was. She was his excuse. And after that, he had Jersey to tease along. He must've loved that, being his lawyer. He couldn't stop himself."

"Yeah, well, it's like that," said McGill, staring deep into his scotch. "Your self, I mean. It's like that." He shook his head once and looked up at me. "What the hell, Michael. Stick around, willya? Stick around and work on the book. Christ, you won't have to put up with me much. The research alone is sure to get you killed."

He swayed in his seat. He laughed. So did I.

"Oh, all right," I said. "If it'll get me killed."

It was just as well. His daughter had graduated from college now and was all but living with me at St. Mark's Place. She got a job at a school in Brooklyn for retarded kids. We began looking for a place of our own. All in all, there wasn't much point maintaining hostilities with the old guy. I had to see him on holidays anyway. It was already getting to be time for Thanksgiving. And then, of course, after that came Christmas.

Christmas came. Charlie and Angela were there at the house in Trent. Susannah and me and McGill were there, and Kate and Kelly. All of us who were there at the beginning were there again. We didn't say anything about it. We were just there. That was enough.

Some things, of course, were different this year. This year the snow fell lightly: just a pretty patina on the trees and the grass, and big whirling flakes swallowed in the black water of the river. And this year we did not tell ghost stories at night. This year, we did not believe in ghosts.

But we had the tree again, and the great meal, and the presents and the nog and the mistletoe and the sleigh ride and the music. And we knew how to keep Christmas well, if anyone alive possessed the knowledge, and we resolved to live in the Past, the Present, and the Future, and let nothing us dismay.

May that be truly said of us, and all of us.

And, as Charlie Rose observed: Doo-wow.

BOOK MARK

The text of this book was set in the typeface
Baskerville and the display in Codex
by Berryville Graphics,
Berryville, Virginia.

It was printed on 50 lb. Glatfelter,
an acid-free paper,
and bound by Berryville Graphics,
Berryville, Virginia.

Designed by Guenet Abraham